Dangerous Love

His lips left her mouth and moved across her cheek to
her neck and shoulder. She felt the warmth of his arms,
the strong beat of his heart, his desire growing as he held
her.

She licked his neck with the tip of her tongue and the
taste electrified her. Val hissed as she breathed in,
gasping involuntarily. Her upper lip pulled up from her
teeth as though it had a life of its own. She moved fast,
as far from him as she could and backed up against the
wall, trembling. There were tears in her eyes.

Vampyr

ATTENTION: SCHOOLS AND CORPORATIONS

PINNACLE Books are available at quantity discounts with bulk purchases for educational, business or special promotional use. For further details, please write to: SPECIAL SALES MANAGER, Pinnacle Books, Inc., 271 Madison Ave., Suite 904, New York, NY 10016.

WRITE FOR OUR FREE CATALOG

If there is a Pinnacle Book you want—and you cannot find it locally—it is available from us simply by sending the title and price plus 75¢ to cover mailing and handling costs to:

Pinnacle Books, Inc.
Reader Service Department
271 Madison Avenue
New York, NY 10016

Please allow 6 weeks for delivery.

_____Check here if you want to receive our catalog regularly.

JAN JENNINGS

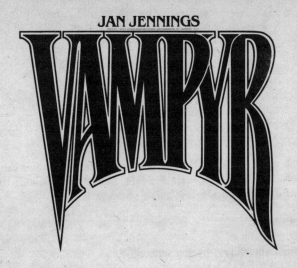

VAMPYR

TOR

A TOM DOHERTY ASSOCIATES BOOK
Distributed by Pinnacle Books, New York

VAMPYR

A Tor Book

First printing, August 1981

ISBN: 0-523-48010-5

Cover illustration by: Don Brautigon

Printed in the United States of America

Distributed by Pinnacle Books,
New York, New York.

VAMPYR

Chapter I

Theo James, M.D., retired, glanced absently through the pages of the medical report one more time before he dropped the thick folder on his desk. The latest page of test results, only a few days old, was nearly a carbon copy of the first from four years ago. It gave the same information and the same guarded prognosis, and, while many of the monthly reports were labeled "In Remission," he knew that sometime in the near future a final page reading "Terminal" would be added.

Theo stared at the plain manila folder, dogeared at the corners and badly worn along the spine. Chronic lymphocytic leukemia, generally striking men forty to fifty years of age, was almost invariably fatal within five years of onset. It was a death sentence in polite disguise; the name typed neatly on the file's index tab was JAMES, THEODORE MD.

He ran his square-tipped fingers through his hair and pursed his well-shaped lips in frustration. Theo was a handsome man in his early forties, of medium height and regular features. He had large inquisitive eyes and a healthful-looking tan that was the envy of the other university doctors. It was ironic, he thought, twisting his mouth slightly to the side, that he had fallen a victim to one of the most malignant diseases within his own specialty.

The chair squeaked as he settled back, resting his fingers lightly on the glossy surface of the mahogany desk. He considered with some apprehension the tangled series of events that were drawing him to the brink of uneasy familiarity with the supernatural, quackery, and a rapidly-approaching evening appointment with the unknown.

When he'd first experienced the alarming loss of stamina that presaged a bout with his disease, he had passed it off as overwork, but a routine physical exam had uncovered the truth. He'd taken the news quietly, with a calmness that was indicative of his determination to stay alive. He had sold his lucrative practice, taken a modest appointment as a consulting hematologist for the university and applied himself full time to researching blood diseases. The papers he had written and published on exotic blood disorders had made him a leading authority in the field of hematology and given him access to the otherwise inaccessible information he sought.

It was all part of his desperate plan for survival. Theo found it difficult to give up anything he cared much about, and life was high on his list. "Forty-two. Too damn young to die," he whispered, glancing around his office, the done-over third-floor landing of his spacious home. Downstairs he heard the click of a door closing and staccato footsteps coming up the steps.

"Poppa?" a cheerful soprano voice called. His

8

daughter, Sarah, exuberantly healthy at fourteen, started talking before she was halfway up. "Is there anything I can do for you before I go out?" She finished the flight of stairs and plopped down in the chair at the end of his desk. She was the image of her long-dead mother: tall, with a gawky grace and golden hair that fell in satiny ribbons over her shoulders. Sarah was so beautiful in her unaffected innocence that it brought a lump to Theo's throat.

"One favor, sweetheart," he said, smiling broadly at her. "I have a six o'clock appointment with a patient. I'm a little tired. Could you show her the way up here?"

"Poppa," Sarah frowned prettily as she spoke. "You said you gave up all that stuff years ago. You don't need any patients. Besides, you've been pretty pooped out lately. She'll just be like that witch doctor you had here last month—another fake!"

"This patient's special."

"What's so special about her? She can't be any sicker than you." Sarah tossed her honey-colored mane of hair back. "She'll only make you overwork and get sick again."

"Her name is Valan Anderweldt, and her condition is very serious. Nothing like it has been reported before. But," he raised his hand as Sarah leaned forward to interrupt and waited until she settled back before he continued. "She may hold the key to my problem. Will you show her up? And promise not to mention that her new physician is having difficulty healing himself."

"Of course," Sarah gave in, brushing her skirt down smoothly as she stood up. She walked around the end of the desk, gave her father a quick kiss on the cheek, said, "I love you, Poppa," and was down the stairs in a clatter of leather soled sandals before he had time to ask her where she was going for the evening.

He shook his head and smiled, wondering briefly whether all fathers felt the same way about their teen-aged daughters. He knew she was spoiled rotten, and he enjoyed letting her have her own way. But sometimes, just sometimes, she acted a lot older than fourteen and, as far as he was concerned, a lot bossier than a little girl should.

He heard the grandfather clock in the downstairs entryway chime six o'clock. Mrs. MacMullin, the housekeeper, spoke and he heard Sarah reply, but he couldn't make out the words. He pulled another file, a thick one, and set it on his desk. It was labeled ANDERWELDT VALAN. The two letters it contained were handwritten in neat, carefully controlled script. One requested an appointment and accompanied a packet of gruesome photographs. The second confirmed the date and time. A faint smile played across Theo's lips while he waited for Valan Anderweldt.

Val was distinctly ill at ease: acutely aware that she might be facing one of the most dangerous encounters of her life, acutely aware of how different she was from ordinary mortals and determined to play her hand to the end. The last few days of decision making had been pure hell for her, but there was too much at stake for her to back out now.

She parked the baby blue Ford in front of Dr. James' house, got out, and leaned against the door on the driver's side for a few minutes, working up nerve to go inside. She stared at the plants along the driveway and along the road in front of the house but didn't see them.

She was concentrating on her heart. It was racing so fast her chest ached. "It's incredible," she thought, "that after all this time I have to beg for help from a human." With great conscious effort she slowed her heartbeat to its normal rate and felt the aching stop. She exhaled and straightened up.

There were eyes watching. Val could sense someone staring at her back. As she turned, stiffly, to face the house, the door opened and a young girl called, "Miss Anderweldt?"

"Yes?" The girl was a lovely child thirteen or fourteen, with a mane of silky blond hair and a red dress that stopped just above her knees. The girl stood poised in the doorway, beckoning with one hand.

"I'm Sarah James. Come on in. Poppa's expecting you." She pushed the door open all the way, watching the visitor with wide-open deep violet eyes. She didn't move as Val approached, and artlessly blocked the door, forcing Val to brush against her in passing. The girl was totally unaware of Val's sudden gasp for breath.

"Poppa asked me to keep watch for you. He's upstairs," she said, closing the door and moving quickly toward the stairs. "Come on up."

Val moved warily, tensely, struggling to maintain self-control. It was all she could do to keep from cringing away from the warmth of the girl. "Touching is so simple for her," Val thought. She rubbed her arms, which were covered with goosebumps. Her tongue was bleeding slightly where she'd bitten it, fighting to master the beast within her that hungered for blood. "It's a good thing I've already had my meal today, or I'd have taken her just now." Val shivered. "I'm so weak willed

11

at times."

Sarah walked up the stairs, leading the way, completely unaware of the turmoil within the slight stranger who followed her, unaware that Val was far from being what she seemed, a well-dressed, attractive young woman with auburn hair and dark green eyes.

Val noticed a heavy medicinal smell in the air as they came up the marble stairs, faintly on the huge second floor landing, then stronger and stronger as they rose to the third floor. It was a mixture of herbs in a chemical base. The only ingredient Val could identify was wormwood. Its bitter astringent vapor masked whatever else was in the air. The odor assailed her nostrils, not unpleasantly, but it went through her like wind in a tree, leaving behind a feeling of relaxation and the sensation of time slowed down.

There were flowers in a vase on the third-floor landing, artificial but nice to look at. They were the first thing that came in view at the top of the stairs and she found herself staring at them with a morbid intensity as though the coral blossoms had some significance in her reason for being there. Reluctantly she pulled her attention away from the flowers.

"Here she is, Poppa," Sarah said and immediately turned, almost bumping into Val on her way back down. "See you later," she called, obviously in a hurry.

Val froze, waiting until Sarah was gone before she looked around the luxuriously panelled office that occupied the landing. When she finally focused her attention on Theo her knees were shaky.

Although he scarcely moved in his chair, Theo had watched her ascent onto the landing with undisguised interest. She was slender, with a willowy elegance that

12

contrasted sharply with Sarah's golden charm. Valan Anderweldt wore a long-sleeved pantsuit of pale blue silk, white kid gloves and the largest pair of dark glasses he'd ever seen. She looked frail, expensive and frightened. He detected a slight tremor in her lower lip as she turned to look at him.

He stood up and extended his hand to her across the desk. She smiled hesitantly as she approached and touched his finger tips. "This may not be easy," he thought, "but it certainly will be pleasant." She was the most exquisite woman he'd ever seen. He found it difficult to believe that she could possibly be what she'd hinted at—what he desperately hoped she was.

Val was aware of the cat-like assuredness of his movements, interpreting it as a sign of strength. She was instantly attracted to him. He was dark-haired and deeply tanned, not what she'd expected from someone with an English surname like James. His dark brown eyes were steady and penetrating. He tried to hold her gaze, but she dropped her head, letting her long lashes shield her eyes from him. She should have been wary, she knew, but standing there in the late afternoon, with the strange odor enveloping her, she felt at ease, and not the least bit thirsty. The only light came from the setting sun, through the windows above the stairs. The alternating streaks of light and dark marched across the steps and flowers but left both of them standing in a pool of partial shadow.

"In your letter," he said, as she settled gracefully into the chair at the end of his desk, "you wrote that you have a serious blood condition that has proven to be very resistant to treatment. I don't believe in vampyrs. You are aware, of course, that I am no longer in active

13

practice. My time is taken up almost entirely by my research and writing. I'm not quite sure what you expect of me." He spread his hands, palms up, on his desk and leaned back. Val smiled; he wasn't rejecting her outright. But the dangerous part was yet to come.

"Perhaps," she began, "if you knew more about the nature of my affliction you'd be interested in studying me. I don't expect or even hope for a cure, doctor. It's knowledge I desire. People like me have been hunted and hounded for centuries. We need help. We know how to control the less attractive symptoms. We're a bit like epileptics or lepers—we can get along without being noticed most of the time, but if we're ever discovered people can't accept us. It's getting harder and harder to hide with all the electronic record keeping. We need secrecy and security. And this Darrell Montana business"—she gestured at the file containing the photographs—"has made matters much more urgent." In fact, I'm scared just being here."

Theo leaned forward and looked at her closely with his knuckles over his mouth, his elbow on the desk and a studious look on his face. "All right. Tell me more."

"Look at me," she said standing up. She pulled off her gloves and jacket and dropped the sunglasses on his desk. "Do I look like a normal, healthy, twenty-year-old woman to you?" She turned completely around, and then put both hands on his desk.

Suddenly she realized that she couldn't smell a thing. The disinfectant had completely stopped up her sinuses, making her voice husky. "Would it surprise you to know that I am nearly seventy years old?" He stared at her and leaned forward, his pupils wide with interest. Val looked away, and sat back down. "It's sometimes called the 'dracula syndrome' or the 'curse of the undead.' I am a vampyr, doctor. It doesn't matter what you believe. I've come to you in desperate need of help. I have to know why I'm the way I am. What is it that makes me a vampyr?''

Theo frowned. "I was rather under the impression that vampyrs can't travel abroad in daylight." There was an obviously sarcastic arch to his left eyebrow. "You don't even have fangs."

"What proof would satisfy you?" she shrugged. "I don't turn into a bat or sleep in a coffin full of dirt from my homeland, if that's what you want. Most of the popular ideas about us are absolutely false. But I am a vampyr. The only thing my system can absorb for nourishment is fresh blood. I must have it."

His face took on a dreamy, faraway look. He sat there absorbed in thought for a long time. She waited.

"And where do you get it?" he asked, suddenly drumming his fingers on the desktop.

"Anywhere I can. If I can stay ahead of my needs, most of the vampyr impulses are easy to control, but if I get too hungry I can't stop myself. The longer I fast, the stronger the urges get, until it's like riding a tiger. You have no idea how incredibly strong my muscles are or how fast I can react. When I'm hungry everything is intensified." She reached out quickly and touched his neck as though to grab it, and just as quickly leaned back at ease in the chair.

He felt her fingers on his neck, as though a fly had momentarily landed there, and saw her enigmatic smile. He was suddenly aware of the power in her fragile-looking body. He was also suddenly aware that he hadn't seen her move.

His reaction was quite gratifying to Val. He jerked back and flushed darkly, then just sat there staring at her for more than a minute. She could almost see the wheels going around in his head. His chin was lowered onto his chest so he had to look up to see her. He looked so virile sitting there thinking about her that she was drawn to him in a way she hadn't felt in years. The chemical odor of the room, the shifting light from the setting sun and the slowness of their conversation all made her feel nearly human; as though she had come home from a long, frightening journey.

"All right," he said finally. "That was impressive. I think there's something here we can look into. What exactly is it you're offering?"

She sighed. He'd accepted her. It had been a lot easier than she'd expected. Now if they could agree on how to work together, she thought, she would have good news for the others.

"I can only offer myself," she said. "I'll answer all your questions and submit to your examinations and any reasonable experiments. All I ask is absolute privacy and freedom. I won't harm anyone and I'll cooperate fully. But if I have to go, I will go. It's my nature."

"Where will you get your blood, then, if you say you won't harm anyone?"

"Blood is blood. Any blood will do. Cattle blood is good, horse is better. There's only one better than human blood though, that's blood from another vampyr. I've tasted vampyr blood once—no one ever tastes it more than once that I know of. I've never even tasted human blood, but I know its smell."

"You can't go around killing a cow every night."

16

"Of course not. I only need about two liters a day. That's nothing to a large animal. It'd probably kill a dog or child or even a weak adult. When we're hungry, it's easy to forget to stop. That's why only very rarely will a vampyr take blood from a person."

"The stockyards."

"What?"

"I can arrange to have fresh blood sent up from the stockyards. No problem. We often do it for serum studies." He nodded his head slowly. "Tomorrow, it's too late for today. How long will it keep and be fresh enough for you?"

"Refrigerated, about three days." Relief flooded through her. The whole thing was falling together far more easily than she'd anticipated.

"You'll be our house guest?" He stood up and came around the other end of the desk. "It could be important to have you here; and much more convenient."

"You'd ask a blood-sucking vampyr to live with you and your family?" she smiled.

He laughed. "If that's all you wanted, it would already be too late." He snapped on the light over the stairwell. They had been standing in the dark. She hadn't noticed that he'd been unable to see her for some time, but his hand had groped for the switch.

"Would you like to stay tonight?" he asked, concerned that she'd change her mind. Just knowing that she was there, real and not another hopeless dream gave him energy he hadn't known in over a year. He didn't want to lose her.

"I have things to do," she said, shaking her head. "My luggage is at the motel. It's been a very long trip for me. I've gambled a lot to come here. Don't worry, Dr. James; I'll be back tomorrow, at about the same time."

"Perhaps dinner before you leave? The housekeeper can set an extra place."

It was her turn to laugh. "Thank you, but I think not. Perhaps it would be wiser instead if you considered what you're going to tell her and your daughter about me. I'll be as unobtrusive as possible, but there's no way to keep them from noticing that the latest house guest is peculiar, to say the least."

He smiled, a gorgeous smile, perfect teeth, tiny wrinkles around his eyes, but he came a little too close as they started down to the first floor and she started to tremble. His man-smell was warm and salty on her nostrils. She held the railing until he was well past.

"Doctor, what is it that makes the third floor smell the way it does?"

He glanced back at her, standing above him on the stairs. "Just a strong disinfectant we use in the lab. Why? Does it bother you?"

"No, on the contrary. It's the first substance in fifty years that has ever acted like a tranquilizer on me. May I suggest that you keep plenty of it around whenever we have to work closely together." She held her breath and brushed past him and on out of the house; fast: vampyr-style.

Theo stood on the steps halfway down to the first floor and gripped the railing in astonishment. Valan Anderweldt had vanished so quickly that he wasn't really aware that she'd gone until after the door clicked closed behind her.

"Incredible!" he whispered, elation bursting inside

18

his chest. "An-honest-to-God vampire."

He went back upstairs, through his office on the landing and into the lab beyond it. He checked the refrigerator, took a single vial from a honeycombed box which was barely half full, and expertly gave himself an injection. The medicine was going down faster than usual, he noted. He dropped the used syringe and its plastic wrapper into the wastebasket.

On the other side of the lab was a modern treatment room. He walked through it on the way back to his office, and checked briefly to make sure everything was in place. When finished, he sat at his desk and stared at the walnut wainscotting with unseeing eyes. There was so much to do and so little time. He glanced down, noticed the manila folders still lying on the shiny desktop and put them carefully back into their places in the file drawer.

"Damn," he said out loud. The end was approaching so quickly. His lips tightened in determination as he rose, clicked off the light and headed down to his bedroom on the second floor. The medicine was already making him drowsy and a bit nauseated.

A sixty-mile loop of four-lane highway encircles the city of San Antonio. Val drove all the way around nearly twice before she got back to the motel, just driving and thinking and still feeling strange. It was more than buying time and safety, she decided. Theo James could very well be the focus and turning point of her life, if he could unravel the secrets of the dracula syndrome.

She spent most of the night recording the day's events in her journal. By dawn she had put her papers away and settled down in the bed. The dead bolt was drawn to seal the door, there was a "Do Not Disturb" sign hanging on the knob outside, and a sealed letter addressed to Salvatore Denoir was waiting to be mailed in the evening.

Salvatore Denoir
Chateau Robinet
Rue St. Ambrose, Paris

Dearest Salvatore,
    I have arrived in San Antonio and things are proceeding according to our plan. Doctor James is a fascinating person and has accepted me with open arms. Tell the others that I am optimistic this time. More later about our experiement. The most difficult thing I'll encounter is having to eat with the family.
    I have rented a postal box: 14 Costa Station, San Antonio, TX. Let me know how you are progressing with Le Guignol. I am interested in finding out how hypnosis affects a vampyr.

Love, Valerie

Saturday, April 5
It was raining. The soft, incessant drumming of the water on the roof made Val nervous. She lay on the rumpled sheets unable to sleep, even though it was nearly noon. The maid had awakened her an hour earlier, ignoring the "Do Not Disturb" sign and banging away at the door until Val got up and let her in.

Val had felt like a harpy; nightgown all rumpled, robe half on, hair disheveled. The daylight had made her squint uncomfortably even though the sky was completely overcast. The maid was ugly, ill kempt and ignorant. "Can't you read?" Val had said, tapping on the sign. "Go away!" The woman had left grumbling.

Now, suddenly, Val felt very much alone. There were no reports or even rumors of vampyrs in the area and only a slight chance of rogues. She shuddered, wishing she hadn't come alone to find the cure for the incurable. She was hungry for company, not for a man. She was more in the mood to be with a woman; one like her close friend, Claire. "We'd talk," Val thought, "and comb each other's hair, and perhaps lie in bed and caress each other's bodies." Val smiled and sprawled out on the bed, letting her robe fall loose. Her skin was milky white with touches of pale blue where the veins were close to the surface. She ran her hands gently over her body.

She had lived long enough to learn that there were many kinds of love and many kinds of pleasure; she was too intelligent to deny something that was natural throughout the entire range of the animal kingdom just because someone, long ago, was ashamed of his perfectly normal sensual nature. She cupped her fingers over her breasts and sighed as she caressed herself.

Doctor James intruded on her thoughts—his smooth tan hands and expressive lips. It was strange, she felt, to think that way about a human who would touch her more than any other had ever dared, and in a way so different from the ways of love. She hoped he would find, hidden in her body, the causes of the dracula syndrome and maybe even a cure. And, perhaps, something more. She rolled over, bored with daydreaming but unable to sleep.

She glanced at her cooler, a gift from Salvatore. It ran on household or twelve-volt current. In one compartment, it could freeze a block of ice overnight that would last for two days away from electricity. The other side had a six-liter capacity. She took the cooler everywhere she went.

She sat up and pulled the robe together over her breasts "My fingers are cold," she said, talking to herself just to hear a voice.

She recalled having heard about a girl, May or Mary —she didn't remember the name—back in the thirties. The girl had a craving for blood that drove her and haunted her. She thought she was a vampyr and damned. She'd put herself into the care of physicians and had died within a year. It was pernicious anemia. Her tormented body was hungering for vitamins, not the souls of men. Val felt a sudden compassion for the long-dead girl, understanding the terror she must have felt, the anxiety and doubts on the day she gave herself over to the healers.

Rain was coming down harder outside, hitting the walkway cover with thunderous force as Val got up and headed for the shower. Her mind was filled with so many conflicting thoughts that she knew she would have to face a mirror.

She had felt secure until Darrell got killed. The vampyrs had found places to hide, things to do, paths to follow. Darrell Montana changed that. "Damn him! He brought destruction down on all of us," she thought. "Oh, Robin, we don't deserve it." She dropped the robe on the edge of the sink, stepped into the shower stall, turned the hot water on, and let the steam roll up around her body before adding the cold.

There was a large mirror in the bedroom. She would stand there and let herself be sucked into her own eyes;

22

then she would find peace. She had done that many times before, thankful that the laws of physics didn't bend for vampyrs. Light rays came and went, reflecting and coursing their straight paths, for vampyrs as well as normal beings. It was the one thing she had clung to in all her years as a vampyr that convinced her that the myths were wrong, all wrong.

Robin had told her, in the first year of their long-ago life together, that the dracula syndrome was an incurable disease, nothing more. She believed him; she could never accept the idea that vampyrs were damned because of their peculiar diet and nocturnal tendencies. She had freely gone with Robin in the vampyr way. "I may be damned for loving him that much," she mused, "but there were a lot of vampyrs who had no choice."

She turned off the water and stepped out of the shower, grabbing a towel as she went. She left a trail of water on the floor as she walked to the dresser, wrapping the too small rectangle of terrycloth around her waist. She stood squarely in front of the mirror and stared into the image of her own dark green eyes, losing herself in the swirling emerald light radiating from the pupils.

Val had become a vampyr when Robin bent her head to drink vampyr blood flowing from his own wrist. With that act she passed beyond mere humankind. Although there was a powerful lust in the heart of every vampyr for human blood, she had told Dr. James the truth; she had never touched it. She had walked proudly through the years, gaining strength from her self-denial.

Claire's most recent mate, Darrell Montana, was the latest victim of his uncontrolled passions. He'd been so sure of his power that he'd drained a Hollywood starlet, letting her die of dehydration and blood loss. Then the police had come to question him, accompanied by a self-styled "vampire hunter," a member of an L.A. group committed to the idea that vampires existed. Darrell had erred; he'd attacked one of the policemen. The policeman fired four rounds at Darrell's heart. Darrell might have recovered if he'd played the part of a helpless victim, but he had lost his control, writhing, hissing and snarling.

The vampire-hunter had driven a wooden stake into one of the bullet holes. Darrell died, and the damage was done—people were once again aware of the ones who walked in the shadows of night, among humans, yet set forever apart.

Val thought of Claire, beautiful Claire, with ivory skin and a Botticelli face. Robin had told Val she was the lovelier of the two, but Val had never believed him. "No one," she'd told him, "with ordinary chestnut hair, hazel eyes, and freckles is going to be a raving beauty, no matter what her lover says."

He'd laughed at her.

She wished he was with her. She wished he were still alive.

She moved away from the mirror and looked out the window, pulling the heavy drape back a few inches. The rain was still coming down, but not quite so hard. "It'll clear off by this evening," she thought, and went back into the bedroom, to her suitcase. She dressed and straightened the room slowly, taking her time and wishing she could be anywhere else. Even Arthur's made-over bordello in New Orleans would be preferable to a thin-walled motel room in San Antonio in the rain.

"Thanks, Doc." The young man took the twenty from Theo, folded it in half and shoved it unceremoniously into his jeans pocket. "I'll be back Tuesday and Friday."

"Fine, I appreciate it." Theo nodded curtly and offered his hand. The young man, a premed student in need of an extra sixty dollars a week, had agreed to deliver six liters of fresh cattle blood from the stock-yards three times a week. He was sandy-haired, grey-eyed, and wore a T-shirt that said "Nowhere but Texas." A round snuff can was trying to escape from a hole in his hip pocket. He shook Theo's hand warmly and headed downstairs, moving soundlessly on sneakered feet.

"What was all that about?" Sarah asked. She was sprawled casually in the chair by his desk, waiting to talk to her father.

"Some blood studies I want to do."

"Oh."

"Did you have a nice time last night?"

"Sure. We went to a movie." Sarah pushed a thick lock of hair out of her eyes. "Did you have a nice time last night?"

Theo sat down at his desk and gave his daughter a quizzical look. "Why, yes, as a matter of fact. Miss Anderweldt is a fascinating person, beautiful, too."

"Stuckup and stiff as a board, I'd say. You really think she's beautiful, Poppa?" Sarah stuck her lower lip out.

"Uh-hum." Theo let a smile tug at the corners of his mouth. He realized that Sarah was unpleasantly piqued to discover that her monastic father could even notice a woman, let alone admit it.

"Are you kidding?"

"Nope. And I hope you can get used to her. She'll be staying here with us for a while."

"What?" Sarah sat up straight.

"That's right, as a patient."

"You've got to be kidding! It'll be too much work for you."

He shrugged and spoke in a flat monotone that invited no arguments. "It's something I have to do."

Sarah sighed in exasperation. "Well, maybe she'll be more interesting to talk to than Mrs. Mac." She frowned. "I don't like it."

Theo curled his fingers over the armrests on his chair. "You will make a special effort to make her feel at home?"

"Sure, Poppa. I'll try, but what will the neighbors think? You and a strange woman living in the same house." Sarah's frown deepened. She stared at a spot on the wall near the head of the stairs.

"Do you really care what they think?"

"Yes, I really care. And, it isn't fair of you to invite her to stay without asking me first! And it isn't fair that you spend all your time up here working instead of taking care of yourself, instead of—"

She stopped suddenly. He knew intuitively what she had almost said—"instead of spending time with me before it's too late."

"Sarah, sweetheart," he spoke sharply, almost harshly. "That's the way it's going to be." He couldn't tell her about the decreasing effectiveness of the chemotherapy or the feeling he had that the end was closing in. Most of all, he couldn't tell her of this, his most desperate gamble with life, or why Valan Anderweldt was so important.

"Oh, Poppa," she cried out, jumping up from the chair. "You just don't understand!" She headed for the stairs and started down. "You just don't care!"

He started to rise, then leaned back and stared at the ink-stained blotter covering the center of the desk. "I love you, Poppa. XXX Sarah," was written in the upper right-hand corner in tiny script. The blotter was frayed and torn along the bottom. He'd kept it there long after it should have been replaced, just to see the words written in her spidery, childish hand.

It would have been simple to tell her everything: about his illness, about Valan Anderweldt, about the fear of dying that gnawed inside his guts. He could not do it. He wanted to protect her from as much worry as he could. "It must be nice," he thought, "to be a vampyr with no worries except where your next meal is coming from—to live forever."

He glanced at the clock on the corner of the desk. A quarter to six. The clock, a small brass globe set on a chunk of marble, always ran five minutes slow. Christine, his late wife, had given it to him on her last Christmas—only a few days before she died in the automobile accident. Sarah had been three that Christmas. Christine had set the hands back five minutes, complaining that he expected too much of her. "Promptness," she'd said, "is the curse of the working class."

Valan Anderweldt wasn't of the working class, but Theo fervently hoped she'd be prompt. He got up, walked to the window overlooking the driveway and stood there watching. At last Val's immaculate light blue car swung in from the winding road.

An old man came into view, walking along the side of the road, just as Val parked the car. It was Pop Warren, the old wino who lived in the toolshed of the house across the street and did odd jobs around the neighborhood. As Val stepped out of the car, the old man bobbed his head with interest and headed her way.

The auburn-haired woman stood frozen, yet poised for instant motion, as the wino shuffled toward her. She was impeccably dressed in a dove-grey pantsuit, beige shoes and matching gloves and bag. Theo thought she looked exactly like a high-fashion model. Only her head moved, turning with deliberate precision as she watched Pop Warren approach.

When he was less than six feet away, rounding the front of the car, she took one step back and tossed her head. The old wino came a little closer and stopped with his hand outstretched. Asking for a handout, Theo decided.

Valan reached up and pushed her sunglasses onto her forehead, as if to see better. The old man's face contorted with horror. He shrank back, mouthing a silent scream, turned and shuffled away, breaking into a run when he reached the downhill part of the road. Valan stepped forward, hesitated, glanced up at Theo's window, looked back once at the old man's retreating form, shrugged, and started towards the front door.

She dodged the small puddles left by the rain without looking down, walking with a slightly undulating motion, her toes pointing slightly outward. He found the combination of her gracefully swaying body and her awkward feet highly sensual to watch, and vaguely reminiscent of a feminine fragility that was fashionable long ago.

Chapter II

The packet of photographs and clippings was lying on Dr. James' desk when Val reached his office and sat down. She recognized it; it was the set she had sent him. Theo pushed it across his desk. She hesitated before touching the papers.

"Did you know Darrell Montana personally?" Theo asked gently.

Val was so reluctant to talk about Darrell that she started to push herself up from the chair, to leave. Theo sensed her unease and lifted his hand, a gesture she realized was a request to wait rather than a command. She settled back.

"Take your time. We'll talk when you're ready." Outside the sky darkened and the rain started again. Val didn't believe in omens, so she took the packet.

The first pictures were of Darrell; one of him defying the police with blood from at least one bullet wound over his heart, one with him lying on his back snarling, with blood all over, and a third with him dead and the stake through his heart. It was in complete contradiction to the newspaper clipping from the *Los Angeles Times*.

DERANGED MURDERER
KILLED IN FREAK ACCIDENT

Darrell Montana, well-known local nightclub owner, sought by police for questioning following the bizarre sex slaying of Kitty Laime, was accidentally impaled on a wooden stake at the Harris Bros. Lumberyard while attempting to evade the police. Witnesses said Montana fell into an open gravel pit onto the stake during a shootout with police. Montana's wife, Claire, was incapable of issuing a statement but said her husband had been acting strangely for some time.

Miss Laime's strangely mutilated body was found at a local motel, in a room registered to Montana.

The final picture was of Kitty Laime full length on her deathbed in the motel. She was nearly nude with her dressing gown open and exposing all her much filmed charm. She looked very relaxed, as though she'd fallen into a drunken stupor. The second showed her head and neck with her wavy blond hair pulled back to expose a small slash on her neck just over the carotid artery. She had a peaceful and satisfied expression on her face.

"That's a typical vampyr mark," Val said. "She died content."

The other clippings described Kitty Laime's short but spectacular career in the porno film industry and some overdramatized accounts of her "brutal" slaying by a deranged sex maniac. "Knowing Darrell," Val mused out loud, "that was an accurate description. He was completely crazy." She slid the whole stack of pictures back across the desk. "We all knew it, but there wasn't anything we could do. What's more curious is that we're

30

all not psychotic. Being a vampyr puts us under a lot of pressure." Val glanced up and shrugged. The doctor was listening carefully. His thoughtful expression seemed to indicate that he was sympathetic to her.

"Besides," Val continued, "she was begging for it. Just look at the picture. It's the ultimate high, making love to Dracula."

He frowned at her last remark, not knowing whether to take her seriously or whether she was being flippant. He hoped she was joking, because somewhere deep inside he was wondering what it would be like to have her; what dangers, what excitement waited for her lover. Then, for no reason at all, he thought of the black widow spider, who waits, irresistible to the male of her species, devouring him after the consummation.

"Suppose," he said, "you tell me the real reason you came to me. This is interesting," he tapped the packet of pictures with his fingertip, "but hardly convincing. You wouldn't put yourself in such a risky position just because this man got killed. You are quite wealthy?"

She nodded. There was a tiny curve upward on one side of her mouth, as though she was trying to suppress a smile. "Money can't buy everything." She shifted her position slightly and fluttered her eyelashes. "Would you believe I'm afraid of the dark?"

He chuckled. "A vampyr afraid of the dark?"

"Actually," she said, "you'd be surprised at the number of public officials who wouldn't dream of taking a bribe. Keeping ahead of the authorities, ahead of hunters like the ones who killed Darrell, trying to control our beasts, and even offering some of our gifts to humankind: don't you think these are reasons enough?"

He nodded, unconvinced by any of the reasons she'd given, but nagged by a feeling that the real reason was somewhere in what she'd said.

"We can start with the tests this evening. Is that all right?"

"Socially, yes. But if someone is hanging around I might have to go hungry too long. Can we manage that?" She realized with a rush of pleasure that he was really trying to help. Whether it was just Dr. James' tableside manner or the strong and pervasive odor of the disinfectant, she wasn't sure. It was eerie that she was able to put herself under this man's protection although she'd known him only one day.

"Remember," she said, "that there are two kinds of vampires, the Hollywood vampires who dress in black capes and go around killing people, and real vampyrs. I am not what people believe a vampire to be. I am a vampyr." She finished forcefully, an elbow resting on the edge of his desk. "I want to outwit mankind, throw them off the vampyr scent, to gain a little more time for my vampyr companions, to let them vanish completely into the fabric of society. A little more time, a little more money, a few more vampyrs in influential positions and the likes of Darrell's murderers will never be able to touch us. It won't be easy, I know, but I want to try."

"I think I can handle it, Doctor. There have been sticky situations before, and I've managed."

He nodded. She sensed that he was pleased. "I'm at the Med School days until three-thirty. We'll start working about five and run until nine or ten. That'll give you privacy in the lab. I want to start with blood, serum, and tissue studies, a complete physical,

32

metabolic rates, things like that. We'll start by finding out the ways in which you differ from normal humans, work on some causative factors, then try some treatments. We'll set things up as we go. A lot of the equipment will come from the school on loan, and we'll take it as we get it.''

Claire Montana
Chateau Robinet
Rue St. Ambrose, Paris

Dear Claire, I hope this will reach you quickly. Something wonderful is happening here in San Antonio. Dr. James has agreed to help us and seems incredibly enthusiastic. I can hardly wait until he's able to produce results. We will, of course, reward him beyond his wildest expectations, if he is successful.

Tell Salvatore not to worry. There is no way we will repeat the errors we made with Lui Renoit. Dr. James will never be a vampyr unless he is successful.

Ciao, Valerie

Sunday, April 6

By midnight Val felt like a pincushion. Her new room didn't have a desk, just the double bed, a dresser, one large comfortable chair, and a vanity with a hard wooden stool. She sat crosslegged on the bed and tried to work on her correspondence, spreading the papers all over the brocade bedspread. But the evening in the examination room had been enough to give her serious doubts about what she'd let herself in for, and she found it difficult to concentrate.

The tissue samples were easily the most painful thing that had ever happened to her. None of the human anesthetics worked in her system, and the bone marrow extractions still ached, even though the skin over the punctures had sealed and was turning pink already. She almost quit after the first one. Only the thought of Sarah in the sitting room directly below the examination room kept Val from screaming. And only the doctor's intense professionalism kept her from quitting.

The examining table was long and narrow on chromed legs and covered with black vinyl. It reminded her of a medieval instrument of torture. The room, although narrow and not very large, was set up with modern equipment. Cabinets lined the walls and there was a waist-high counter all along one side, everything white and chrome except the table. Val hadn't expected to find a setup like that in a private residence.

Theo sensed her surprise when he opened the door to usher her in. "When I gave up my downtown office years ago, I had my personal equipment put in here. It comes in handy now and then."

"Yes, I suppose it does." Val kicked off her shoes and stepped on the scales that stood by the door. "One hundred and thirty-two pounds and holding," she said.

"Your weight stays pretty constant?"

"Yes, except for the long sleeps, then it drops. I've been a hundred and thirty for over forty years."

"And before that?"

"I gained nearly twenty pounds the first ten years. I was a skinny kid." She stood still while he measured her height.

"Five foot six," he muttered while he wrote the information onto a manila-colored chart. "No way," he shook his head and came over to the scales. "Let me see that." He fiddled with the riders, the little weights that slide across the bar at the top of the scale, but when

34

he was finished she still weighed one hundred and thirty-two pounds. Then he pinched the back of her arm, not hard, just squeezing a bit of flesh.

"What are you doing?" Her puzzlement was equal to his. Obviously he'd found something about her weight that was unusual.

"Skinfold test. It's an indication of the amount of fat a person has. You weigh about twenty pounds more than someone your height and build should weigh."

"I'm not fat."

"That's the problem. Where do you put it? You're just . . . ." He paused, thinking. "Can you swim?"

"Barely," she replied. "And badly. When I was a kid we swam a lot. I can't any more. All of us have trouble. We have to thrash around just to keep from going down. It's usually easier to sink to the bottom and walk out."

"That's it," he straightened up and smiled. "Your density is all off. Normal people float without even trying.

"It seems I've read something about vampyrs being unable to cross flowing water unaided?" He arched his eyebrows.

"Yes, that's a fairly common supposition about us, but as usual it's not true. It's just difficult; not impossible."

"What if," he asked, "the vampyr didn't know how to swim or was afraid of the water? Wouldn't he stand and fight?"

"Probably, and get killed in the process. There are a lot of human beings who can't force themselves into deep water."

"Exactly." He started writing another note on the

35

chart. "Strange that so often those old legends have some basis in fact."

"Twisted truth. Do you have a secure place to put those records?"

"A concealed safe out in the hall. It's guaranteed to be burglarproof." He put the chart on the counter. "Now, up on the table."

That's when the hurting began.

Val was terrified to lie barechested and vulnerable in front of a strange man, even if it was for scientific purposes. She couldn't breathe when that long and sharp instrument went into her sternum. It wasn't the pain; the pain was almost bearable. It was something deep in the back of her brain, the primitive survival part. She kept picturing the needle going in deeper and deeper until it pierced her heart. She knew it was stainless steel, but the beast within her kept crying: silver, silver! "That's just dumb," she scolded herself. "None of us has been done in by a silver bullet in centuries."

Theo poked his head through his bedroom doorway and looked down the darkened hall. Sarah's room was dark, but Val's light was still on; a narrow shaft leaked out beneath the door. He wondered whether she was restless. She'd been so quiet and controlled during the tests; he'd found himself frowning whenever he noticed himself staring at the marble perfection of her body.

The knowledge that she was inhuman and seventy years old was irreconcilable with her incredibly youthful appearance and gentle manner. The physiological differences were there: the unusual density, the blood anomalies, and the ability to move so fast she seemed to

36

vanish; all were outside any normal human parameters. They provided mute proof that she was different. And she did drink the blood—privately, quietly, alone in the lab.

She wore cotton shirts and blue jeans around the house and he thought she looked as elegant in them as she had in the designer clothes she left hanging in the closet. All she would have to do, he knew, was give him the slightest encouragement; then, vampyr or not, he would touch her as deeply as he could.

Fear was involved, but it was a fear of something far worse than a vampyr's bite.

As he undressed for bed he wondered whether Christine would approve of what he was trying to do, decided she wouldn't and turned off the overhead light. Christine had seldom approved anything he did, unless it was her idea, or unless it involved giving her money to spend. Still, he'd loved Chris and understood her. With Valan it was different. She was an enigma, an unknown except for one thing. Theo was quite sure Valan had access to unlimited money. If Valan could be bought, the price would not be reckoned with cash.

Monday, April 7

Monday's tests were repeats of Sunday's, without the bone marrow extractions. They watched each other closely, the vampyr and the doctor. He was the insatiable scientist, with a bit of frenzy coming through his cool detachment every once in a while. He was in a hurry. But it didn't show in his work, only in a hint of tightness around his mouth and a darkness in the skin just beneath his eyes. Val assumed he hadn't slept well.

She wanted to ask him why he had embraced the idea

of accepting her as a patient so easily, but she felt it was obvious in the way he fussed around her that it was the mystery, the challenge that drove him. There was tension in the air around him; not anxiety, but a sharp sense of vitality and awareness. She liked it and was growing to like the feeling of lethargy the airborne antiseptic scent brought to her. "It must be much the same for people who use drugs habitually," she thought.

When he was working he was silent, withdrawn, and Val sat crosslegged in the corner on the floor and watched him. There was a friendly silence, one that grew naturally between them.

"Dr. James," Val asked when curiosity finally overcame her, "were you expecting me when I came to you?"

"Of course. You had an appointment."

"No, I mean me, and what I am." He put down the box he was transferring from the counter to the shelf and turned to look at her.

"In a way, yes." He slid his hands into the pockets of his lab jacket then shook his head. "I didn't actually believe that vampyrs really existed before you brought it to my attention rather forcefully. It isn't something educated people are prepared to believe. But, yes, there's a bit of the romantic in me. I wanted to see for myself. I was looking forward to it."

"And you weren't afraid?"

"You're the most incredible creature I've ever met; incredibly beautiful, healthy, more alive than anyone I know." He pulled his hand from his pocket and waved it with the fingers widespread, as though he was describing a landscape panorama. "I find it hard to express. I am attracted to you as an extremely desirable woman. But, I hesitate to touch you. I don't know . . . ."

"What to expect?" She finished his sentence. "You're right, you know. With us it's hard to know what to expect. You've touched me and nothing has happened. But the next time, a different way, a different context, who knows?" She shrugged.

"There are secrets locked in your body that I have to discover and disclose." Suddenly he was the professional again. Something in what she'd said touched a nerve in him. She wondered what it was.

"And that knowledge is worth any risk?"

"Yes," he said with finality. He turned back to the countertop and finished tidying up, then met her at the door. He asked, "Why did you come to me?"

"Curiosity, hope." She paused while he flicked off the lab lights and closed the door. "The desire to meet someone like you and not have to worry about my beast overcoming me if we were to kiss."

She left him standing there on the landing and went down the stairs, vampyr-fast, like a hummingbird. She didn't pause until the door to her bedroom slammed tightly closed behind her.

"I think we said too much tonight," she thought, leaning against her closed door. It wouldn't do to seduce the good doctor. She knew from past experience that if she let herself get carried away, if she let him look deeply into her eyes, he would lose the distant objectivity, the scientific detachment that was absolutely necessary for success.

They'd tried before. Claire and Arthur had enlisted the aid of Lui Renoit, a half French, and half Indo-

Chinese. Lui had been a fine doctor, a brilliant research scientist; until Claire, beautiful Claire, couldn't restrain herself. Val paced across the room to the balconied window. Luie Renoit, as a vampyr, was barely one cut above a rogue. He was, as far as Val knew, in India, where he ran a sterilization clinic and informal blood bank. What a waste. She looked out the window at the dark valley below and promised herself that, whatever else happened, that wouldn't happen to Theo. If he ever became a vampyr it would be after his research was successful.

Tuesday, April 8

When the tests were over for the evening, they sat for a long time in the office. Sarah had gone to bed, and the housekeeper was in her quarters watching television. The mindless sound emanating from it occasionally filtered upstairs.

"Where did it start?" Theo said suddenly.

In a way Val had been expecting it, the desire to know more about vampyrs, and she'd decided to tell him as much as possible without endangering any of the group. So she nodded and curled up in the chair.

"Most of the old ones think that the syndrome started in China before recorded history."

"China? What about Count Dracula and Transylvania?"

"That's pure fiction. No truth to it at all. The original person that Count Dracula is based on was a madman named Vlad Teppes or Vlad the Impaler. He was blood-thirsty and completely insane, but he wasn't a true vampyr."

"What about the Chinese?"

"The Chinese used to bury their dead in stone crypts above ground, or in caves. The culture required the living to honor their dead ancestors with gifts and food, so the cemeteries were fairly nice places, probably better than the homes of most of the poor people. Evidently the earliest vampyrs were driven out of their villages and took up residence in the caves and crypts. They were private, dry in the rainy seasons, and better protection in the winter than the thatched huts every one else had.

"Even though they weren't dead at all, the idea got started that they were walking dead. I would suspect that back then that was enough to keep people away."

"And?" He was leaning forward over the desk, resting on both elbows, his white lab jacket swinging open.

"Vampyrism spread south into India and north across Russia to Europe. Dutch colonists brought it to America. There was more truth than fiction in the legend of Rip Van Winkle."

"Really, now," he asked. "How could a vampyr survive a long journey in a sailing vessel without killing everyone on board?"

"Estivation."

"Huh! I haven't heard that word used in years. Not since my first biology course in undergrad school."

"Estivation, summer sleep. We don't hibernate unless the temperature is well controlled. The energy requirements are too great. But it's handy for emergencies or long voyages."

"Can you really go twenty years, like Rip Van Winkle?"

"The longest sleep I know of personally lasted just over a year. There are stories of others that have gone longer, but it's quite possible for us to starve to death."

41

"Last night you said something that intrigued me. You referred to something as 'your beast.' What did you mean?"

"Everyone has a beast. Some are small and insignificant. Some are huge and dominate completely. It's whatever there is inside a person that makes him act irrationally. I can't explain it much better than that, except to say that with us the beasts are separate and always aware, waiting for a chance to take over and use the powers all vampyrs have. It's like having two souls in one body, one hopefully good and one with seriously magnified flaws or even hopelessly malignant. Sometimes it's hard to keep the beast under control. When there is a lot of stress and the real personality is distracted, the beast tries to take over. It happens to humans, too. For example, when a man kills his wife in a jealous rage, and can't believe what he's done when it's all over. With us it's more immediate, closer to the surface. That's why usually only the well-adjusted person can make it as a vampyr."

"Are your beasts all alike?"

She shook her head. "They take many forms. Mine is a hungry beast. I don't withstand starvation as well as a lot of vampyrs. If I miss a meal, it starts to take over within hours. There's nothing I can do about it except get blood quickly. I think it's because I was always a bit hungry as a child. I am afraid of the dark, but my beast loves it."

"Fascinating," he said. And that was the last thing he said for a long time. The lean strong fingers of his neatly sculpted hands played with a pencil stub, absently rolling it back and forth on the bare desktop. It was long after midnight before they retired to their separate rooms.

Wednesday, April 9

Salvatore Denoir
Chateau Robinet
Rue St. Ambrose, Paris

Dearest Salvatore,

Results seem a long way off. Theo, I call him that now, says the tests are going well, but slowly. There are lots of abnormalities in the blood and tissues—nothing definite yet. He seems far more dedicated and intelligent than Lui ever was. There is much hope, I think.

We worked on blood pressure this evening. I tried to explain how it's done but he just kept shaking his head. "It's not possible," he muttered over and over. It was amusing to drop my blood pressure to nothing and stop my heart, then sit there talking to him as if nothing interesting was happening. He fussed around, whacking the gauge and checking everything over and over. His brow wrinkled engagingly; he'd stand there rocking back and forth on his heels with his hands in his hip pockets and his jacket all wrinkled up.

His features are regular, well proportioned in a classical way. He shows emotion easily when we are alone, but he often wears a guarded mask in front of others. I like him very much. Perhaps "like" is not a strong enough word. He is sincere and dedicated to his work. During the day he handles leukemia patients at the university. The team he heads has made remarkable progress.

Perhaps you will have an opportunity to meet him someday. I think you'd like him very much. He would make a good vampyr. He is very intense and concentrates closely when conversing with anyone. At first I thought he was trying to hypnotize me, the way he frowns and stares, but it is just his way of giving his undivided attention. He is the same with his daughter, Sarah. I don't look into his eyes more than a single

43

glance at a time. This puzzles him. But he doesn't say anything about it. He waits, I think, for me to tell him.

Give my regards to the others. Tell them I miss them all and will come to visit soon. It's been a long five years since I've seen Paris and we've been together.

Ciao, Valerie

Some day, she thought as she folded the thin sheets of paper, perhaps she would look into his eyes. Then they would know the truth about each other. It was a difficult thing to do, to open up that way. She had done it so many times before. It was hard, especially if it didn't go well.

She stuffed the letter into an envelope, licked the flap to seal it, and made a wry face as she tasted the glue.

Thursday, April 10

The telephone rang late in the evening when they were just finishing in the lab. Val was still squeezing a lever that measured the strength in her hand. The results came out on a small drum wrapped with graph paper. The zigzag line of her achievements was even and uninteresting. As far as she could see, nothing much was happening; a most boring evening; squeeze and release, squeeze and release for an hour and a half. Except that after the first ten minutes, Theo's eyes had dilated and he had started taking notes. He went to his bookshelf and looked up something. He was totally absorbed in whatever he found. Val sat there watching the line forming its identical and never-handing peaks and valleys.

He answered the telephone when it rang. "For you," he said, half turning her way. They were both a bit surprised.

She shrugged. "Can I stop this?"

He nodded. "That's enough for tonight. You can use the phone on my desk." When she left the lab he was taking the graph paper off the drum, and his fingertips were shaking slightly.

"Hello."

"Valan? This Valan speaking?" It was a black woman's mellow voice, a stranger to her.

"Yes."

"Listen, honey, this phone clean?"

"There's someone on the receiver in the kitchen." Val could tell by the little static hum. "It's probably Mrs. Mac, the housekeeper." They waited silently for a few seconds, the strange dark voice and Val, until whoever was downstairs replaced the receiver.

"You don't know me, Valerie. That's your real name? My name's Pearl. Pearl from L. A., but—I'm living in Chicago now. Got out just in time, too. Lady name of Claire asked me to call you. Some folks are going to bother you, all right."

"You know Claire?"

"We old friends, you might say. Her husband that's dead made me what I is today."

"I see."

"Listen, honey, you got problems."

"Are you a member of the group? Are you organized?"

"You want to know where I'm coming from." She laughed heartily. "What your group do with the likes of me? No, all I got is Claudius. That's why I'm calling. Claudius joined that L.A. club, the vampire hunters. Ain't that something?"

"Is he a vampyr?"

"Oh yes, and a professor out there too. He's going to

45

call you as soon's he can. There's something you got to know about Darrell Montana's address book."

"Yes." Val said with a sinking feeling.

"It's gone. And three people whose names were probably in it are dead, his friends."

A chill ran through Val. "Vampyrs?"

"No, just folks, made to look like accidents. We got to get that book back. Claudius is trying to find it. You be careful down there, now, you hear?"

"Yes, of course," Val replied. "Thanks for calling. I'll be looking out."

"What was all that about?" Theo asked from the doorway of the lab as she hung up the phone.

"Just a friend from Chicago calling to see if I'm still OK."

"And?"

"Nothing much." Val frowned. "I'd like to stop for tonight." She found it too difficult to concentrate on both the work and Pearl's message. "How could Darrell have been such a fool?" she thought.

Chapter III

Friday, April 11

The evening session in the windowless lab seemed to last forever. The incessant hum of the air conditioner in the attic just overhead and the brilliant sameness of the fluorescent lights distorted Val's time sense. She was hungry and getting restless. Her body could tell, even though her mind was uncertain, that it was past her usual mealtime. They had been doing saliva samples, and she was thankful that she didn't have to talk much. It gave her an opportunity to look around and examine the lab.

It was larger than the examining room and had wide spaces around the tables. Most of the counter space was clear. There were a few trays with wire racks full of small bottles, an incubator, and a few other pieces of machinery Val still didn't recognize. But most of the equipment was kept neatly stored in cabinets along the wall.

All she had to do was sit with a U-tube hanging out of her mouth while a suction machine collected the saliva. Her mouth was dry, so it took a long time.

"It's worse than going to the dentist," she mumbled, "and I haven't done that in sixty years." Finally, she pulled the tube out of her mouth. The collecting jar was nearly full of the thick liquid.

"Am I finished spitting up?"

Theo looked up from his notes. "For tonight," he said as he took the tubes and disconnected the pump.

"Good," she said, licking her lips. Val was ready, more than ready, for her meal.

"Tell me," he said, looking intently at her, "would a religious symbol bother you? Repel you?"

"The cross? Of course not. That's an old wives' tale." She shrugged. "I suppose it might have bothered some of the vampyrs in medieval times when the power of religious suggestion was a lot greater than now. But none of the others that I know are affected by crosses or holy water or any of that stuff. Garlic is terrible smelling. Don't you think so?"

"Yes."

"But it's not much worse for me than for you. It wouldn't stop a vampyr for a moment, but it might make one want to hold his nose."

"How about silver bullets?" His tone was serious now, and he had turned his back to her. She couldn't see his face. He was busy stacking trays and wiping off the counter.

"It depends on how many and where they hit. We're no more affected by them than lead ones," she replied wondering what he was leading up to. "Why are you so interested all of a sudden in what it takes to do me in?" She moved over and stood behind him, just a few feet away. For a moment her trust in him wavered.

"Valan," he said in an odd tone of voice. She

48

shivered from it as he turned around and took hold of her shoulders. "Valan, I'm not sure I can protect you. You've been quieter since that phone call. I can't help but think something is wrong."

He tried to pull her close to him. She was moved by what he said, but she put her hands on his chest. "Theo, I'm not defenseless. There's a lot you don't know."

Theo shook his head. "I feel responsible for keeping you here, for you, I feel . . . I feel very much for you."

He pulled her hard against him and kissed her lips, hard. His tongue pushed against her clenched teeth. The human smell of his skin flooded her and she felt her blood pressure dropping. Her hands formed fists as they came together and she slipped them around him, under his arms and clung to him almost fainting.

His lips left her mouth and moved across her cheek to her neck and shoulder. She felt the warmth of his arms, the strong beat of his heart, his hardness growing against her. She licked his neck with the tip of her tongue and the taste electrified her. Val hissed as she breathed in, gasping involuntarily. Her upper lip pulled up from her teeth as though it had life of its own. She moved fast, as far from him as she could and backed up against the wall trembling. If there had been windows in the lab, she probably would have gone out one of them. There were tears in her eyes and that gave the room an unreal appearance, all sparkling and wavering with rainbows around the light fixtures.

"Theo," she said, shaking her head, tears starting to run down her cheeks, unchecked. "I'm sorry. I can't help it." She slid down the wall until she was sitting on the floor with her arms around her knees and her head bowed, almost touching them. When she finally looked up as he was standing beside her with his arm out-stretched. He handed her a plastic bag of cow's blood from the refrigerator.

"You haven't eaten today," he said, squatting down next to her. She took the bag and held it loosely in her hand. It seemed dark and strange lying there so cold and fluid, as though the sack itself was a living thing.

"Go away." She knew he wouldn't, even though she told him to. There was something magnetic between them at that moment, almost tangible, binding them together.

"No." He shook his head.

"I don't want you to watch. You promised me privacy."

"We're in this together now," was all he said. And he stayed there on his heels until she was finished. Then he sat beside her and kissed her again, while there was still blood on her lips. He held her there for a long time. She found it to be easier than she expected in the heavy atmosphere of the lab. It was comforting, the warmth of his body, the strength and firmness of his arms. She relaxed and leaned her head against his chest and listen-ed to the sounds of his heart and the blood rushing through his veins.

Saturday, April 12

The late afternoon sun rode brilliantly in the clear sky, making Theo squint as he peered glumly at the valley behind the house. The paved and terraced patio was one of his favorite places to sit and enjoy an after-noon drink. Stately pecan trees in the yard shielded the patio from most of the glare from the sun, but the hill-side below, with its rocky outcroppings and scraggly mesquite trees, was already drying out in anticipation of the coming summer heat.

The nausea was back in full force, eating at him like worms in his gut. He wondered how long he could hold out with another bout in the hospital. He toyed with the prospect of telling Valan and discarded the idea immediately. If she knew how sick he was, she'd leave. He had no illusions that she cared enough about him yet to save his life. It would take time.

He clenched his teeth as he got up and went inside. The whole situation was out of control. No matter what cards he played, he was in grave danger of losing the game, and the stakes were too high to back out now. He felt dizzy. The sickness was coming down hard. He had to get his medication, soon.

The third floor seemed too far away. He made it to his bedroom and slumped limply in the upholstered chair at the side of the bed. His fingers shook as he picked up the phone and gave the house bell one long buzz, the signal for Sarah to answer. He rang twice more before she picked up the receiver and spoke, mumbling her greeting.

"'Lo."

"Sweetheart, go up and get my medication and a syringe. I'm in my room."

"Let me put my sandwich away. You OK?"

"Just hurry, babe."

"Sure, Poppa, gotcha." She replaced the receiver, and within a few minutes he heard her quick steps going by as she ran up to the lab.

He relaxed, letting his head rest on the back of the chair. His eyes were closed when she came in, and he didn't open them until she'd prepared the syringe, carefully squeezing the last air bubble out of the needle.

He unbuttoned his left cuff and pushed the sleeve up.

"Let me do it, Poppa. I'll use your other arm. That left one's a mess," she said. "It has as many needle tracks as a junkie's."

He held out his right arm, passively, and let her push the cuff back and jab him in the forearm. "I didn't feel a thing." He grinned at her.

"I'm an expert." She dropped the used syringe in the wastebasket and pulled the bedspread back. "Lie down."

"Yes, boss," he said and moved to the bed, settling on the sheet with a sigh. "Glad you're here today."

"School's a drag. I'd rather stay home with you and Valan."

"What do you really think about her now?"

"I was really jealous at first, Poppa, but she's neat. We talk sometimes."

"She's not to know I'm sick." Theo felt his eyelids flutter. As usual, the medication was making him drowsy.

"You don't need her, Poppa," Theo heard his daughter say, "as long as you have me."

"Just you and me, babe," he whispered, unable to argue.

"Sure, Poppa. I'll check on you later. Got to eat my sandwich." She left, closing the door gently, and he drifted into an uneasy sleep. The last thing he was aware of was Chris's picture smiling vacuously down from the bureau. He decided to pack it away and concentrate on the living. Just before he drifted off to sleep he saw Sarah's child-wise face in his mind and resolved that, no matter what else happened, he'd never give her up.

There was a new moon, and the night was dark with a rustle and whine in the wind that promised adventure. Small, silver-dark clouds moved quickly, sailing by unseen. Val wanted to be out there, in the unknown, with the things that walked alone in the night.

Theo was sleeping. She could hear his occasional movements as he tossed restlessly in bed. Val was quiet, waiting. She longed to be walking in the night. That was odd, she knew. Usually she was afraid of the dark. She couldn't decide what was making her so uneasy.

Sunday, April 13

Val played sick and slept until lunchtime when Sarah brought her a tray. The girl was smiling, happy.

"We're going for a pizza," she said. "So I can't stay and talk."

"That's nice."

"Just me and some girl friends," Sarah said. "It'll be fun."

She left and Val flushed the sandwiches down the toilet, left some toothmarks on a cookie and went for a walk.

There had already been a hint of the coming summer season in the air, with a wave of heat rising now and then, but mostly the days had been mild, the nights cool and easy for Val to be awake in. Even in the warmth of the afternoons there were breezes coming in her windows. But this afternoon was hot. Even with a large-brimmed hat and dark glasses, Val was uncomfortable long before she reached the air-conditioned haven of the post office. She kept looking for shade. The trees were different from those in the northern forests. They grew spidery and lean, with thin leaves and open spaces skyward.

She found only one letter in her box, written in Salvatore's ornate Florentine script.

Cheri,

Valerie, it sounds too good to be true. I suggest you pry into this doctor's soul as soon as possible. It is not a natural thing for a human to welcome one of us with open arms. Scientific devotion is a worthy motive, but I am not as easily convinced as you seem to be. Please, my dear, be most careful.

I have heard rumors of a new power, Georges, a vampyr from Canada. He waits like an uneasy volcano. I have been told that he is most ambitious.

Potchnick, or le Guignol, as you humorously prefer to call him, has come and gone like the wild creature he is. We had several sessions, where I tried to reduce his murderous tendencies. Only time will tell if our idea, to hypnotize him into gentleness, will succeed. It is a sad thing indeed when a vampyr cannot control himself. But Potchnick is old and learned his manners from a society far more barbaric than ours. He has become quite set in his ways over the centuries. We must be patient and not expect too much.

Corey wishes to communicate with you, and Javier wants backing to relocate into the United States. I have sent them your latest address. Corey has questions about the German gold, whether or not he should sell it. I would advise you to have him keep the gold and use cash for the real estate he wishes to purchase on our behalf. Gold will always be gold. The money of any country is merely paper on its way to ashes.

Ciao, Salvatore

Just after midnight Val stepped out of the shower and stood alertly poised, head tilted, listening for sounds that weren't there. She felt a tension building throughout the house, like the brilliance just before a lightning storm, when the air became charged with excitement. She knew, however, that it was the people within the house who were charged.

She lay down, nude and damp from the shower, on the bed and cradled the back of her head in laced fingers. Her arms were pulled tautly upward and the pulsating beat of her heart drummed placidly in her ears. She dreamed of Robin, his cold sure hands and fiery embraces. There had always been the same brilliance and excitement radiating from him, charging everyone nearby. It was strange, she thought, how the mood of the house made him seem so near.

He'd always stood tall and lean, his skin pale and smooth, unmarred by the sun and weather. He was saturnine and sophisticated, always impeccably dressed and always moving with an air of complete confidence and power. She'd met him at a debutante ball in honor of New York City's finest daughters. Val had been a gate crasher, looking for a wealthy husband. He had been looking for a quick thrill to renew his faded interest in life.

There were dark shadows under his eyes even then, yet he was the most magnificent man she'd ever seen. His eyes were sensual, heavy-lidded, and knowing. He looked untouchable, wealthy beyond measure and it wasn't, as she later found out, an act. He had wealth and power. A word from him in the right places toppled governments.

The mothers of giggling debutantes swarmed around him, offering their daughters like so many gypsies selling pigs. He turned them away with such grace and finesse that Val laughed at him in his pleasant predicament. Then laughed at herself and her ten-cents-on-the-dollar, second-hand black satin gown. It was a designer original, but not designed for Val. Most likely the original owner was dancing in a newer gown that night, somewhere in the ballroom. It fit her perfectly, though, hanging in graceful folds that accentuated her fashionably slender body.

It didn't matter how beautiful she looked, she still felt like an outsider, such an imposter that she was embarrassed even to think of having a glorious man like that. She stood up from the ledge she'd been sitting on and turned to go. That's when he noticed her and their eyes met. It was ten years before she ever left his side. And then it wasn't her idea.

His eyes were blue, but coal black in the depths, and the depths—it was like looking to the end of the universe. They sucked out her soul. He came to her from across the ballroom, from across eternity, and took her hand. Without a word they danced as she had never danced before or since; as though they were already one being. Her feet were not her own. His arms were part of her, holding, caressing, yet as light as mist on her waist.

They went to his home, a tall gothic house, new and splendid. They made love on his fourposter bed with the heavy drapes sealed around them. She knew what he was before the final kiss and offered her neck willingly. She said she would not live without him. So be it.

His lips were delicate, silken, sensual on her neck. She held his head to her neck until her fingers grew cold and slipped away. She felt then that she had been born for that one night of ecstasy; to die on those satin sheets.

She fainted then, from the loss of blood, and her next vision was of him standing by the bed. The heavy drapes were drawn back, and he was bare to the waist. His body was lean and white with faint scar lines running all over his chest. He'd pulled on his trousers and gone downstairs while she'd been unconscious. He held a gleaming kitchen knife in his right hand and as she watched he cut his wrist. As dark blood dripped from the deep slash he dropped the knife and gently forced her mouth open.

She moaned in terror and loathing when he thrust his wrist into her mouth, but she couldn't turn away. He held her head with his other hand. She gagged on the first salty taste, then drank, eagerly. It was finer than the grandest liquer; sweet and irresistible.

The soft pain, the lassitude she'd been fainting from, the shock from the loss of blood, the terror; all vanished. Suddenly she was more alive than she'd ever been—ravenous. She drank until the blood stopped flowing, then licked his slit wrist. He stood over her brooding and silent, smiling his sardonic smile.

"I've given you the gift of eternal life, my love," he said. "It's up to you to pay the price."

She knew she would be with him still but for the fact that he had no longings that no living thing or actual place could satisfy. Not even the power and the riches he'd accumulated could hold him; a discontent of the soul, he had said. He had been dead now for nearly forty years.

She forced herself to relax muscle by muscle, draining the tension from her body. Then she picked up a novel from the bedstand. Reading was good; it kept the incubus of memory away. She read until nearly dawn.

Monday, April 14

"Theo, what was so exciting about that test we did?" They were in the lab, late in the evening, and Theo was getting things put away.

He looked up and shrugged. "Which one?"

"You know," Val continued. "The one where I squeezed a lever and made that endless zigzag graph."

He got the paper out of the file and showed it to her. The up-and-down lines were very nearly even all across the page. Then he did the test himself, silently setting up the apparatus and alternately squeezing and releasing the lever. After a few minutes the valleys and peaks grew shallower, until there was only a flat line traveling across the paper.

"Fatigue," he said. "This is normal for everyone from the very weak to the very strong. No matter what a person's physical condition, the line flattens out within a matter of minutes, due to a buildup of waste products in the tissues. Somehow that doesn't happen to you. Do you ever get tired?"

"Not from work or exercise. Just when I'm sleepy or bored."

"That must be nice," he said. "Never fatigued or ill. It seems like I'm exhausted all the time lately."

"You work too hard; maybe we should slow down."

He shook his head. "Every minute with you is too valuable to waste. You can think in terms of years or even longer. I have patients at the University Hospital who measure their lives in minutes."

"It's hard to argue with a philosophy like that."

Valerie,

Get away from that place as quickly as possible. There is, unfortunately, a possible link between Darrell and you. When I was allowed to collect his personal effects from the police, his pocket address book was missing as were the papers he carried in his wallet. If he had your name or alias in that book you can be sure our enemies will have it.

A friend of mine from Los Angeles with connections there will be contacting you. Please listen to her. She is most reliable.

Have you decided to buy that estate north of Chicago? Salvatore says you haven't made up your mind yet. I have someone in mind to manage it if you are interested.

Ciao, Claire

Claire Montana
Chateau Robinet
Rue St. Ambrose, Paris

Claire,

It isn't possible for me to leave here. We are making wonderful progress, and I am absolutely taken by Theo. We have discovered why vampyrs are unable to swim and it has nothing to do with a curse of St. Christopher as the monk Modesto claims. The next time I say you're dense, it won't be a joke. Vampyrs are heavier than humans in the same way steel is heavier than wood. Steel sinks and wood floats.

It is difficult to rationalize the attraction I feel toward Theo. He is about a head taller than I am, dark-haired with leanly molded features. But beyond his physical handsomeness, he seems to have little in common with the men who have been close to me. Their souls burned with the searing flame of power. When they were kind or gentle it was a conscious thing, beneath which an awesome strength lay thinly buried. Theo is different, Claire. Kindness and gentleness come naturally to him. But he is not a vampyr. That is the greatest difference.

Pearl has been in contact with me, but her friend, Claudius, hasn't. Pearl would be perfect to manage the Chicago estate if that's what you had in mind.

59

Claire, darling, stay away from humans. If you pick any more like Darrell or Lui Renoit, we are going to be in serious trouble.

Ciao, Valerie

Tuesday, April 22

"Have I or have I not been a perfect guest?" Valan asked, pushing her plate toward the center of the dining-room table.

"Still hungry?" Sarah asked. "You can have my pudding. I'm full." She reached across the table and set her dish of butterscotch pudding between Val and her father.

"You've made it seem like a vacation for me, just being here," Theo said. She had been the houseguest exemplar, quiet, unobtrusive and inordinately amusing.

"It's been a busy, fruitful and pleasant time. I'm totally disarmed."

"If you two don't mind, I have homework to do," Sarah said, pushing her chair back with the calves of her legs as she stood up.

"Sure, sweetheart," Theo said as she headed for the hallway.

Mrs. MacMullin bustled in and refilled the coffee cups. "You ate a good dinner tonight, doctor," she said on her way out.

"How long has Mrs. Mac been with you, Theo?"

"Since Chris and I were married. Fifteen years." Theo shook his head. "Seems like yesterday that I stood up at the wedding." He lifted his cup and blew on the dark liquid.

"Is it difficult for you to talk about your wife?"

Theo slumped back in his chair. "It happened so

60

suddenly and so long ago." Theo frowned. "It seems like yesterday."

"What happened?" Val asked, gently prying.

"She died in an auto accident on New Year's Eve."

"There's a lot more to it than that, isn't there?"

"She was beautiful and used to having everything."

"And you let her have anything she wanted, just as you do with Sarah."

Theo nodded. "I loved her so much I never could say 'No.'"

"And as long as she got whatever she wanted, she loved you in return." Val spoke softly.

Theo frowned again and lifted his cup, but before he took a sip, he rested his elbows on the table and supported the cup in front of his chin. "I suppose so. I sort of knew it all along." He drank and set the cup back down.

"Sarah was two that year, and I was just getting my practice going. Money was a little tight. Chris tried to be careful, but she borrowed from her father and ran up a lot of bills anyway. It was hard for her to change.

"That night we went to the party quarreling about money. She flirted around, and we argued. I was going to take her home but she really threw a tantrum in the parking lot, got in the car, and took off.

"Then she tried to pick a fight with the car and the road and lost."

"So." Val reached across the table and touched his hand. "All these years you've been feeling guilty about it?"

"No. I've had plenty of time to think about it. There was nothing I could have done to change her or the financial situation. If it hadn't been New Year's Eve it would have been some other night. I loved her and did the best I could. No regrets.''

''So she got what she asked for.'' Val leaned back. ''If your conscience is so crystal clear, why haven't you gotten married again?''

''It's not natural, you say, for a healthy young widower with a small child to stay single?'' Theo shrugged. ''Mrs. Mac takes better care of us than a wife or mother could. I haven't been exactly celibate, either. But after the way Chris treated me and after I see the marriages my friends have—always fighting, bickering, tearing each other apart—who needs it?''

Val raised a finger and started to say something, but Mrs. MacMullin came in and started clearing the table.

''Sir,'' she announced. ''There was a call today, from a Dr. Marsh in Los Angeles. He said to tell you he would be stopping by for a visit at the end of the month.''

''Did he say why?''

''No sir. He did mention that he wanted to meet Miss Valan. I couldn't tell, sir, but he sounded like he wanted to stay a few days here at the house.'' She bustled out with a tray full of dirty dishes.

Theo was frowning, his brows pulled together in puzzlement. He glanced up at Valan. She was sitting frozen with dread.

''Do you know him?'' Theo asked with one eyebrow arched slightly.

She shook her head.

''Marsh is a biochemist. We've corresponded before, about some of my articles. But how does he know about you?''

Val shook her head again, unable to answer. She'd

never heard the name before. The thundering panic of her own heartbeat was roaring in her ears; all she could think about were the warnings from Claire and the mysterious Pearl.

"Vampyr hunter?"

Val didn't answer. She got up from the table and walked out of the house. Although he listened until after midnight, he didn't hear her return. In the morning, when he left for the hospital, she was asleep in her bed.

Chapter IV

Val was meditating on the floor of her room, sitting in the lotus position in the medallion of the small Kirman rug by the bed. The balcony doors were open, and a slight evening breeze stirred the curtains.

"It is pleasant to feel it coming, the relaxation, the control it brings," she thought. "With my eyelids almost closed and a half smile caressing my face I sit here concentrating on the air currents eddying around me. Soon there will—"

"Valan?" A female voice called her name. It didn't register in her mind until she heard her name the second time and a hand rocked her shoulder. "Your door was partly open."

"Hmmm," Val mumbled and came back to reality with great reluctance. It was Sarah, in her pajamas. There was a worried look on her face.

"What are you doing?" She asked, plopping down on the rug in front of Val.

"Just meditating, trying to get in touch with the universe. What about you? It's nearly two o'clock. Don't you have school tomorrow?"

"Yah, I couldn't sleep." She pushed her blond hair back from her pixie face. "I wander around a lot at night. I see your light on sometimes. You don't mind?"

"No, I like company. The days are too tiring. My sleep gets quite irregular," Val answered, but Sarah wasn't really listening. Something else was occupying her mind. Val waited.

"Poppa says I worry too much," she finally said.

"Do you?"

"He says there's no point in worrying about something if you can't change it, and if you can change it, do it; don't waste time worrying. But I worry anyway."

"What is it you worry so much about?"

"Poppa. He works too hard and gets too tired. Sometimes he . . . . " She paused for a moment, staring off absently to the side. There was something she was almost going to tell Val, but she changed her mind. Val could see the alteration of expression on her face as she decided not to let Val in on her secret. Val got the impression it was something Sarah had been asked not to tell.

"Anything you can do about it?"

"Not much." She grinned at Val. "I worry about you, too. Poppa says you're really very sick, and I'm not to bother you."

"Don't worry about my affliction. I don't think it's terminal." Val laughed, amused by Theo's excuses for her odd behavior.

Sarah sniffed the air and wrinkled her nose. "Why are you using Poppa's disinfectant in here? It stinks."

"It works well in there," Val nodded toward the partly open door of the bathroom, where a two-liter

66

bottle sat uncapped under the sink. "I don't think it stinks. It rather reminds me of racehorses."

"Racehorses?"

"The grooms wash their legs with liniment to keep them fit to run. It smells a bit like this." They talked of racehorses for a while and Sarah finally went off to bed, leaving Val sitting on the Persian rug thinking back many years before, to the first time she had ever seen racehorses.

They had been glorious vibrating creatures, all lean and shining with taut muscles rippling and nostrils flaring. She'd been with Robin for less than two years when they went to watch the night races at the Syracuse Fair Grounds. They'd gone to wager on a dark horse named Sudden Prince in the eighth race. It had been Robin's idea. Some lout had annoyed him bragging about the favorite, so they went out to watch.

As the seventh race was ending, Robin stood up from his seat in the front row box. "Come along," he told Val, "we have to talk to the horses." He guided her through the clutter of folding chairs and the throngs of people milling about behind the white rail fence.

The horses were waiting in the paddock by the track.

There were men yelling at each other, making bets and boasts, but Robin and Val ignored the throng and pushed their way to the rail. Sudden Prince stood near the fence, only a few yards away. He was a fine and intelligent creature, but had never won a major race. Touts had told Robin that he lacked the desire to win and would always be a second-place horse. The mahogany bay stallion was restlessly pawing and nodding his head. He tossed his snaffle up and down, catching it on his lower teeth until Robin caught his eye.

Then Sudden Prince froze, staring at the man who was not a man.

"Talk to him, Valerie," he whispered to her, sliding his firm arm around her shoulders. There was a strange, knowing smile playing on his lips. "Tell him he must run like the wind for us."

She did. Without words, Val called him to her will. When the bugle sounded, the magnificent beast turned toward the starting gate with a faraway look in his limpid eyes. He won his mile and a quarter, two lengths ahead of the place. The odds were eight to one.

It was the first time she had ever used her eyes that way, bending Sudden Prince to her bidding. It was the one vampyr trait, the pathway of communication, that set them apart from humankind more than any other, the talking with eyes. If people had it perhaps they would understand vampyrs, Val didn't know for sure. She only knew that she'd found it to be a power within her so strong that even Robin had only guessed at its strength.

Robin had given her the winnings. She'd never seen thousand-dollar bills before.

Friday, April 25

Claire Montana
Chateau Robinet
Rue St. Ambrose, Paris

Ma Chere Claire,
There is a full moon tonight and I am restless. I walk abroad in daylight and act as human as anyone. I eat dinner with the family. It's getting on my nerves. I hate to throw up every evening, but that's better than

stomach cramps all night with a belly full of food my system can't handle. I'd rather bite a snake than stick my finger down my throat one more time.

Poor Theo, he knows what I'm doing. He is kind and careful but there is pressure on him too. He is anxious and trying hard not to let it show. He even snaps at his daughter. Sarah understands, though. In a way I envy her. She's quite beautiful, with a heart-shaped face and pixie eyes. She told me she was the spitting image of her mother. There is a picture of Theo's dead wife on his dresser (Sarah says) but I haven't been in there yet.

I probably will see it soon though. Theo wants me. We dance a careful dance with our emotions. I still won't look into his eyes. Perhaps it will be different someday.

Give my love to everyone.

Toujours Amies, Valerie

Val was still restless, unable to concentrate, as she sealed the letter in an envelope. It was past midnight and her mood grew like a fever. She was almost ready to go out the window when she heard footsteps on the stairs. Sarah was home from a party.

They went for a walk in the moonlight, Sarah and Val. Sarah chattered about her date, openly, as they walked along.

They walked all the way to the bottom of the hill and back in a little over an hour. The pavement was still warm under Val's bare feet and a bit of a breeze was blowing. It rustled the leaves and brushed against their faces.

It was pleasant and uneventful until they got to the bottom of the hill where there was a cul-de-sac and a small park with benches and an overflowing trash can. The ground was covered with pea gravel that crunched underfoot, and the street lamp was hidden overhead by the foliage of several large oak trees.

They sat down for a few minutes on one of the wooden benches to enjoy the view of the city lights in the distance. Val was relieved to get away from the house, and the dulling effect of the disinfectant that clogged her nostrils and clouded her mind. Her senses sharpened more and more the longer they stayed in the night air, until she felt they were nearly at their normal strength.

A pair of raccoons, a mother and son, shuffled around the back of the trash can. Sarah didn't see them; the shadows under the tree were deep even though the full moon illuminated the street quite well.

The raccoons knew Val and Sarah were there and were quiet and careful. Val wanted to ask them whether or not they'd seen others like her around the neighborhood. She didn't, though, with Sarah watching.

"I like the night air," Val said. "It's cleaner at night than in the daytime."

"Me, too," Sarah replied, scuffing the gravel with her toes.

The coons went off, noses to the ground, busy paws checking under each rock in their path for stray bits to eat. Then Val saw the figure of a man coming up the side of the street.

"Who's that?" she asked, pointing him out to Sarah. It was the old wino who had been terrified of her.

Sarah stared at the wavering pedestrian until he came close enough for her to make out his features. The moon, nearly overhead, shed more light than the street lamp.

"It's just Mr. Warren. He lives in the toolshed of the Bannister house across the street from us. He's sort of a gardener. Mostly he just plants bottles in the trash cans." She whispered the last sentence because Mr. Warren was approaching their bench.

"Good evening, girls," he said in a hoarse voice, broken from years of hard drinking. He staggered a bit on the gravel and walked with one leg stiffer than the other.

Val stood up. She had to see what was in his mind, to know why he'd run from her before. It would only take a moment, she thought, and Sarah wouldn't even notice what she was doing in the heavy shadow of the oak tree.

"Mr. Warren," Val called softly and held out her hand, palm up, with the fingers slightly curled. He came a step closer and looked up at her face. In the split second before she caught his eyes, a terrible grimace of fright and pain crossed his face. He recognized Val as a vampyr as only another vampyr—or the victim of a vampyr attack—could do.

"You!" he whispered.

Then, as Val reassured him with her eyes, he relaxed and stood there passively. She searched his mind. It took less than a minute. "Rogue," Val whispered and released him. A rogue had attacked him.

"I have something for you."

"Yes, Mistress," Val handed him a five-dollar bill from the hip pocket of her jeans.

"I always carry something for those who need it."

"Yes, Mistress." His voice was still hoarse, but not breaking. Sarah looked back and forth between them, but didn't say anything.

"Go in peace," Val said. He shuffled away, his back a little straighter, his head a little higher.

"What was that all about?" Sarah asked.

"He looked so sad," Val said. "I just wanted to give him something. Let's go back. Maybe we can get to sleep now."

They went back, up the hill, following in Mr. Warren's wake.

Val was disturbed by what she'd seen in Warren's terrified human eyes, a vision of a vampyr, ravenous, overwhelming. It had come out of the darkness with a swarthy face, coal-black eyes and long misshaped yellow fangs; a terrifying, forced, and overpowering encounter. There had been no permission asked, no sharing of spirit, the way Val would have done with even a cow.

"There are rogue vampyrs here," Val thought, "uneducated and uncontrolled." As soon as she could, she knew she would have to investigate them. She had checked before coming, and there were no known vampyrs in San Antonio. That vision, the memory of that hideous dark face, haunted her as it did Warren. She shuddered, thinking of it, and wondered how any responsible vampyr could give a thing like that eternal life.

Theo was waiting for them in the living room when Val and Sarah got back to the house. He'd fallen asleep on the couch there, waking to the strains of the "Star Spangled Banner" as the television station signed off for the night. "I was worried," he said, rising to meet them.

"We're all right," Sarah said. She yawned and fluttered her long eyelashes at him at the same time.

Theo frowned at her. He'd been frantic when he'd wakened to find the house empty. He couldn't help

72

imagining Valan luring Sarah to her death. The idea that he didn't trust Valan was a shock to him. He had flirted with the danger within her and it hadn't frightened him. But, Sarah was different. He was only worrying about Sarah, he rationalized.

"Go on to bed, pet. I want to talk to Valan." He blew his daughter a kiss as she went off. "Sweet dreams. See you in the morning."

"I'm sorry, Theo," Val said, slumping down on one of the chairs. "Sarah is so innocent. I didn't mean to worry you." She sighed. "I was getting cabin fever." She smiled up at him, obviously managing to look wan and contrite at the same time. He didn't know whether to feel angry or relieved. "It was a lovely night," she whispered. "So lovely now with the full moon."

"Why did you take Sarah?"

"It was her idea to go." Val spoke sharply. He was acutely aware that she knew his thoughts. Her eyes narrowed as she watched him. "I told you, when we first met, that I'm afraid of the dark. I never go out alone at night unless something is terribly wrong. Then it'll be my desperate beast, not me, that does the prowling."

"God knows what I was thinking," he said. He wanted to apologize but the words wouldn't come.

She got up and left the room, moving so quietly that, if he hadn't been watching, he wouldn't have known she was gone. He sat woodenly for a long time after he heard the click of her bedroom door closing. He'd known how risky it was just having her in the house. He'd seen enough of her powers to know how dangerous she could be if she wanted to be. He wanted her, he wanted her vampyrism, and he wanted to live.

But he wasn't sure it was worth endangering Sarah.

Val stood with her hands on the window frame and stared out at the purple-shadowed valley. She wasn't surprised at Theo's reaction. Anything else would have been distinctly abnormal. She felt depressed. Disappointed, she decided. It was really disappointment. She brushed a tear from the corner of her eyes. She'd expected more from him, an impossible amount, she knew.

She heard his footsteps sounding in the hallway, they paused outside her door. Then he knocked twice.

"Valan," he said, when she opened the door. "Are you all right?"

He stood close to her with one hand on the door frame by her shoulder. She hadn't been indoors long enough for the soothing disinfectant to take the edge off her senses and he seemed very alive and warm. His breath was slightly labored, his heartbeat a little fast. She could hear it. The warmth, the pungency of his scent excited her. She drew back.

"I'm sorry," he said. "It's a matter of trust. On one level I trust you but, somehow, where Sarah is concerned . . . ." His jaw was set, and the fine lines at the corners of his eyes were deeply outlined. She could tell that the apology he was trying to make was not coming easily for him.

"It's OK," she said, touching his cheek and running the tips of her fingers back and forth across it until the muscle there relaxed. "It's just that people attack without trying to understand anything about us. I thought you were different. No wonder we're so defensive." She shook her head. "It's been the same way for centuries. Maybe I was wrong in trying to change it."

"I completely lost perspective, Valan. There's no way

I can reason when that happens. Sarah is the only human in the world that I really give a damn about."

"I'll go away if you want. I won't jeopardize your family. We have to trust each other completely."

"No! Don't even think of going."

"Why not?"

"I have to know about vampyrs."

"Why?"

"The secret of eternal life. If it could save my patients . . . ."

"How sad."

"Why?"

"I can't help you that way."

Theo cocked his head and looked at her with a puzzled expression. "Don't you just bite someone and infect them with it?"

"No, Theo." She smiled. "It's a gift freely given. But there must be mutual respect and absolute trust. It's dangerous and quite painful. Perhaps, someday, we'll talk about it." She reached up, to touch his cheek again. "You really look tired."

"I am." He slouched against the doorframe, covered her hand with his, pulled it up against his lips and kissed her palm. It was a dangerous moment for him. Val's mouth watered with desire, her tongue ran across the edges of her teeth. Then it was over. He loosened the hold on her hand and as she let it fall to her side he turned away and went to his room.

Until just before dawn, Val sat crosslegged on the floor. Then she slept.

Monday, April 28

Theo slumped wearily into one of the low Danish-style chairs that formed a sterile row in front of the nurses' station. He barely noticed that the University Hospital corridors were quiet in the mid-afternoon lull.

Susie Macklin, his favorite patient for nearly four years, had died just after lunch. Her small body with its spindly limbs and swollen belly waited, sheet-covered, on a rolling stretcher, for an orderly to wheel away. The elfin child with huge brown eyes and nearly bald head was the latest casualty in the battle against leukemia, and it was a personal defeat for Theo, leaving him drained and acutely aware of his own vulnerability. Susie had been tiny, even for a seven-year-old, and had exuded cheerfulness and complete confidence in his ability to cure her. All through the painful treatments, she'd managed to smile trustingly up at him.

The image of her face, the smile on her lips, as she slipped into the terminal coma kept flashing in his mind, but it was Valan he thought about, and a conversation they'd had one night after the tests were done. They'd been sitting comfortably in the near dark of his third-floor office when he'd asked her about Susie.

"What if . . . ," he'd said, then paused, unsure how to even begin talking about the child. Valan had waited patiently, sitting with her fingers dangling gracefully over the arms of her chair an her head tilted back against the wall. He could even recall making out a slight throbbing in one of the bluish arteries on the side of her neck. "There's a little girl," he had begun again, "at the hospital. She's dying of leukemia. The team has tried everything. We can't control it." He had looked away from Valan. The only light came streaming across the office floor from the open lab door. He had wondered why it was so difficult to talk about the child. Then, he had realized it wasn't Susie he was reluctant to

76

talk about. He had been hesitant to ask Valan for a favor, unsure how she would react.

"Susie is seven, brown-eyed, and angelic, Valan. I feel as though I'm losing a daughter. She's been in and out of our program since she was three." He had paused again, and stared at the brass clock on the corner of his desk. It had read five minutes to midnight, and the grandfather clock downstairs had begun to count off the hour. "Midnight," he'd thought. "But up here it's only five minutes to midnight." For four years he had measured the course of his destruction against Susie's.

"What if," he had repeated, "there were a way to make her a vampyr? Would it save her life?"

Valan had been silent for so long he couldn't tell what she was thinking about. Her gaze had been directed toward the ribbon of light snaking across the floor. Finally, she had spoken, her voice so soft that he had strained to hear her.

"Over four hundred years ago a new vampyr, Thelma, rescued her child from the plague. She just couldn't bear to watch her little girl die; so the child, Constance, became a vampyr. She lived nearly four hundred years as a nine-year-old." Val had chewed her lower lip and glanced up at Theo. "Thelma made her daughter into a vampyr and saved her life, but we all knew it was a mistake, and we never do it anymore. You see, the little girl vampyr never grew up. I met her once. It was pathetic to be so old and wise and frozen in a child's body."

"Where is she now?" Theo had asked, a crazy desire to meet the child vampyr flitting through his mind.

"She committed suicide. Perhaps it was best."

He'd known that night that Valan was right. But

77

now, as he sat there waiting for a man in a pale green cotton uniform to take Susie, he was reluctant to accept Valan's gentle refusal.

"Afternoon, Doctor," a nurse said, her uniform rustling stiffly as she walked by. Then the orderly arrived and wheeled the rolling stretcher away.

Theo got up and spent the rest of the day working harder than he had in over a month. At four-thirty he left, walking across the gently sloping lawn to the parking lot, and never looking back at the glass-checkered walls of the hospital. He was so drained emotionally and physically that he had trouble concentrating on the traffic. The drive home seemed endless.

A little after six Val heard the sound of Theo's Corvette drawing up at the side of the house. She was on the stairs when Theo came in, slammed the door, and dropped his suit coat onto a hook in the hall. He entered the living room with an expression of deep sadness on his face. "Susie's dead," he said. He lay down on the couch with his arm over his eyes and fell asleep almost immediately.

He was sprawled on the couch, with his head lolling sideways and one hand curled over his forehead like a small child's. Val sat across from him and listened as his breathing grew relaxed and the haunted look faded from his face. All of the worry signs softened, except for the dark circles under his eyes. They formed sooty shadows in the soft yellow light of the Capiz lamps on the end tables. For a while Val felt at ease, almost secure, just being there.

Toward midnight, she grew restless and left Theo lying on the couch. She'd touched his shoulder and

78

called his name several times, but he slept as though drugged, without movement. She pulled a knitted afghan over his still form and went up to the lab. The door was securely locked. "Too many drugs," Theo'd said. She couldn't open it without leaving marks. So, with a sense of morality that puzzled her with its intensity, she went back to her room to wait. She proudly refused to go looking for the key. The one moment of faltering trust on Theo's part had affected her more than she cared to admit.

Thoughts of Susie and Constance engulfed her as she tried to forget her growing hunger and the hopes that he'd wake up and come feed her.

"For everything there is a reason," she whispered, sinking down on the Persian rug beside the bed, "that's in the Bible. It's true for humankind but for us there is only one season. We live in it forever." It was because of Constance that they tried never to choose the very old or very young. Val would never have to know what it would be like to grow old and settled or feeble and grey. She had always thought it would be a blessing not to grow old until she met Constance, but then she had realized the goodness and growth in the changing ages of man, a fullness of the life cycle; the seasons coming in a time and completeness that she would never know. She stared out of the window, her mind rambling. In spite of the strong scent of the disinfectant, her senses were getting sharper and more alert as her hunger grew.

The moon was still full. She could sit there no longer. The beast within her thirsted. She had to go.

She locked her bedroom door, slipped out the window, and paused at the edge of the balcony.

There was heavy moisture in the air, a primeval smell of earth and mold and things alive. She shivered, fearful of the night. No one else was stirring. The ranch-style houses in the twisted little valley below were silent. The night sky glowed dully with a diffused violet aura from the street lights. Then she stepped over the railing of the balcony and went down the brick wall, like a lizard, her chest pressed against the roughness of the bricks. She held her breath momentarily as she entered the darkness, trying to conquer her fear of the shadows. It didn't matter that she controlled a fortune almost beyond measure, and power beyond human understanding. It didn't matter that she could see in the dark nearly as well as she could in daylight. It was the night itself that frightened her—irrational fears born in the nights of her long-distant youth.

Her fingers with their carefully sculpted nails were so pale and slender that she sometimes looked at them as though they belonged to someone else. Yet one frail-looking finger tucked into the space between two bricks would support her entire weight almost indefinitely.

All she wore were jeans and a dark blue shirt. The night air caressed her face, and dew was already covering the grass. Her shadow was long and lean in the moonlight. It stretched ahead of her as though it was leading, feeling the way along the ground. Her elemental, primordial yearning grew. Somewhere she would find life to drink from. Her thoughts ran together, incoherent and blurred. Visions of Sarah and Theo loomed side by side with specters from the past. Her head seemed to float, disembodied above her throbbing body, a vehicle for her rapidly sharpening senses as her beast inexorably took control. Then her fears of the darkness vanished; her beast knew no fear, only survival.

She slipped around the house and down the hill where the road curved and the gravel was thrown up in a long crescent wave by passing cars, then over the back and down toward the ranch houses. There were clouds in big clumps overhead that moved westward in a ghostly armada.

Her bare feet were nimble over the loose shale. The slabs of rock were large, like flagstones, and the whole hillside was covered with them. They were thrown about at random and stifled all but the hardiest grasses. She was aware of everything, yet unable to control her movements. Her body flowed smoothly down the slope. There were things moving in the nighttime coolness and she felt them all.

She was drawn irresistibly to a particular house at the bottom of the valley, the last one before the hills gave way to the city. The lights were out in the back of the sprawling brick house, but not in the front.

The dog started barking long before she reached the back yard. He knew she was coming toward him and could sense something unusual about her. A tremor in his snarl betrayed his uncertainty. She stood just past his range of vision and studied him. He was a large dog, like a wolf, big and grey, with a mane of silver around his neck and down his chest. He growled and barked. His ears were laid back tight against his head, and his hackles were raised; he smelled of fear and rage. His long fangs glistened in the moonlight.

The man of the house came to the back door and yelled at the dog to shut up. He stood outlined in the light. "Damn mutt," he said and turned away. The light went out.

The dog had stopped barking for a moment to snarl fearlessly at the man. He was nearly as large as Val, almost a hundred pounds, she estimated, but with all his thick coat it was hard to judge. He was chained, she saw.

She stepped soundlessly out from behind the bushy hedge that surrounded most of the back yard. He froze, standing so still that for a moment he nearly vanished in the darkness. Then slowly, as he stared at her, he relaxed and dropped lower and lower until he was lying down and whimpering so softly that even Val could barely hear it; little sounds from deep in his throat. She approached slowly, holding his eyes with hers, and shared his pain.

His life had been hard, full of punishment he never understood, days of neglect, and years of wearing a chain. Val promised him freedom. His long tail thumped in the grass soundlessly. His tongue lolled wetly to one side.

He rolled onto his side as she knelt beside him and parted the long hair of his neck ruff with her fingers. The fur was greasy, full of dirt ground in by the heavy leather collar.

She snicked the skin with her teeth and drank what he eagerly offered until her needs were satisfied. He gazed at Val adoringly. When she was finished she knelt beside him and stroked his flank. He was so thin under the thick hair that his ribs were easy to feel. There were tears in Val's eyes as she regained control of her body. She was certain the dog would die, and for that she was sorry. But it was the beast within her that she held accountable for such an unnecessary death.

The collar was hard to open so she tore the leather between her fingers, rending it, dropping it broken to the ground. "At least if you die you will be free," she whispered. She felt good from the drinking, and at the same time she was depressed thinking about what she'd done to the dog. She climbed back up to the road and, when she reached the pavement, stood there looking back over the valley. It was the only memorial she could offer him.

From behind her on the road she recognized the sound of footsteps on the pavement. The darkness seemed to close in around her. She started walking up the road.

Theo came jogging up to her and stopped at her side. His shirt was rumpled, and a part of the tail was hanging out in the back. He rubbed his eyes and the back of his neck, trying to wake up.

"Where were you?"

"I was out walking." She pointed along the pavement.

"There's blood on your lips."

She closed her eyes and turned away. Her shoulders were shaking.

"Valan," he asked softly, "Why were you out walking again?"

"You fell asleep, Theo. The lab was locked. I had to come out. I couldn't help myself." She started walking back to the house. "I'll leave now. Thanks for trying."

Her shoulders slumped a little. The experiment hadn't lasted very long, she thought. She'd have to start it all over somewhere else. It seemed as though failure was all vampyrs ever knew in their efforts to reach humankind.

She felt wounded, defeated. She hunched her

shoulders and held her left elbow with her right hand, as though the whole side of her body was broken.

"Valan, wait," he said. "I can't let you go." He caught up to her and put his arm around her shoulders. They were still trembling. "I put you into a no-win situation," he said gently. They walked back to the house together.

Val was at peace in the pink dawn, for Theo and she had come to terms of trust, and the dog was lying in the back yard, watching her window. His head was on his paws and his tail straight behind him, but there was joy in his expression. He was weak, but he was free.

Chapter V

Tuesday, April 29

Theo stayed home and indoors all day. He sat in the living room most of the morning and pretended to work on a manuscript, but he found himself staring morosely out of the window, the pages of his paper scattered where they'd fallen, unnoticed, from his hands.

He wondered how precarious his control over Valan really was, and how much longer he could keep her in the house. As long as he produced results in the lab for her, as long as his health didn't deteriorate any further, she'd probably stay. Then again, Dr. Marsh would be arriving tomorrow. What was his connection with Valan? That was the big unknown.

Wednesday, April 30

Curiosity overrode Val's fear as she awaited the arrival of the mysterious Dr. Marsh. She glanced around the living room one last time to reassure herself that there were many avenues of escape. Then she waited, with one hand on the window sill, and watched until the yellow taxi pulled up in front of the house.

A phone call to Corey had drawn a complete blank. Dr. Marsh was, apparently, nothing more than an unknown, unpublished biochemist with good academic credentials.

He arrived just before the sun went down. He climbed out of the taxi and stood like a magnificent ebony statue in the glare of the setting sun. He was well over six feet tall and appeared to be in his late forties. There was grey in his hair, but his dark face was unlined and calm.

Val had nearly panicked when Mrs. Mac took the call from California and announced the impending arrival of Dr. Marsh. Now she stood frozen with tension as Sarah answered the door.

"I've come to see Dr. James," the strange voice intoned slowly.

"Who are you?" Val heard Sarah ask.

"Claudius Marsh. He's expecting me."

"I'll get him. Wait here." Sarah's words came out in quick staccato, but Val barely noticed. Her knees had gone weak with relief as she realized that Dr. Marsh was Pearl's friend. She walked to the doorway and leaned against the frame, fully aware that there was a smile bending the corners of her mouth. She ignored Sarah, who brushed past her on the way upstairs.

Claudius put his hat on the hall table, and as soon as he saw Val standing in the doorway to the living room he turned to face her. They looked into each other. Almost immediately his eyes flickered away, then came back and held. Val saw that he had a beautiful soul, full of sharing and well being, but with a darker side with hatred for the unseeing and selfish people. It was there, almost concealed, but he underestimated her power. She smiled. It was better to know more, she thought, than a stranger really wanted to reveal.

As he came to her, with one hand reaching out to take hers, Theo appeared at the head of the stairs and came down quickly, two steps at a time. His face was tight with worry. Val glanced up, aware that Theo would tackle Claudius if she gave him any sign of distress.

"Theo, meet Dr. Marsh," she said, smiling at him, and turned back to the tall black man. When Claudius kissed the back of her hand, she felt like floating right off the floor.

"You know each other?" Theo frowned, perplexed.

"We have mutual acquaintances," Claudius said in a rich baritone. There was not a hint of anything but good education in his accent. "I've wanted to meet Miss Anderweldt for a long time. This unpleasant business trip is a cloud with a silver lining. I must say that she is everything I had been warned to expect—and more. But unfortunately my time is limited. I'm expected back in to Los Angeles tomorrow."

"Stay here tonight," Val said, hoping that she and Claudius could talk all night. "Are you satisfied?"

Claudius shook his head and flashed a guarded look at Theo, who was still standing on the first step with one hand clutching the newel post.

Theo felt the corners of his mouth tighten involuntarily as he realized Valan was referring to Claudius' daily need for blood.

"Come with me," he said and turned and started back upward.

The carefully measured tread of the vampyr was close behind him on the stairs. Theo was afraid with a fear that formed a knot of pain just under his breastbone; he struggled to analyze it. By the time he led the way into the lab and opened the refrigerator door for Claudius, he'd decided it was the black man's physical bulk, the ominous force he embodied, more than anything else that made his blood run cold.

Claudius' amber-tinged eyes lit up when he saw the neat stacks of plastic blood packs on the refrigerator shelves.

"Help yourself," Theo said, as casually as he could.

"Thank you," Claudius took two of the cold bags, weighed them in his hand and reached for another. "Do you have a glass?"

"Of course," Theo turned and reached for a tumbler in the cabinet over the sink. His lips were tight. He hadn't expected this, the thought of Claudius drinking blood from an iced-tea glass disquieted him. Valan usually just bit a small hole in the corner of the bag and sucked out the blood, neatly and inoffensively.

"She's quite unusual," Claudius said, taking the glass and setting it on the counter. He pulled the corner off one bag and poured most of its contents into the glass. "How much do you know about us?"

"Vampyrs? Not a lot. Why?" Theo felt caught off guard by the question. He had a feeling that Claudius could read his mind, even though he was certain it wasn't possible.

"Curiosity."

"Why don't you just hypnotize me? Valan said any vampyr could do it with a glance."

Claudius drank deeply, draining the glass, then he set it down carefully. "Because she said no one was to interfere with you and your family." He poured another bag of blood into the glass.

"What do you mean by that?" There was a tinge of anger in Theo's voice. Something was going on between Valan and Claudius that hinted of a closer relationship than they had admitted.

Claudius swung around to face Theo, peering at him closely, yet, Theo noticed, Claudius never quite met his eyes. "You really don't know who she is, do you?"

"I know Valan Anderweldt isn't her real name, if that's what you mean."

Claudius shook his head and smiled. "You'll find out soon enough." He lifted the glass as if to make a toast. "You have a very powerful ally, my friend. Do not abuse her." He drank and set the glass down. "Now, before we rejoin the irresistible lady, tell me about your work."

It was ten o'clock before they came down from the lab and Theo rapped on Val's door.

"I must tell you," Claudius said as soon as he settled into the easy chair by the window, "the real reason that I'm here." His tone of deference toward Val was obvious, almost obsequious, Theo thought. He recalled Claudius' cryptic remark about Valan being a powerful ally.

Val was sitting crosslegged at the head of the bed, with the pillows tucked behind her. She'd put aside the letter she'd been writing when Theo had knocked on the door, and she was listening with rapt attention to Claudius. "Yes," she said softly, in a tone Theo interpreted as granting permission to speak more than curiosity for what he was going to say.

Although it was still early in the night, the house was quiet around them, spreading a protective web of silence

89

over the words about to be said. Theo closed the door and sat down at the foot of the bed, facing both Val and Claudius.

"Ostensibly, I'm here to attend the protein synthesis seminar." He got a brief nod of acknowledgment from Theo. "But, in actuality, my cohorts in the vampire hunters society wanted me to use the seminar as an excuse to check on you, Dr. James. They have Darrell Montana's address book and in it there was a clipping from one of your articles." He looked at Theo. Theo shrugged.

"Do they know I'm here?" Val shifted her hips to sit up straighter.

"No, but they suspect a vampyr will be in contact with Dr. James. I'm supposed to warn him." He bowed his head toward Val. "I'm sorry, Val. I'll have to tell them about you." He spoke deferentially, apologetically. "You see, they don't trust me completely yet. I can't lie about something they can check on so easily."

"It's all right." She raised her hand up, palm outward. "What exactly do you have to tell them?"

"Your name, the one you're using now—and it is in that address book—and a description." His eyes were full of sorrow when their gazes met, and she read deep reluctance in him to betray her.

"You cannot compromise your own safety," she said, knowing that he would if she told him to. "Are they really that dangerous?"

"Yes," he said simply. "They captured a young vampyr, Jill, and starved her to death, deliberately. They tried to force her to eat food. Of course, she couldn't. And she wasn't strong enough to escape. She went into irreversible estivation and died."

"How'd they catch her?" Theo asked, his first words since he and Claudius had entered Val's room. He was mentally comparing Val's speed to a normal man's and found it difficult to believe a vampyr could be trapped involuntarily.

"She had tried to commit suicide by jumping out of a tenth-story window. They got to her in the hospital before I did. That's when I joined their group. I was trying to help." He shrugged his broad shoulders in resignation.

"They got her boyfriend, an old rogue named Salty, when he tried to rescue her. He escaped into the sunlight. You know the rest." He bowed toward Val again.

"How many are there in this hunting group?"

"About twelve. The number varies. They are quite dedicated and serious about wiping out vampires. They have a lot of money.

"You have two options, Valan, either go now and avoid a confrontation or stay and . . . who knows."

Theo left them, reluctantly, at midnight. The circles under his eyes were almost purple. He wanted to stay but was too tired to do so. Val didn't encourage him. She and Claudius had things to talk about that weren't for human ears. He was their first topic of conversation.

"Valerie, what's wrong with him?" Claudius used her real name as soon as they were alone. She stared vacantly at Claudius' finely chiseled head, not quite understanding what he was getting at.

"Nothing. He's just more of a scientist than a doctor at heart, I suppose."

"I've read his work. I felt I had to before I came

91

here," Claudius said, nodding. "I agree. But that's not what I meant. He isn't well physically."

She shook her head. "He's usually full of energy." Claudius raised his head until their eyes met briefly.

"Be careful, Valerie. I can afford you some protection from the hunters. That's what they call themselves. But it's a risky business dealing with human beings on an intimate level. It doesn't pay to trust them. Make him one of us if you have to. Then there would be no betrayals."

"His life is too complicated. It wouldn't work. He has his daughter. I doubt that he could accept the change."

"Possibly not." Claudius rubbed his forehead with the tips of his fingers. "I understand what you're trying to do here. We all appreciate your risk on our behalf, even though my people have never belonged to your group. Dr. James showed me some of the results. It could mean a whole new existence for us. But the thing that's obviously growing between the two of you is beyond that."

"He's very attractive," she said, thinking that Claudius was either disapproving or jealous.

He shook his head. "From what I know about you, only the most powerful vampyrs have ever attracted you. He doesn't seem to fit."

She shrugged, but didn't try to refute him. It was an interesting point, one she'd have to think about at length. Just what was the attraction between Theo and herself? Claudius was right. Theo, with his quiet, rational, and unassuming manners, didn't fit in with the other men in her life: Rovin, Salvatore, or even Claudius.

With Claudius she felt a force of attraction as soft and inexorable as gravity. It would be interesting, she decided, to have a friendly contest of wills with him. Perhaps the group would find itself with a new leader. "It's time, you know," she said, "for all of us to let go of human differences. What we are now is more important than what we were."

"Do you think your fancy friends believe that?"

"Have you given them the chance to get to know you?"

"You have a point."

"Think of the advantages if every vampyr had access to our resources."

"I will." He got up from the chair and sat on the edge of the bed next to her.

"All you have to do is ask," she answered simply.

"Of course."

They held hands briefly before they parted. It started as a handshake and turned into something much deeper for both of them, a kinship, but there were other commitments important to each of them. She knew he longed for Pearl.

"I have to fly back to Los Angeles in the morning."

"We will meet again some time."

"Yes."

Thursday, May 1

Claudius flew back to California. Theo and Sarah went to the airport with him. And as the plane took off, Theo relaxed, as though a great burden had been lifted from his shoulders.

In the evening, at the end of dinner, an argument broke out when Mrs. Mac asked Sarah, "When will you be back from your slumber party?"

They were sitting at the kitchen table having hamburgers with chips on paper plates.

Sarah said, "Maybe tomorrow." She took a bite of her hamburger. It was already half gone, with little crescent bite marks along one side. "These are good," she said to Mrs. Mac.

"Maybe? You have school tomorrow," Mrs. Mac said as she took another handful of chips.

"So what?" Sarah snapped, pointing her half-eaten burger at the housekeeper.

"No need to be rude, Sarah," Theo said, wiping his mouth and leaning back in the wooden chair. "You need to be in school. Finals are coming up."

"I hate it!" she pouted. "Everyone's been talking about you!"

"That's enough," Theo said, sitting up a little straighter in his chair.

"Well, it's all over school that you've got a live-in girl friend. They talk about us behind my back."

"Excuse me," Val said, starting to rise. "I don't care to listen to this."

"Sit down, Valan," Theo said, momentarily turning her way. "Please." He lifted his hand with one finger extended to Sarah. "First of all, young lady, what you think is going on, isn't. Second, it's none of your business. Third, you are not responsible for the bad manners of your classmates."

"It looks bad. That's all, Poppa. I'm just trying to protect you." Sarah almost sounded contrite.

"When I need protection I'll ask for it."

"That does it!" Sarah yelled, slamming back her chair. "I don't get any consideration around here. I'm

94

leaving now." She stormed upstairs, leaving the half-eaten hamburger on her plate.

"You were a little hard on her," Val said.

"I don't know what to do with her sometimes," Theo said, as though talking to himself. "She gets like this when she doesn't get her own way. But I don't know what's eating her tonight."

They sat, picking at the remains of dinner, until Sarah's wooden-soled sandals were heard coming down the stairs. Then Mrs. Mac got up and brought a plate of doughnuts. "You're just going to let her go off mad like that?" she spoke while she was setting down the plate.

Theo shrugged. "If she stayed, she'd have to act like a member of the family. I haven't got the energy to force it."

"Really," Mrs. Mac said sarcastically. "You let her do anything."

He grinned at Val and shook his head ruefully. "Maybe I do give in to her too much."

"Sarah," Mrs. MacMullin called, "come have a doughnut before you go."

The wooden-soled sandals clacked slowly back into the kitchen, and Sarah sat back down. "Sorry." She hung her head. There was a bit of moisture in the corners of her eyes. She took a doughnut and ate it silently.

"Really, sir," Mrs. Mac said, "it does look a bit odd, even with me and Miss Sarah here, to have such an attractive houseguest. Now we know she's a patient, but she looks young enough to be Sarah's friend. Others do gossip."

"Let them talk," Theo said.

"Why don't you marry her, Poppa? I approve."

Sarah coolly licked her fingers to get the last sweetness of her doughnut and tossed her honey mane back. Mrs. MacMullin clucked at her. Val stared, wondering at Sarah's complete about-face.

"Look," Sarah continued, shrugging innocently. "Valan's nice looking, fun to be with, and won't cost as much as that wolf out back to feed." They all laughed. The dog was making friends fast. Sarah had found him out in the yard, fed him two pounds of chopped sirloin, and given him a bath with her own shampoo. His coat gleamed dark and metallic now. "Anyway, Poppa," she continued, "if the two of you aren't sleeping together already, you soon will be. Make an honest woman out of her."

Val laughed at Theo, who was frowning and flushing darkly at the same time. He glared across the table at her. "Modern children," Val said, "have no respect for their elders."

"All right," he said with a bit of mock severity. "Valan, marry me, please. Make an honest woman out of yourself."

He was serious, Val realized in astonishment. "Some proposal," she replied lightly. "Whatever has happened to romance? You two con artists act like you're in cahoots." She paused for a moment, then, in an effort to gain more time to think, said, "I'll give you an answer in the morning, Theo. There are many things to consider."

"Fine," Sarah said, pushing back her chair. "OK, Poppa, that gives you tonight to work her over. I've got the party at Diane's. 'Bye." And she left.

"Where did that dog come from?" Theo asked as

they closed up the lab an hour later. Val had just finished her meal and felt lazy and relaxed.

"He followed me home," she said. "Can I keep him?"

"Why did he follow you home, Valan?"

"He was chained to a tree, beaten and half-starved, Theo. He saved my life. I gave him his freedom. It was a fair trade. He's just grateful."

"The way that dog looks at you; it's worship." He shook his head. "Very strange."

"He's looked into my eyes, Theo, and seen my soul." She said it without really thinking of the consequences.

"Is that why you never look at me?" He spoke in his gentlest voice. "So I won't see your soul?"

"Partly." She hesitated, but it was too late to stop. "I look into souls, too. It has to be a sharing process."

They were silent then, until they were downstairs in front of her door. Instead of going his separate way he took her hand and led her to his room. She looked for the picture of Sarah's mother that should have been on the dresser. It wasn't there. Instead there was a gallon jug of disinfectant on the night stand by his bed.

"I've been set up," she said as he took off the cap.

"It's been sitting here almost a month." They both laughed and sat together on the chaise lounge by the window until the fumes were noticeable.

"Valan." He took her hand.

"Yes."

"Look at me." He lifted her chin and turned her head toward him, cupping his tan fingers lightly over her pale cheek. Their eyes met, and she felt the same swirling vortex that came when Robin saw into her eyes for the first time. Suddenly, Theo and Val knew each other very well. They sat there staring into each other, lost in a universe that held only them.

She perceived the fear of debilitating illness and death that drove him in his quest for knowledge. She didn't probe beneath the open parts of his mind, content to bask in his desire for her as a woman. There was no avarice or treachery in him, no betrayal. She let it go at that, savoring what she felt and dimly aware that if there were darker aspects within his personality, she didn't want to know about them just then.

After a while, she couldn't judge how long, he drew her to him and held her tight. There were tears falling on her neck. "Valan, Valan," he whispered from a place so deep inside him that she clung to him, trying to find it. She knew then that she had made him hers, and she wanted him. There were tears in her eyes, too, when he lifted her in his arms and carried her to the bed.

She was heavier in his arms than he expected, and he was aware that she was holding her breath. She lay totally relaxed, almost submissive, with her head resting on his shoulder. When he settled her quiescent form on the bed she lifted her slender arms, encircled his neck and lightly pulled him down with her. Almost automatically, he bent over her face, intrigued with her acetone-sweet breath.

"Don't kiss me or touch my lips," Val whispered. She caressed his mouth with her fingertips, without fully opening her green eyes. He realized it was a warning, a gentle command, the one condition she was putting on their love-making.

Later, while they lay twined together, he could hear her teeth grinding within her tightly clenched jaws, and, though she smiled lazily up at him and moaned with delight at all the right times, she never spoke or opened her mouth. It was a subtle but constant reminder that she was more than merely human; that she struggled to control something aroused by their physical closeness, something beyond the moral side of her nature.

Chapter VI

Friday, May 2

Val slipped away in the hours before dawn and left Theo sleeping soundly. Her thoughts occupied her for a long time in the silence of the night. When all the tangled events of yesterday were analyzed, she still was uneasy. The night was warm and heavy, the air still. There was dew already glistening in the grass. Wolf was waiting for her when she stepped out onto the patio. He wagged his long grey tail ingratiatingly, swishing it back and forth, nearly brushing the ground with the tip of it.

There were brick steps leading down to the back yard at the edge of the patio. From there the yard dropped off, sloping gently down the hill toward the valley where all the fashionable ranch style houses sat crammed together on tiny lots. She sat on the steps and waited for dawn. Wolf lay beside her with his great head on her lap.

There were so many things to think about that the false dawn had come and gone before she went back to the house, the seat of her jeans damp and clammy from the dew off the bricks. No one was stirring. Her bare feet were silent on the marble. There was a promise of heat to come filling the house. She thought Mrs. Mac might decide to close up the house today and turn on the central air conditioning.

She showered, and, feeling much cooler, put on her nightgown and robe. As she stepped out in the hallway, sounds of pots banging in the kitchen rose to greet her. She went to the window seat at the end of the hall to wait and watch the sun come up. Her emotions were still in a state of confusion.

Theo came out of his room, fully dressed in his usual grey suit, one of a closetful. He was perfectly groomed, ready to face the day, looking fresh and rested even though he hadn't had much sleep the night before.

He sat at the other end of the plum-colored velvet cushion, crossing his legs so he could twist around to face Val. The light was beginning to stream in through the window onto her face; he reached for the pull cords and drew the drapes.

"You're an angel of loveliness in white lace," he said, confident that he'd won her over.

"An angel of death," she answered. "Theo, if I were a young girl, inexperienced and unwise to the ways of the world, if I were only a girl, I would accept you and be deliriously happy. But this isn't a dream world. And," she continued, "I can't accept you on your terms. It wouldn't work, trying to pretend everything is normal according to human standards. We'd both wind up miserable."

"Name your own terms, then, Valan. I'll try to go along with whatever you think you need." He reached out and wiped a tear from her cheek. She hadn't even realized it was there. "All right?"

She nodded. "I can stay for a while, but not more than a few years. After a time people will notice that I don't change. I must be gone before they have time to wonder."

"I've thought about that. When you have to go, I'll go with you. By then there'll be nothing to keep me here."

"And I would watch you grow older." She shook her head.

"Make me a vampyr." She was disconcerted. She searched his face. He was serious about what had started out as little more than a diversion for her.

"You don't know what you're asking. Could you see Sarah growing old and dying while you dance in the capitals of the world, eternally young?" She covered his hands with hers. "Could you endure being hunted and hounded by every maniac with a thirst for adventure?"

"At the risk of sounding corny, if it means keeping you, yes." His earnest declaration came too fast for her.

"It isn't really that simple." She sat back, leaning against the wall. "There are others involved."

"Take me to meet them and get it over with."

"I'll see what I can do." She was stalling. She felt certain that making him into a vampyr would be a mistake, as it had been with Lui Renoit, who lost all interest in research when he became a vampyr. Yet, at the same time, she was so strongly attracted to him that she wavered, undecided, unable to keep her resolve firm, let alone say the words that would destroy the fragile relationship between them.

"Theo, would you be offended if I went away for a while? I need time to think."

He frowned. "I don't understand. But if you need it,

you've got it. Promise you won't go right away." She nodded. But it was easy to see that he wasn't pleased. It showed in the way he walked away, after kissing her cheek so lightly that she barely felt it. His shoulders were squared back and tight, not swinging smoothly the way they usually did.

The phone rang at almost the same time he drove off for the day. Mrs. MacMullin answered it downstairs in the kitchen and buzzed Val's room. It was Sarah, calling from her friend's house.

"Well," she asked, breathlessly. "How'd it go?"

"Badly, I'm afraid," Val said. "Sarah, I have to have time to think. I'm going away for a little while, but . . . ." The receiver clicked sharply. "I promise I'll come back," Val whispered to the dial tone.

Saturday, May 10

"I have a lake cottage about an hour's drive from here. It's yours as long as you like." Theo sensed that Valan was standing somewhere behind him, but he didn't turn his head to see. He'd come out to the patio when daylight faded, and had sat brooding in the gathering darkness, waiting for her to wake up. He knew he was dangerously close to losing her and that was intolerable, totally unacceptable. He had never been able to give up anything important without a struggle.

The idea of letting her use the cottage had come to him as the only possible way of letting her go away and keeping her at the same time. The cold fury he'd felt, when she'd announced she had to leave, had dissipated. He knew it had been born of helplessness. He wondered if she'd sensed it and interpreted his anger as a weakness.

104

"It's not on a lake, actually, it's on a reservoir. The dam blocks a deep canyon in the hill country."

"Yes," she said, moving in closer behind him and resting her hand on his shoulder. She'd come like a wisp of wind; the simple word and touch warmed him. "Wolf will go with me."

"I'll drive up every other day to bring you supplies."

"It isn't necessary."

"I know. I'd just like to see you." He didn't add that he wanted to be sure she was still there, to talk to her, to sway her decision.

"Don't worry," she said, almost as if she was reading his mind. "Whatever I decide, I will come back, at least to tell you what I have to do." Her voice was emotionless, distant, as if she'd already gone.

Sunday, May 11

The front of the wooden A-frame cottage was glass and overlooked the lake. The loft, which occupied half of the second story, held the main bedroom. Everything else was downstairs. Val had never been in an A-frame before. There were odd angles everywhere, and that took getting used to. Looking up two stories from the living room to the peaked ceiling gave Val an unexpected feeling of vertigo.

It was quiet over the lake as the sun went down. There were a few fishermen still out. Fireflies glowed in the grass along the shore. Val pushed the sliding glass doors open to let in the evening breeze, and the house cooled off rapidly, making the evening much more pleasant than in town where the air hung humid and heavy on the skin throughout the night.

There was something about the climate that Val found unearthly. She was used to cool summers and snow-filled winters, to Colorado and Oregon. She had been in Oregon when she decided to enlist the famous hematologist, Dr. James. It had originally been Claire's idea, and the group had argued for a long time: Allow a human to become privy to vampyrs and their problems? Val had pushed for it, and Claire had too, after Darrell's death. Then the others had reluctantly agreed to let Val try.

She looked out across the water, where the last fisherman was trying, without success, to start for home. Finally, the engine caught and he went off with a roar.

The house was perched over the edge of a rocky slope, the side facing the lake supported by sawed-off telephone poles. There was a deck that hung completely over the water. She could fish from it if she cared to; others had. There were fish scales on its wooden floor.

The smell of the lake, the cool evening breeze, all the sounds on the waterfront, reminded her of the years she'd spent in the Oregon mountains, far from the bustle of Paris. She'd delegated all of her business responsibilities to Salvatore, said goodbye to the group and escaped for a while from a life that had become too full of tension.

She had loved the clear Oregon air and reveled in the keenness of her perceptions. Then, when she had been in Oregon nearly five years, she had begun to see the lines growing deeper on people's faces. She had known she had to go.

She envied them, the ones who spent their whole lives in one place. But her way was to move on in four or five years before folks became suspicious. Keep a low profile and use money to buy time and privacy. Money was one thing vampyrs had plenty of. Just work hard for a while and save everything with a vengeance, then sit back and let the money take care of you. She felt sorry for people who couldn't live long enough to enjoy what they earned. Somehow it didn't seem right.

The moon was rising. There was a small boat tied to the small dock in front of the cottage. She could see it from where she sat crosslegged in the living room. It was pleasant to watch the water lapping against its sides and hear the little chuckling sounds the waves made. It distracted her, though, from the things she had to think about.

She wondered what would happen if she and Theo were ever to come together unguarded by her watchfulness and the dulling disinfectant. She'd never been so attracted to a human before. It was something she didn't understand or quite know how to keep under control.

Wolf watched her as she thought. He sat by the fireplace like a warm blue steel statue. He'd spent all day at the foot of the bed, quietly waiting for her to awaken. Now, as the moon rose, he grew restless. His blunt claws clicked on the hardwood floor as he paced back and forth.

A firebreak started not far from the cottage, across the road and about a hundred yards down. There were several of them streaking up the slopes, forming scars on the mountainsides. The state workmen had bulldozed a strip about fifty feet across, like a rough road bed, wherever there was a lot of wild land dense with trees or brush, to help control forest fires. The breaks were rocky and uneven. Only the hardiest off-the-road vehicles could use them. Val and Wolf chose to walk along the center, out of the night shadows. She wasn't afraid with him at her side.

They went to the crest of the hill and sat, side by side, on a patch of grass and watched the heavens go round and round overhead.

Val saw the sky as a clock marking the hours as well as the millennium. She tried to measure her own time by staring at the stars, but couldn't.

"If I were to marry a human, for the joy we feel together, what price would we pay when I have to leave him?" She rubbed Wolf's head. "He wouldn't be happy as a vampyr. There's a quality of toughness missing in him. Missing or buried so deep he might not be able to call it out, even as a matter of survival."

She pictured the others—Salvatore, Claire, Javier—all the ones who were closest to her, and she doubted that they would approve. Even Javier, who stayed apart, coming only when she needed him, would look at Theo and laugh at his gentleness.

The breeze picked up, blowing the dog scent away from her and bringing the perfume of desert grasses and dry dirt floating in the night. Wolf growled, licked his nose and whined as a skunk meandered across the fire-break not far below them. She dropped her arm over the dog's rough back, then sighed and stood up, stretching her arms out, embracing the sky. The clouds were making wispy silver tangles over the lake. A dark grey buck emerged from the brush downhill and stood silhouetted against the water. She smiled as it saw her and froze. Then she went to the waiting beast.

Tuesday, May 13

Theo arrived late, long after sunset. He brought a cardboard box of supplies in from his Corvette, and fell asleep on the sofa before he'd even finished his sandwich. The shadowy circles were back under his eyes. He'd brought along only his shaving kit and intended to leave in the morning as they'd agreed.

She liked having him there. Whenever he was near she got a warm feeling of security, something she'd rarely known since she was very young. Her mother had made her feel that way when she'd taken Val onto her lap and held her hands in her workworn fingers. "Make something fine out of yourself," she'd said. "Never work the way I've had to." They had been poor, incredibly so by today's standards; and toiling in the cloth mill, Byrstin's Bolt Goods, was her mother's lot. She had worked up to eighty hours a week to earn barely enough to feed and clothe the two of them. Even then she had done without things for herself to keep Val in school. Her hair had been prematurely streaked with grey and her face, once very much like Val's, creased with worry lines. But they had been sure about their love for each other.

"Perhaps Theo and I have found that sureness about each other," she mused. "It's a good feeling to have."

Val's mother had been impressed that Robin chose her daughter, and pleased beyond measure with the little house he'd given her. It had been nothing to him, a small pittance from his pocket, but far surpassing the greatest hopes she'd had for her old age.

Val liked to think he had done it out of kindness.

It seemed to Val that lately her thoughts jumped back and forth from the immediate present to the distant past as though the answers to her problems were there. Perhaps?

Wolf stood on the deck staring out over the water. She tucked a blanket over Theo and went up the hill again with Wolf.

Wednesday, May 14

Theo left shortly after dawn. Val was painfully aware that something was wrong with him. He looked so tired, as though just moving around took extra effort. He'd given himself an injection. She saw the hypodermic when she went by the bathroom. It was one of the plastic disposable kind that has a slender needle. The needle was bent in half, and it lay on the top of the litter in the trash basket. He'd made no effort to hide it, as though he'd wanted her to find it, but when she took his arm and rolled up his sleeve, he stood silently and offered no explanation. There were numerous puncture marks, all recent.

"Why?"

"Just vitamins, Valan. I'm rundown." He pulled down the sleeve and buttoned the cuff as if to close that topic of conversation at the same time.

It wasn't vitamins, she knew that. But she sensed he wasn't on mind-altering drugs either. It was disturbing.

Dusk was settling in over the lake and there was patches of mist around the rock outcrops that came down to the water's edge.

Friday, May 16

Theo arrived at the cottage a little before sunset and served Val breakfast in bed. He said she was ravishing wearing nothing but a sheet tucked around her, just under her arms. He looked much better, she decided. There was a bit of the old zest back in his eyes. She liked his eyes, dark brown and searching. The upper lids were heavy and rounded which gave him a very sexy and knowing expression. That, and his habit of watching things intently, she found fascinating.

"Sarah says she misses you. There's a new boyfriend, I think she wants to tell you all about him." He sat on the edge of the bed with one leg tucked under and one dangling off the side.

She smiled and nodded. "How are the tests coming? Have you had time to get any results?"

"A little. It looks as though you have the regenerative powers of an infant. The cell turnover rate is ten times greater than in normal adults. Protein metabolism is way up. There are lots of other things, but that's the gist of what I'm finding. I'm beginning to suspect a virus that may have caused some sort of chromosomal changes. I'd like your permission to have a blood sample examined by a couple of colleagues of mine who will be discreet: a virologist and a geneticist. It would help explain quite a few things, such as why you don't age. Your immunological support system is incredible. One drop of your blood kills any foreign life form I can find to put in it."

"I don't understand a whole lot of that, but does it mean there may be some sort of controls I can use?"

"Possibly. It's really too early to tell. I'd also like to isolate whatever it is in the disinfectant that affects you."

"You're encouraged?"

"Definitely." He smiled. "It looks good for you. Perhaps for others too; if we can control your syndrome perhaps we can save some of the people who are needlessly dying each year from cancer and other diseases. It's a thought. But that's way in the future." He unbuttoned his cuffs with a distracted look. "Wouldn't it be something if one of mankind's most feared predators turned out to be his savior?"

"Has anything else been happening in town?"

"Two men from Los Angeles stopped by the house today."

"Oh?"

"They stayed for quite a while. They're members of the Vampire and Werewolf Hunters Society. They told me they have over two hundred members, world-wide." He talked while he was tugging off his maroon tie, first loosening it with his fingers then throwing it on the chair beside the bed. His shirt followed.

"That's not what Claudius told us."

"Maybe Claudius doesn't know as much about them as he thinks."

"Do they have any official status, or are they just private citizens snooping around?" Val asked as he got up and headed for the bathroom.

"Nothing official, but they've both got a bit of that look in their eyes."

"Which look?"

"The look of a fanatic."

"When will they go away?"

"They insist on seeing you first, Valan."

"Can't you tell them that I am quite nervous and easily upset?"

"I did." He stuck his head around the corner of the bathroom to answer. "They promised they wouldn't upset you. The leader of the two, a Martin Nicholas, seemed a bit embarrassed even to bother you. The other one, a fat man named Tom Smith, announced that it's the policy of the Society to check up on every lead. They said that Claudius OK'd you but they want to have a look." He ducked back into the bathroom. Val went around the upper level and finished closing the drapes.

She was back in bed when he came out, wiped his face on a hand towel then threw it on the back of the chair.

"I didn't take time to shave this morning," he said. "There's something strange about Tom Smith, though."

"Other than his obvious alias?"

He nodded. "More than that. I can't put my finger on it, though. He was grossly overweight, and wore a black suit that was shiny at the knees and elbows."

"Is he crazy?"

"Beyond the obesity, not that I can see. He seems to be sincere, concerned. The other one is not very sure of himself." He went over and sat beside Val on the bed.

"I will not be badgered."

"Will you see them? I think it's best to face them and get it over with." He touched her face, running his fingers lightly down her cheek.

It was against her better judgment. Her instincts said run. But she wanted to please him. She replied, "Only if they give us a list of the questions they will ask. Only if you are there with me. I'll do it only because you ask it. If it goes badly don't question what I do. I will protect myself."

"Monday, then, come in about eleven. All right?" She nodded, and the conversation turned to other more pleasant things.

Val knew she was in love, and nothing else seemed to matter. When he clicked off the last light and came to her, glowing with warmth, across the wooden plank floor, she didn't try to think anymore.

Monday, May 19

Sarah ran out of the house to meet Val. She bounded down the steps, arms akimbo, and grabbed her around the waist without warning. Val was taken by surprise and almost bit her. It was a close call for Sarah, but she was completely unaware of the danger. Theo, following closely behind her, turned pale, but it was over in a moment.

The list of questions Theo had given Val seemed harmless enough. The men had specified noon for the time of the meeting and the patio behind the house as the meeting place. Val was wary, ready for anything. All of her belongings were packed into the trunk of a rented car parked at a shopping mall not far from the house; all except for five thousand dollars in a little bag in her bra. Even though she trusted Theo's intentions, she didn't trust the vampire hunters.

The day was overcast and easy for Val to bear as long as she wore her oversized sunglasses. Once the hunters arrived, they all sat in the white wrought-iron lawn chairs on the back patio and sipped tea.

Tom Smith wore a long chain around his neck, with a large gold crucifix dangling over the thickly padded flesh of his chest. It was obvious to Val that he believed the cross would protect him. She stifled a smile at the thought. He sat mountainously self-contained in his rolls of fat. He wasn't pleasant to look at. The other one, Martin Nicholas, was small, thin, and had a large Adam's apple. They were both armed with handguns in bulging shoulder holsters. No doubt the guns carried silver bullets. They were polite and seemed a little ill at ease with their task, but determined to carry it through.

Tom Smith began. "We asked for this interview because we received an anonymous tip that you are a vampire. That might sound preposterous, but we feel we have to check out all the possibilities. Vampires are a real threat to mankind." Smith ran his finger around the inside of his collar as he spoke. He was perspiring heavily, even though the temperature was only in the seventies.

Mrs. Mac wheeled a cart with snacks out onto the patio. "You'll need something, if you're going to skip lunch," she said, and bustled away.

"Have you ever had any experience with a real vampire?" Val asked Smith. "I don't even believe in all that supernatural mumbo jumbo."

"We have two well-documented cases within this last year," Smith replied. He took a plate of finger sandwiches from the cart and put them on the table in front of himself. "We can show you the files if you wish."

"What is it that makes a vampire?" she asked.

Nicholas waved his tea glass, slopping a bit onto his hand. "The need for blood is the only thing we've established. There don't seem to be too many other common factors. They vary in characteristics. Some can tolerate sunlight, some can't. Some can move with blinding speed, some can't. Some can hypnotize their victims, etc." He shrugged. Val looked at Smith. He shrugged, also, mimicking Nicholas' attempt at nonchalance. The huge layers of flab quivered all over his chest; he reminded Val of a hippopotamus wallowing in a swamp.

"About the only thing we know for sure about vampires," said Nicholas, his Adam's apple bobbing with each syllable, "is that they are practically indestructible. Just about the only way to do them in is with great physical trauma, cut off their heads or drive stakes through their hearts."

"You're not going to dismember me to see if I'm a vampire, are you?"

"Of course not."

"Have you ever talked to one?"

"No." Smith shook his head. "The one I had contact with refused to talk to me."

"Then you really don't know anything about the way they think or the way they feel, assuming there actually are vampires?"

"It doesn't matter," he replied a bit smugly. "They are undead and damned. We are doing them a favor by releasing their immortal souls to God's glory." His eyes rolled heavenward. Val nearly sniggered.

"I'd be a bit more convinced if you'd discussed things with a vampire, before you're so presumptuous as to drive a stake through his heart."

"They are vicious, amoral, irrational. They are evil incarnate!" He waved his hand. "There can be no dialogue with such things."

"Then why are you talking to me? What is it that made you think I'm a vampire?" Val shuddered.

"The blood in this lab mysteriously coming and going all the time, for one thing," Nicholas said, thrusting his chin out. "We've already checked this place out."

"I'm a hematologist," Theo said easily. "I use it in my research on blood serum. I've used the stockyards as a blood source now and then for years. What else?"

"We've been watching the house. She stays up all night and roams around in the dark, then sleeps all day."

"That's not true. Here I am," Val said, sipping a glass of iced water from a small pitcher Mrs. Mac had provided especially for her. "I get very tired and rest a lot. I also sleep late in the mornings. So do millions of other people who don't have to drag themselves out of bed at daybreak. They aren't even ill."

"That brings us to our first question. Why did you come here, to this doctor?"

"I've been to four other doctors who've been unable to help me. My medical records can be verified if you like," Val said, knowing that the documents, though completely fake, were thoroughly backed up with files planted in carefully selected places. Money does wonders, she mused. "Dr. James is trying to find out why I get so anemic periodically. It messes up my life."

"The next question is for you, doctor. Why did you take this case? You've been out of practice for several years."

"Curiosity." Theo spoke bluntly.

The questions went on, Smith and Nicholas following the list of questions they had given Theo. Finally Nicholas leaned back and dropped the paper onto his lap.

Val relaxed, lulled by their apologetic attitude and confident that she'd carried off the deception. The interrogation would soon be over. They would shake hands all around and the hunters would leave. "Do you still think I'm a vampyr?" she asked.

"Of course not." Smith smiled an easy gold-toothed smile. "Just one more thing. Could you try to identify this for us?"

He placed a box on the table. It was about the size of a cigar box, but made of metal and much heavier. His motions were smooth in a practiced way. An unusual grace, she thought. Then she noticed that the pupils of his eyes were huge, wide with interest and excitement. "When there is a secret, eyes will always betray it." The words of caution, once spoken by Robin, filled her. She left the box setting on the table without touching it and glanced at Theo. He looked puzzled.

Smith sat back and pressed the tips of his blunt fingers together, forming a steeple over his protruding belly.

"This wasn't on the list of questions," she protested and started to stand up. There were beads of oily sweat dotting Smith's forehead and upper lip. Something was definitely out of order.

"Wait," Nicholas said, holding his hand up. Val settled back, tense.

"No," she said shaking her head. "I want no more of this. It's making me very nervous."

"It's nothing," he said, reaching for the box. He fumbled with the catch. She didn't realize until he had it nearly open that he hadn't turned the box around. Whatever was in it would be directed toward her.

The lid came open with a blast of light and flame. She moved fast. The acrid smoke burned her nostrils; the light robbed her of her sight momentarily. She couldn't help herself. Looking back later, she realized the explosion was probably harmless, but her instinct for self-preservation was all powerful, and she was terrified. The chair tipped over behind her and its metallic clang on the pavement echoed dully in her ears. She was around the house and in the Ford before the others were able to stand up. The engine turned over, roaring as she gunned it. Gravel shot out as she raced down the hill. The landscape passed by, colorless and blurred until her eyes recovered. It was like moving in a phantasmagoric nightmare.

Val started trembling only when she pulled into an underground parking place in the mall. They hadn't followed her; she sat there for a few minutes pulling herself together. It was all over. Nothing left to do now but run; run and disappear. Her fast vanishing act was proof enough for anyone that there was something positively different about Valan Anderweldt. Her head fell forward until the steering wheel supported it entirely. All around shoppers were coming and going on their way to or from cars. No one paid any attention to the slender woman blowing her nose.

"'Abandon hope all ye that enter here.' That's written over the gates of Hell," Val whispered. For her it was written over the portals of that shopping mall in San Antonio. She had abandoned everything she'd found in the human world: Theo, Sarah, and even Wolf.

Chapter VII

Tuesday, May 20

Val walked through the mall, slowly, window shopping as she went. There were throngs of people strolling in the air conditioned arcade; women pushing strollers and couples leaning on each other. She matched their pace, flowing with them like a leaf on a slow current and with barely more consciousness than a leaf of what was happening around her.

The rental car was still where she'd left it, at the edge of the mall under an oak tree. The driver who had delivered it, a thin young man with black hair and Asiatic features, was more than pleased when she'd handed him a crisp twenty-dollar bill. He hadn't even suggested that she give him a lift back to his agency. He had just smiled, tipped his cap and wandered off in the direction of the bus stop.

Hot air flowed out all around her when she opened the door; the car smelled of something sour and of stale tobacco smoke. The edge of the seat on the driver's side was frayed. She frowned. The rental car was definitely second rate, but it would serve the purpose. It would get her to the airport in plenty of time to catch a flight to Dallas; another to New Orleans, and on to New York before sunset.

It would have taken an expert or a magician to follow her. She changed clothes and wigs at each airport and had booked each flight separately under different names. Everything was paid for with cash. In Dallas she got all new luggage, brown leather this time, and shipped the baby blue to a thrift shop found in the Fort Worth Yellow Pages, with no return address. The cooler was crated and sent to a curio shop in New York City. It would be picked up later.

The whole run was smooth, much more so than Val had anticipated. And she was able to pass the time thinking, because the planes were nearly empty. "Perhaps experience in getting lost counts for something. When they get to the Ford they'll find it has been registered to Sarah, and she'll find a set of keys for it on her vanity where I left them."

Val had left a short letter to them both in the glove compartment. She wanted them to know that she had decided to stay with them for a while and was sorry it could never happen. From the moment of the explosion Valan Anderweldt had ceased to exist. If things had gone differently, they never would have seen the letter.

The plane touched down at New York's International Airport with the thud of wheels hitting the pavement, the whir of the engines braking down. The whole fuselage shuddered, reluctant to come out of the sky. Val—"Ann Turner," now—was glad the flight was over. As far as she was concerned airplanes were definitely not the best way to travel. Fast, yes, but not the best. It had to do with the speed. Whenever she had to go more than a few hundred miles that fast it would throw her internal clock completely out of whack. Then the stars looked funny, and she'd get hungry at the wrong times.

Corey Madison was there to meet her at the terminal gate. He took her arm without even making small talk. Her skin seemed ghastly pale against his darkly tanned hand.

Corey was one of the lawyers who represented Val's business interests. He had a chauffeur, dressed in pin-striped suits, and never asked questions that were not his concern. He was always available and could provide any of Val's friends with foolproof, alternate identities whenever necessary. While Corey was capable of handling clandestine or illegal operations for his clients, he was the only human Val trusted completely; he and his father before him. For that he earned a million dollars, American, a year.

Val often wondered what he thought of her. She'd even asked him once. He'd just shrugged and said, "rich and invisible." He was right.

Within twenty-four hours Val would have a new passport and would be on a flight to Paris. In the meantime she rested at his home, a four-acre, three-house compound on the east coast of Long Island. The sound of the surf could be clearly heard when the windows were open. She found it soothing to her shattered emotions.

Wednesday, May 21
The other passengers on the transatlantic flight dozed off about midnight, and Val spent the night reading a

book. She planned to estivate for a while at the "safe house," the ancient chateau on the northern outskirts of Paris. The neighbors there thought it was a private club. However, they had no idea how exclusive the membership of Chateau Robinet really was. No human had stepped foot inside since the end of the war.

The house was dark red brick, three stories tall, with stone window mouldings, balconies, and porches. There was an attic above the third story and a multitude of cellars below ground. The whole place was immaculate, and was tended by three French vampyrs who were devoted caretakers. They lived in the gatekeeper's cottage. The entire property was surrounded by a seven-foot brick wall broken only at the main entrance. A rush of relief swept over Val when the ornate iron gates clanged shut behind the car.

"Home at last," she said as the car pulled up and stopped in front of the front porch. The early morning sunbeams were just hitting the grey slate shingles of the roof, causing them to glisten metallically.

Salvatore, who was driving, nodded and said, "It's been a long time." He'd met her at airport customs at four thirty in the morning and silently offered his arm. They had barely spoken on the way to the house.

"Nearly five years."

"Your rooms have been made ready. You'll want to go right up?" He helped her out of the car and they went into the house together. He treated her as though she was terribly sensitive and fragile, although he knew that wasn't true. He put her in a chair in the hallway and went back for the bags.

"I won't be needing the rooms right away, except to store the luggage," she said when he came in with them.

"Oh?" He arched his brows.

"I need to sleep for a while. Is anyone else up there?"

"Only Potchnick."

"Le Guignol?"

"Yes, he's estivating in the back of the attic."

Val shuddered. "I hope we won't meet."

"You're much more powerful than he is. You shouldn't worry. Anyway, he plans to sleep until December. There was some trouble in South Africa. He's hiding."

"What did he do this time, massacre an entire village the way he did in Mikros?"

"He didn't kill anyone personally. He was selling guns to rebels." They went up to the second floor to her suite, Sal leading the way with both arms full of luggage. He pushed the door open with his foot and set the bags down on the sheepskin at the side of the bed.

"It hasn't changed a bit," she sighed.

"I'll leave you now, the sun is almost up." He came to her by the door, and they hugged each other closely, her cheek tight against his silk shirt. It was good to feel his familiar arms around her. "It's been difficult for you?" He made no effort to let go of her.

"Yes."

"Would you like me to stay today?"

"No." She shook her head but made no effort to move away.

"Is there someone else now?"

"No, it's over; all except the pain of it." He dropped his arms and they stepped apart.

"Until this evening?"

She shook her head. "Until the full moon."

"I'll still be here." He left her then, slim and graceful

as always.

"As always," she said after he'd closed the door and was gone. "You are here whenever I need you. We are complete opposites. But we have been closer than friends ever since Robin died in the gardens of this chateau."

She took only a pen and notebook up to the attic and used them to get her thoughts together, to unwind, to get in tune with the motions of the earth.

The attic was huge and windowless, with fourteen small cubicle-like dormitories where vampyrs could sleep in complete darkness and solitude for weeks at a time without being disturbed. While Val slept, discreet inquiries would be made. She wanted to learn more about the Vampire and Werewolf Hunters Society. "Corey will take take of it properly," she mused. "He always does."

Her cubicle was just under the eaves at the front of the house. It had been freshly painted white and was immaculately clean. She got into bed and began to write.

I will estivate for a month and wake when the moon is full again. It's nearly full now. Sometimes I think that we are the normal ones and humans are the freaks. They can't feel the tides in their blood and cannot measure the passing of time by the rhythms in their bodies. Don't they sometimes feel that they are only partly awake, partly alive? I don't regret being the way I am, but I miss Theo, his warmth and the way he cares about me.

I am ready; clean and cool. The bed is hard and smooth with one thick feather comforter. That's all that is necessary. The less to irritate the skin during the long sleep the better.

As I start to relax, my mind is slowing down. The

cares I brought to this small room are fading. Soon I will sleep. And down the hall, in the furthest cubicle, lies the most infamous of us all: Potchnick. He's old, four hundred years or more and very photoallergic and long in the tooth, as we all get with great age. Only the Countess Carlotta claims to be older. No one knows who made Potchnick a vampyr. He came out of Poland at the end of the first world war with blood on his hands that he refused to wash off, and madness in his mind. He's a dark man with black hair and heavy brows that form a thick line above his deepset eyes. His arms are hairy and his cheeks always blue from his beard. Whenever I see him, I am reminded of the Russian Rasputin. But that is impossible.

Personally, I think he is the cause of most of our bad image. Potchnick has a nasty habit of sneaking around in underdeveloped regions and killing the inhabitants until he gets run out. Sooner or later he'll get caught. I don't think any of us will be sorry. We tolerate him because he makes no demands on the group and never makes converts. He doesn't have particularly strong power either. That's the main reason he's still alive. None of us have ever been threatened enough by him to go in and kill him while he's asleep. It's been done before.

I have just dined on the blood of rabbits; a great delicacy. They keep several hundred on the property. It takes seventeen or eighteen to donate enough for one meal without harming them. It's hardly worth the effort. But delicious.

She licked her lips and smiled faintly, anticipating forgetfulness, then slept.

Monday, June 16
There was a hand on her shoulder, shaking her. "It's too soon," Val thought, struggling to go back into warm unconsciousness. "The moon's not full . . . ."

The hand persisted; a feminine hand.

"Valerie," a voice echoed its way into the silence. "Wake up. It's important."

She tried to twist away wondering why Sarah was trying to wake her up. The shaking continued, even harder. "Wake up, Valerie."

Val sighed and gave up. Her eyes came open slowly, unwillingly, dry and scratchy. The room was dark except for a small taper glowing calmly on the stand at the head of the bed. Thank goodness, she thought. Sarah hadn't turned on the overhead light. That would have been unbearable.

It wasn't Sarah at all. Claire's cameo face hovered over Val like a wraith. Her gown, long-sleeved and black, blended into the semidarkness of the room, and in Val's waking confusion all she saw were hand and a face, separate entities in space.

"Go away," Val mumbled.

Claire let go of Val's shoulder. "Val, I've a letter for you from someone named Sarah James."

"How . . . ?" It seemed to be incredible. Had she not covered her trail well enough to stop a fifteen-year-old child from finding her?

"Come on, let me get you up. You can read it once you've broken your fast." She had to help Val sit up, supporting her neck and back with a black-clad arm. Val felt terrible. Every muscle and joint ached. There seemed to have been rats or something worse nesting in her mouth, from the taste of it.

Claire reached back to the night stand and handed Val the brimming golden goblet that had been sitting there. By the time she had finished it she was wide awake, shaky but alert, and the rats had completely moved out of her mouth.

Usually when she woke up after a long sleep it was like waking from a nap; she felt hungry and full of well being. She'd never been wakened out of time like that before. It felt worse than fighting off the hangover from a weeklong drunken orgy.

Claire handed her a thick envelope postmarked San Antonio, and addressed to Claire in Sarah's spidery and immature hand.

"How did she get your name and address?"

"Read it."

Dear Claire,

I am writing because you must be a friend of Valan's. I found your letter to her the day after those horrible men frightened her away. It was in the cushions of the chair in her room. I took it and hid it. I was cleaning her room because I didn't go to school. I was too upset to go that day.

I am sure you must know how to get in touch with her. It is very important. Please give her this letter. She has to read it.

Yours truly, Sarah James

P.S. Claire, no one else knows that you wrote to Valan. I destroyed your letter. I hope that was the right thing to do.

There was another envelope; this one still sealed. "Valan Anderweldt" was written across the front in large block letters. Val's hands shook as she tore it open.

Dear Valan,

Poppa and I got your note. Thanks for the car, even though I can't drive it until next year when I get my provisional license. We both love you very much, also, and wish you could come back. Poppa explained the whole thing to me, about your being a vampire and all that. It doesn't matter. No one ever listened to me the way you did. And no one ever made Poppa so happy, not even Mom, and she was terrific.

The real reason for this letter is Poppa. He is very sick again. You didn't know it because it's supposed to be a secret, but he has had chronic lymphatic leukemia for nearly four years. Most of the time he can keep it controlled with the drugs he takes. It is a special kind of leukemia that grownups get. It's about the easiest to control the symptoms of, but it is almost always fatal within five years.

That is why he would get so tired sometimes. They discovered it during a regular physical all the doctors at the University have to take. That's when he quit his practice so he wouldn't have to work so hard.

But he kept working with the university and at home all the time to find a cure. That's when you came to us. I think with a little more time he might have had one; a cure, that is.

When you left, he hired a detective to find you and another to make sure the vampire hunters have gone away. The detective got a list of most of the members and we know where they are. I made a copy for you—it's enclosed.

Anyway, when the first detective couldn't trace you past where you left the car, Poppa just seemed to give up.

This is the most important part. His leukemia has been in remission or partial remission for a long time but all of a sudden he is losing weight fast. He doesn't seem to care. Mrs. Mac and I put him in the hospital this morning for new therapy. He is very sick. The doctors told us not to expect too much success this time, because the symptoms are pretty severe.

What I'm getting at, Valan, is only you can save him. Please come back. Just for a few minutes even, and save Poppa.

When I mail this I'm going to the hospital on the bus

and tell him that you'll be coming next week. I pray that you will. Every minute I pray.

I included a map of the hospital and an X marks Poppa's room. Visiting hours are six to eight but the doors are never locked, and not very many people are there late at night. None of the vampire hunters are here now.

Love, Sarah

P.S. Wolf misses you.

Val handed the letter to Claire. "Read it," she said. There were tears running down her cheeks. She felt very empty, as though everything of value was slipping away.

"You'll go back?" Claire asked, when she finished the letter. "You really love that human? You will do it?"

Val nodded numbly.

"OK, listen, you get yourself ready. I'll go get your flight through. Tell Sarah we all appreciate the list. There are over a hundred and eighty names on it." She waved the list as she sailed out the door.

The letters dropped fluttering from Val's hand to the floor while she sat on the edge of the bed with the comforter wrapped around her. She let the tears come as they would. She tried to make plans and was doing a bad job of it when she heard footsteps on the stairs. Salvatore came to the open door of the cubicle.

"May I?" he asked, hesitating at the threshold. She nodded and he came over and sat beside her, slipping his arm around her back. "What happened? Claire came flying down looking quite upset."

"The letters," Val stared down at the floor while he reached over and scooped up the scattered pages. She buried her face in his soft woolen jacket while he read them.

"Get ready," he said, squeezing her. "We'll go as soon as we can." By the time the realization that he was going with her had sunk in, he'd already gone back downstairs to arrange things.

Friday, June 20

And so Val returned to San Antonio, this time with Salvatore. He had been a person of the night for nearly thirty years. They dodged the sun with a layover in New York and arrived at three in the morning. The rental car and motel room were waiting for them.

There were two things they wanted to do: visit Theo and, since no one in the group could think of any vampyrs who might be in San Antonio, there was a strong possibility that an untrained and unpredictable rogue was in the area. They wanted to find him.

Val and Salvatore rested all day in the motel room, a modern place with one wall made entirely of glass and drapery; barely dark enough for Sal. As soon as it was dark he drove Val across town to the University Hospital. All she felt was dry-mouth anticipation. Sarah's map was accurate. She waited in the rental car and played with the glove compartment, popping it open and shut just to hear the noise.

"He's there, Valerie," Sal said to her when he came back down. "There, but not for long. It would be best to hurry if you are going to do it."

She nodded mutely as he helped her from the car. The corridors of the hospital were clean, bare, and sterile; the walls echoed their softly clicking footsteps. They took the stairs to avoid the nurses' stations, gliding quickly from floor to floor. The fewer people who saw them the better. Visiting hours were nearly over and the

132

clocks over the elevators were clicking audibly, but no one paid any attention to the late comers. The corridors seemed endless. Each time they turned a corner Val strained for a glimpse of Sarah.

Finally Val saw her. She wore a red dress and was sitting on a bench at the far end of the hall. Both of her legs were tucked under her; she was staring out of the window. There was nothing out there but a parking lot.

"Sarah," Val called softly. She jumped up and started to come. "No," Val told her. "Don't come any closer. I'm very thirsty."

Sarah stopped in midstride, a little fearful. "Valan, I'm so glad you came. I'd almost given up hope." She stretched her hand toward Val wistfully.

"It's all right. How's Theo?"

"Not good." She shook her head. "The doctors say only a few more days at the most. It's gone into pneumonia."

"Is there any one around who will be likely to bother us?"

"No, they know he's dying so they all stay away." She spoke with bitterness. "They don't care any more."

"How will you get home tonight?"

"I'm not going home. That creep, Nicholas, has been hanging around again. He came back when he heard how sick Poppa was. He thinks you'll try to contact me at the house. Uncle Bart's there, Poppa's big brother from Houston. He doesn't know anything."

Val nodded. "Salvatore, will you sit and talk with her while I see Theo?"

"Of course," he said, rather urbanely. "Lovely child." He took her arm and led her back to the bench. Sarah went with him, staring up at his handsome face

133

and trying to pull away. He let her go. "Don't be afraid," he said as they sat down on the plastic-covered couch. Sarah had moved to the end of the cushion, as far away from him as possible. "I'm not hungry." He smiled one of his most personable smiles. "It'll be all right. Tell me, have you lived in Texas all your life?"

A smile played at the corners of Val's lips. "He could make a stone talk, he's that charming," she thought, turning to enter Theo's private room. There was a large red-and-white no-smoking sign on the door. The door itself, heavy and hard to push, locked easily behind her. The night lamp over the bed washed the room with yellow light. Theo was asleep. His hard, whistling breathing filled the air. There was very little other noise; the constant hum of the central air conditioning and the chugging of a pump somewhere nearby. His features were alien, changed by his illness, an irrefutable declaration of his morbidity.

His body, pitifully thin, was covered to his chest with a rough, white hospital sheet. Only his left forearm was exposed, and there were restraining straps around it, securing it to a board. His fingers, bony and large-knuckled, curled over the end of it like something from a novelty store. Val couldn't help frowning when she saw all the needle marks. There were three separate tubes in his arm, and signs that there had been others. It was the arm of a stranger.

Gently, she pulled away the coarse muslin sheet. The sturdy body that had held her so easily only a month ago, was reduced to a wasted wreck. She'd seen people who had been starved to death in better shape than he was: the protruding bones, the tight dry skin, the shrunken flesh. She could have lost her fingers in the hollows between his ribs. There were cutdown shunts implanted in his side and ankles. Tubes seemed to be running everywhere.

She was completely stunned. It was impossible, her mind declared, for such a change in so short a time. He stirred in his sleep; she dropped the sheet back over him and looked at his unfamiliar face. It was grey, even in the yellow light, with little beads of sweat on his forehead and upper lip. His cheeks were sunken. A pink plastic tube taped to one side ran into his nose. They hadn't shaved him in several days. Had it been anyone other than Theo, she would have been repulsed. Oddly enough, between her thirst and her love for him, she felt an irresistible attraction toward him and a strange eagerness to do what she had to do.

She looked around and found a new razor blade on one of the nurse's trays. She unwrapped it; it fitted nicely into her right had. She reached for the edge of the sheet and lifted it enough to slide carefully in beside him. She didn't want to disturb him.

"Valan," his hoarse whisper caught her by surprise.

"Yes," she answered.

"I knew you'd come. Sarah said you would." His eyes fluttered as Val kissed his dry and tasteless lips. His consciousness seemed to fade away. She moved her lips to his neck, just where the jawbone curves up, and licked him there tenderly to locate the pulse under the stubble of his beard. She kissed him hard, pulling a bit of the skin into her mouth. The high oxygen concentration near his face was exhilarating. She felt curious, as though she was floating. The hospital odors, his familiar scent, the closeness; everything felt good. She sighed and pulled away slightly to savor the moment.

"Do it," he whispered. His right arm came up and around her back weakly.

With a swift stroke her teeth cut deeply into his neck and she drew out the poisonous blood that was killing him. It tasted pale, thin and lifeless. She drank until his heart and breathing slowed, then quickly slashed her wrist where the thickest blue vein stood out and forced it into his mouth.

He gagged once, then sucked greedily, drinking faster than the natural flow provided. Val's arm ached as he pulled her life blood out. Finally, when she began to feel a little weak, she stopped the flow of blood. They lay together then for a long time. Within minutes his cheeks seemed to fill in and his color was less pallid. He grew stronger.

"Get this mess of stuff off me."

"No," Val said smiling. "You're going to have to wear it until Monday. Then you can claim a sudden remission. If you don't, they'll be suspicious. Pretend it's a miracle. They'll all be happy. It's not so unusual. It's happened before, lots of times."

"The miracle is you coming back," he laughed. "But how can I show my appreciation tied to this bed with tubes in one end and out the other?" He actually laughed.

"Spoken like a true chauvinist. You'll just have to wait a while." She touched his lips. "We're leaving now. It isn't safe for me to be here very long. Your old buddy, Nicholas, is back in town and harassing Sarah. We'll be together soon." She kissed him once again, this time hard on the mouth, then slipped away.

Val and Salvatore were back in the motel by midnight. He was restless. She was nervous. They drew

136

apart into separate worlds by mutual agreement. He went out to drive around the city. Val took a long hot shower and settled down to think.

Saturday, June 21

Salvatore made it back to the motel just before dawn with a great screeching of tires. He sauntered into the room and sank into the easy chair with an elaborate show of calm.

"Damnable city." He flicked imaginary dust from his lapel. "Or don't these people believe in night life? Do you realize, Valerie, that in this entire city there aren't enough people out at night past midnight to form a decent party?"

She shrugged. "I can always find something to do."

A narrow shaft of light pierced the drapes. He stood and adjusted them before kicking off his shoes beside his bed. "To bed, old girl, ere the dawn finds us abroad. Hang out the sign."

Chapter VIII

Sunday, June 29

Each night they dressed in jeans and old shirts, sneakers and gloves, and went out walking in the downtown area. Parts of the city were old, with main thoroughfares laid over cattle trails. Indian missions from hundreds of years before, built over campsites from even before that, nestled among modern glass and chromed buildings. The whole town had been built to accommodate a lazy river that wound and bent back upon itself. Stores used the river for their access. People climbed down stone steps to walk along its banks. Val found it charming.

They walked there at night until the bars and cafés closed at one and two in the morning. Then they wandered on to the bus station to watch the transients settling into corners for the night. Toward three o'clock, Salvatore would move the car to the market and they would sit there for a while.

Nowhere did they find the signs they were seeking. Exhausted, they would return to the hotel only to start again the next night. The creatures they visited in the countryside were quite gentle and came to them willingly.

They saw the barrio, where Spanish was the only language and poverty the way of life. They were not accosted. The people there kept their violence to themselves. They walked to the far east side where the black population lived. Nothing, save a few curtains hastily raised and dropped as they passed by, marked their passage.

The city was silent after dark compared to some like New York or Hong Kong where the overpopulation problem has been attacked by using space in the time frontier, twenty-four hours a day. San Antonio, in the center of vast open places, had no need to crowd its people, no need to use its space to the fullest. There was always more land available.

It was not an industrial town where day and nightshift workers were always coming and going in a constant eddying flow of humanity. Here, the night worker was the occasional sight; the all-night café waitresses, the janitors in the large office buildings, the lonesome policeman on his beat.

For Val it was a nice place. For Salvatore, boring.

Val had heard nothing from Sarah or Theo, no news good or bad, and she was burning to know how the effects of the change were taking hold on Theo. It would be fast at first, she knew. Then as time passed, the changes would come more and more slowly. The final change, the photoallergy would not occur until near the end of his normal lifespan.

She wanted Salvatore to call Sarah. She had little patience to wait any longer.

"Sarah, this is Mr. Night." Salvatore spoke with a light European accent. "I'm a friend of your father's. We met one evening at the hospital?"

"Of course. How are you?"

"How's your father?"

"Much better; he's home now, convalescing."

"Is he able to receive callers?"

"Uncle Bart is here. Poppa told him everything. They're very close. Uncle Bart came from Houston as soon as he could when he heard Poppa was sick."

"Is everything all right?"

"I think so."

"I see," Sal's voice suddenly became stern. "Sarah, if you or your Father need help, you must let us know. We have all the proper resources at our command. You have my number?"

"Yes. I'll call tomorrow. Say 'Hello' to Valan for me."

"Of course," he snorted as he replaced the receiver. "Valan, indeed. Valerie, that makes two humans who know about us because of your doctor.

"Come along, my dear, it's time we went out for the evening."

Night heat poured into the car when Salvatore opened the door for Val, palpable and unpleasant. They had used the air conditioner all the way down to the yards. Now the odor of the pens was overwhelming, the smell of cattle and dung, of scalded hides and entrails from the packing plant next door. Poor creatures, calmly eating their last hay, looked out through the wooden slats of the fences and snorted with their slobbery noses.

"I don't like it," Val said. "It's too risky coming

here. Nicholas may be watching for me."

"Look, that jerk is like all fanatics. Easily bored, and not very bright. He's watching your doctor's house. That will keep him occupied. Come along. If we're going to find your rogue we have to check out the concentrated blood supplies around here."

"I know," she sighed. He was right.

They waited until clouds darkened the sky before they crossed the street to the pens themselves. Monday was the main day of activity in the yards, with the weekly auction and all the buyers and sellers moving stock in and out. Those that remained were destined to be moved to the slaughterhouse in a day or two.

The place was a labyrinth of tiny corrals and alleyways interconnected by swinging gates. Above it all ran a catwalk where the buyers and sellers could stand and argue the merits of their offerings. Some of the animals lay asleep in their pens; others moved around restlessly, tossing their horns and eyeing the strangers with white-cornered eyes.

There were three men there, night watchmen, but they didn't look up. They were too busy prying a cow out of a corner where she'd had the misfortune to wedge herself as she'd rolled over in the mud.

None of the animals looked at Val with recognition in their expressions. "Poor dumb brutes. If they could speak," she whispered, tugging at Salvatore's sleeve, "surely they'd prefer our methods to those who claim we're the monsters. Our methods aren't nearly so final."

"Humph."

They refreshed themselves in the pen of a gigantic grey bull of the Brahman type. He was taller at the hump over his shoulders than Salvatore and had veins like ropes hanging loosely in the folds of his huge dewlaps. He stood calmly watching them with his great brown eyes while they stroked him and drank. He did not mind when they took even more for their use tomorrow. Val sensed that he knew his doom was close, and that he preferred the lassitude the loss of blood would bring.

They were followed back to the motel. Val was sure of it. She saw a strange car sitting in the parking lot; not a tourist's or traveler's car, but one with local license plates, dented bumpers, and worn paint. Not the sort of car that would be driven by any one staying at a luxury motel.

There was a man behind the wheel, just sitting there holding on to the steering wheel; a Mexican. Val was curious and wanted to go over to him.

"Wait! He'll come to us if he needs to," Salvatore said, apparently unconcerned, and pulled her along towards their room.

He called a friend who called a friend who called . . .

The car was registered to Herminia Garza of San Antonio and had been reported stolen last week. "Interesting," he said when he hung up the phone.

Val noticed that she was chewing on her lower lip, a bad habit from early childhood.

Sal examined his handgun and put it on the nightstand.

The stranger sat there in the car until almost dawn, then drove away moments before the sun came up.

"The rogue?" Val asked.

"Perhaps."

143

Tuesday, July 1

Sarah called from a pay phone late in the afternoon while Salvatore was singing a fractured Italian aria in the shower. Theo seemed to be fully recovered. Uncle Bart was willing to cooperate. Their neighborhood was quiet. There was no sign of Nicholas, or of fat Smith.

The stranger was there again, parked in the same place, watching. Just after dark Salvatore silently approached and placed his lean fingers through the car window onto the man's shoulder. He was stocky and dark, apparently forty. It all came out in a burst of rapid Spanish. His name was Jesse, Jesse Moreno. He had been made a vampyr by his grandmother's lover when a young man. It had happened in the wild hill country in northern Mexico, where only Indians descended from the Aztecs lived. He said there were many like him there. He had spent many years digging for gold and never found any. Then he had come to the United States to make his fortune. It was a slow process for him. He was ignorant, English was difficult. He couldn't read or write but he was always a hard worker. He was actually nearly ninety years old. Jesse wasn't sure exactly. The years ran together in his memory.

When Val looked at him full in the face for the first time, his features shimmered and blurred until she glanced away. She looked back at him; it happened again and disturbed her greatly. Finally she decided to look and not turn away. When she stared at him and his features shifted again, melting away, a yellow-fanged monster stood staring at her instead of a benign and somewhat apologetic Mexican. Just as suddenly, the fiery-eyed visage vanished, and Jesse was there, completely unaware of what had happened. Val realized that the transformation from man to beast and back again had occurred only within her mind. Jesse was the vampyr who'd attacked the old wino, Mr. Warren. Nothing like that vision had ever happened to Val before and it was a long time before the effect wore off.

Jesse went with them that evening. They had decided to rent a house, get out of the dreary motel, and had made an appointment with a real-estate agent. Jesse sat in the front seat with the agent, Mrs. Volney, and leered at her with a yellow-toothed smile.

"Five acres come with the house," Mrs. Volney said. She spoke with quick, high-pitched chirps. She moved like a bird, too, with rapid gestures. The little Datsun she drove wavered and jolted along, leaving Val slightly nauseous. Jesse unnerved her. She constantly darted glances at him.

"The fence is stone, six feet high, all around the perimeter. The alarm goes off in the house if anything over fifty pounds hits the top. The previous owner was a lawyer; didn't trust anyone." She clucked her tongue as the car's headlights swept over the front of the building. "Two-car garage, here; enclosed, too. That's rare in these parts." She pulled up in front of the red brick house with a lurch. Val gritted her teeth. "But the house is lovely. Two stories, trees everywhere, a wide circular drive, huge wrought iron gates and perhaps best of all, no close neighbors."

"It looks like a northern house," Salvatore said as they unbent themselves from the cramped seats. The gaslights along the drive and in front of the house provided dim illumination but left most of the grounds in soft shadows.

"The original owners were from Pennsylvania."

Sal stood looking up at the narrow windows with approval. "Doesn't get much light."

"Oh, lots of shade around this place," answered Mrs. Volney as she jingled her huge keyring, sorting through them twice before she selected one. "Saves on the utility bills. Though heaven knows anyone who can afford this place shouldn't have to worry. Wait 'til you see the interior."

She unlocked the heavy carved wooden door and ushered them inside. Jesse wandered off to look at the gardens, muttering something about beautiful flowers. The downstairs was furnished in pearl grey and dark red.

"Very elegant," Val said, touching the back of a velvet couch.

"All the furniture comes with it. That's why the deposit is so large."

"Why is the house furnished?" Val asked. "Isn't that a bit unusual with such a large piece of property?"

"Well, I'm not supposed to mention it, but the people who lived here were killed in a plane wreck. It'd queer a deal for most people to find out that the previous owners were killed. You look like sensible folks, though.

"Seven bedrooms upstairs and an unfinished attic, two large sitting rooms here, a kitchen, dining room and a basement you wouldn't believe existed in Texas."

Later Salvatore and Mrs. Volney sat down to discuss terms. He got it for a quarter less than the asking price. Val wanted to pay cash, but Salvatore said it would look suspicious and wrote a check on one of Corey's accounts for the entire six months' lease plus the deposit. Even at that Mrs. Volney's face paled visibly when he handed her the little blue piece of paper worth fifty-five thousand dollars.

She gave him the keys and took them back to the motel. They would get their luggage and move in.

Wednesday, July 2
Jesse stayed in the utility room behind the heating system in the basement. He liked the darkness. It reminded him of home. He looked at Val the way Wolf did as he thanked her for letting him stay.

"He'll have to go, you know," Sal said when the stocky Mexican had left the living room and returned to the cellar.

Val nodded. "He'd never fit in with the rest of the group." She stroked the velvet armrest of her chair. "It would be unkind even to attempt it."

"Well?" Salvatore crossed his legs, leaned back leisurely and waited.

"There are two solutions. The first is unthinkable."
Salvatore nodded.

"The second—send him somewhere, some place he can speak the language and do useful work."

"Send him to Don Alba." Sal waved his hand as if the problem were so minor that it was inconsequential.

"Javier? in Rio?"

"Of course."

She nodded. "Will you take care of it?"

"Always at your service." He smiled.

Salvatore had a brief conversation with Jesse, and longer sessions on the telephone with the airlines. After he had spoken to Don Alba in Rio de Janiero, he returned to Val.

"All set. He goes tonight, lays over in Panama City. Don Alba will pick him up in Rio. Happy?"

She smiled at him and nodded but her thoughts were miles away in a white brick house. She wondered where the hunters were. She wondered what Theo was doing, when he would come, and whether things would be the same between them.

Thursday, July 3

While Salvatore left to take Jesse to the airport, she roamed the house alone, examining each room minutely, looking for momentos of the family that had preceded them, but all she found were a button and a toothpick in one of the hot-air registers. She put them on the coffee table in the living room and sat on the sofa to wait.

"Val? I'm back. By the way," Salvatore called from the doorway, "I forgot to tell you. Theo is coming tomorrow evening."

"To stay?" She looked up expectantly.

"Don't know." He waved through the door and started upstairs. "He says the hunters gave up. Left today. Called Sarah and apologized for their suspicions; said God had called them to Georgia on a new chase. Fanatics! Pea-brains, everyone." He went on upstairs.

She sat there with one foot tucked under her and chewed her lips, and tried not to think about Theo.

Chapter IX

Friday, July 4

The sky was dark and there was a storm brewing, sweeping quickly out of the east. Cold gusts of wind eddied around Theo, and leaves scuttled like live things across the drive. Even the trees felt it, dancing their slow waltz in rhythm to the wind. It was a heavenly night of rich earth odors and strange sounds outside. Theo wondered how he'd endured the living death of his illness for so long when life was so beautiful all around him. And he felt young, strong and powerful as he'd never felt before, and Valan was waiting for him, inside this house. He heard the click of the front door as it started to open. Their waiting was over. His lean hands clenched with anticipation. He wanted her. The door flew open with a mighty crash, pulled by the wind.

The sky was heavy and rolling. Lightning lashed the clouds in fury. She stood with the wind tearing at her yellow silk skirt, pulling at her hair. He came up the steps two at a time to greet her: like the hero in a wonderfully trashy romantic novel.

She was smiling, her perfect teeth glistening; he

picked her up and swung her around and around on the porch. Then into the house he carried her, like a bride. He reveled in his renewed strength, the man smell not yet gone from his body. Outside the first huge drops of rain spattered on the drive.

The house felt uninhabited. The halls were silent. Salvatore, with a knowing look on his face, had retired to his room for the night. He was reading the Bible, again, he claimed.

Theo and Val spent the night with love, sharing the feeling of oneness as they moved together, warm and comfortable despite the wild symphony of the rain outside. The other beds they'd shared were only a prelude to the ways they now found to please each other.

He was vampyr now, and that made all the difference. The muscles of his arms were harder as he held her, his breath slower, deeper as he measured the vital signs within his body. Val's face when she looked at him was so tender that he felt he was holding a virgin bride in the first blush of love, eager, yet hesitant to let herself go. Then when he anointed her body with his lips she matched him kiss for kiss. It felt marvelous abandoning themselves to each other. There was no more holding back, no more need for her to protect him from her all too greedy appetite.

They were the same and drank from the same sweet cup of life. The first time they had made love—it seemed so long ago—she had made him hers. Tonight, with whispered words and passionate embraces, he made her his.

He slept then, not yet used to the night. His restored body lay across the satin sheets, and the smile of a little boy played on his lips. Faint red scars still marked his arms, his side, and his ankles. They were the only signs of the illness he'd conquered.

When he woke, they made love again. "Does it ever stop?" he asked. "I feel like we could go on forever."

"No," she smiled, smiling lazily up at him. "We could go on forever."

"You said one time that vampyrs never get tired."

"Um hum." She looked like a satisfied kitten, eyes closed, lips slightly parted and turned up at the corners.

"I never dreamed . . . . " He rolled onto his side and stared at her, one hand propping up his head. "We could actually make love forever."

"Until we get bored or sleepy or thirsty." She moved her head just enough to look at him through barely opened lashes, and he realized she was teasing him.

He frowned. Something wasn't quite right but he couldn't put a name on it. It was as though he wanted something.

"When was the last time you ate?" she asked. He wondered if she'd read his mind, but her eyes were closed, and she was lying there in pale perfection like a marble statue.

"Yesterday. Sarah brings it. I eat it."

"When was the last time you were hungry?"

He dropped back onto his pillow and looked at the ceiling. "Before that night . . . . "

"The night you became one of us. You're not hungry, but you crave something, and the need for it grows stronger all of the time."

"Yes," and his throat constricted with revulsion. She meant blood.

"You should start now, before the need is so great you lose control."

151

"The beast?"

"Perhaps." She sat up, touched his arm lightly. "You never know about your beast until its turn comes. Some of us can almost starve to death without letting go. Your beast will wear your strongest desire." She got up, put on her robe, a long filmy negligee, and left the room.

He wanted to put it off, to delay taking the first sip of blood that would seal his fate, but he knew she was right. He would only be postponing the inevitable. He'd tasted blood before, almost daily, in the course of his work. It had never bothered him; in fact, the minute differences in the taste of a drop of blood were reliable clues in research. Yet the idea of quaffing a liter of blood like so much orange juice was hard to accept.

Val came back, padding lightly on the bare wooden floor. She was carrying two full glasses on a silver tray. The blood was dark, almost gelid. He closed his eyes again.

He heard her set the tray on the night stand, then move away. Then the smell of it hit him, assailing his nostrils with its sweet wine, salty meat, essence of life.

He started trembling uncontrollably. The vibrations started in his throat and spread in waves until his whole body shook. A dull roaring started in his head, the sound of it blocking out everything else. Then the spasm was over, but the roaring persisted. When he opened his eyes and sat up, there were steam clouds rolling out of the open bathroom door.

He took a deep breath and exhaled, grateful that she hadn't been there to see him lose conscious control of his body and humbled by the power of what had ruled him for a few minutes.

"I think I threw a fit, just now," he said, when she

came back into the bedroom. She'd put on a pair of jeans and a T-shirt and stood at the side of the bed absently rubbing her damp hair with a towel.

"Everyone does. You'll be all right now. That was just your insides gearing up for the first meal."

"Would it have been worse if I waited longer?"

She nodded. "Some rogues who don't know what is happening go berserk at the first smell of blood. It can be pretty bad. A few even try to commit suicide." She perched herself on the bed beside him. When he took her hand, his fingers were still shaking.

"What's a rogue?"

"A vampyr that doesn't belong to a group, or that didn't have any help at the beginning or one that is anti-vampyr. You know—working against us and humankind."

"I'm ready," he said, pulling his legs up to sit cross-legged in the tangled sheets.

She reached to the tray and handed him a glass. "Drink this one now," she said. "It's all you'll need."

"Don't you want yours?"

She shook her head and smiled. "They were both for you."

"Were?" He turned and stared at the glass on the tray. It was empty. He realized that the taste of it was on his tongue, but he had no recollection of drinking it. Being a vampyr obviously had drawbacks he hadn't anticipated.

"To the fulfillment of dreams," he said, nodding to his glass.

"To the acceptance of reality," she replied.

"It's the same thing," he said. Then he drank, and knew the blood was right for him.

Thursday, July 10

Val and Theo were playing cards on the kitchen table when Salvatore came in from hunting and dropped his bulging green knapsack on the drainboard. It landed with a heavy thud.

"There," he said. "Done for the night." He started pulling dark bags of blood from the sack. "We'd better start planning to move. It's too dangerous to stay here much longer."

"Why?" Theo pushed the cards together toward the middle of the table. "The only one who knows where we are is Sarah."

"That's right," Salvatore said. "What if she decides to come here? Can you protect her from yourself?" He picked up two of the bags, weighed them in his hand and went to the refrigerator.

Theo was silent then, thinking of how abruptly he'd lost control at the first scent of blood. He loved Sarah, wanted to be near her, to be responsible for her, to be there when she needed a father. Even though his brother Bart had promised to take care of her, Theo found it almost impossible to let go. "Val?" he finally asked.

She nodded. "I have to agree with Salvatore. I like it here, but he's right. We have to go before an accident happens." She gathered the cards and shuffled them. "It won't be for long, six months perhaps."

Monday, July 14

Salvatore brought Val the last of the mail that they'd receive there. He had closed the box at the post office; the mail would be forwarded to Corey until Val settled somewhere else. Val finalized the papers on a ranch in Colorado, OKed the half-interest purchase of a California-Japanese computer company, and took care of several other business dealings, all easy. The only letter that disturbed her was from the monk, Modesto.

Dear Valerie,

I sincerely hate to bother you in the middle of your grand experiment, but Gaston has gone a little too far. His Children of Rhapsody Church is an abomination in the eyes of God. His novices wear white robes on the street, but there isn't a virgin in the lot of them. They sell tracts promoting free love, communal sex, and passive resistance to civil law. The rest of the time they practice the martial arts on each other. Does that sound like a responsible religious group to you?

They even had the gall to ask me, as the oldest and most religious person present, to be their honorary priest. That was the ultimate insult. Do you know what they do on the altar at each service? Needless to say, I declined.

Gaston claims to have your blessing for his entire operation. Really, Valerie, your business arrangements have always met with my approval before, but this is asking too much of me. I doubt that Robin would approve. Please reconsider your sponsorship of the Children of Rhapsody.

Pax, Modesto

Br. Modesto
Temple of Rhapsody
San Francisco, CA

Dear Modesto,

Your letter has come at a most inopportune time. Therefore, my answer will be brief. First of all, Robin has been dead for forty years. Second, I think that he would have been amused by the Children of Rhapsody. Third, Gaston stands to clear a quarter of a million dollars next year and will use the money to finance a safe house and monastery of sorts north of San Francisco. Fourth, as to their religion being an abomination: they haven't gone on holy wars and slaughtered thousands of innocents in the name of God. They are able to find room to welcome even you into their company.

Dear friend, I have always, and always will, value your advice; but this time you are back in the eighteenth century. You gave up your brown robe long ago in order to wear modern clothes, but it still shrouds your mind. Try to be tolerant.

Valerie

When she reread the letter she'd just written, she decided not to mail it. Modesto had always been too fine a person to deserve rude treatment from her for a mere difference of opinion. She blushed inwardly and decided to keep the letter. It would remind her that she was quite capable of hurting him unintentionally.

She owed him an eternity of gratitude. It was Modesto, who, centuries ago, had saved Robin from a death that would have severed his journey through time to Val. There was no way to reverse the everflowing current of time or cut across from one point to another. Without the gentle monk they would have been like creatures imbedded in amber, forever separate.

She had met Modesto for the first time in the spring of the third year she spent with Robin.

That year Robin and Val had sailed from Southern France, with a crew of four humans, to Rome and across the Mediterranean to Port Said. He still owned the yacht *Bewitched* then; a hundred and twenty feet of varnished glory. She moored two hundred yards off the ship channel at the mouth of the harbor and waited for a broken-down launch with a sputtering motor to pull alongside. There was only one passenger, a lean man wearing a white linen suit which was wilted from the heat. He was grey-bearded and bald. It was Modesto.

He came aboard tugging a heavy khaki duffel bag. It was nearly half full of natural pearls from India. The matched sets were carefully stowed in his socks and the rest, all loose, were rolled up in his underwear, shirts and towels. There was over a million dollars worth of pearls in 1927 American money, and he poured them like so much salt out on the bed in the master suite.

A necklace of huge matched pink pearls dropped out of a checkered argyle sock with a hole in the toe. Val reached out to touch the rosy gems. "Absolutely gorgeous!" she whispered.

Modesto laughed. "She has good taste for a beginner," he said to Robin in a hoarse voice.

Robin nodded and picked the necklace up, weighing the glowing spheres in his hand for a moment. Then he twisted the egg shaped gold clasp apart and put the pearls around Val's neck without a word, just a kiss on her shoulder.

"A rani once wore that," Modesto said. "It's over a hundred years old, but you'll have to wear it to keep it alive."

"What do you mean, to keep it alive?" she asked.

"They come from living things, the oysters," Robin said, "and they lose their luster if they're not used, just like friendships."

"That's it," Modesto said, shaking out the last garment in the bag. It unfolded into a shapeless mass of dull brown material. He took off his linen suit without any false modesty and pulled the rough wool over his head. It turned out to be a full-length robe with a separate cowl that covered his shoulders. He tied the waist with a length of dingy white rope. His face took on a calm and satisfied expression. Val gave Robin a sideways glance, one eyebrow arched.

He smiled faintly. "He was a real monk at one time."

"What happaned?" She looked closely at the lean, brown-eyed man. She could tell now that he wasn't actually bald, even though he appeared to be. The top of his head had been shaven. Little patches of stubble were visible on the shorn area, indicating at least a day's growth.

"I never left the church. She left me." Modesto spoke softly and deliberately, without a hint of bitterness or recrimination. "There doesn't seem to be room there for folk like me." He reached into the deep pocket in the side of his robe and pulled out a rosary and a large pearl in the shape of a sitting Buddha. "An interesting curio." He handed it to Val. "Artificially made by implanting a statue in an oyster. "Keep it." Then he sighed. "It's a long story, Valerie."

She looked down at the rotund Buddha in her palm. It was larger than most of the pearls, perhaps the size of a dime. Then she stuck it in her pocket. It struck her as a strange token for a monk to have.

"Let's go up on deck and watch the harbor lights for a while," Robin said and started to take her arm. "I won't see Egypt again."

Modesto's bony face froze at Robin's words. He turned and raised his hand very slowly, as if to bless them, then dropped it on Robin's shoulder. "Then you've decided; chosen a time to die?"

Val gasped.

"Some day," Robin replied. "Not long from now, when there is nothing new left for me to do. I'm getting

158

weary, old friend.''

Val gritted her teeth, saying nothing, but resolving to find things for him to do forever. Then they climbed out onto the deck of the *Bewitched* to watch the moon rise over the water.

They were planning to sell the pearls in London and buy gold. Robin, leader of the group, had begun selling almost all of their paper assets and luxuries, and buying real estate, precious stones and noble metals. Val thought he'd lost his senses, but, of course, he was right. After the 1929 crash the group was even wealthier than before.

As the sky lightened with the rising moon, heavily laden vessels creaked past in the night on their way in and out of port, and the talk wandered to times long ago.

''We first met in about 1710 or '12, I don't recall the exact date,'' Robin began in response to Val's idle question.

''I would say 'met' is a rather fanciful term to describe our first encounter,'' Modesto interrupted. ''I chanced upon him lodged solidly under a rock, and there are certain times that I heartily wish I'd had the good sense to leave him there.''

''I'd come across the mountains into Northern Italy early in the spring, when the ground was thawing slightly in the daytime and freezing solid again at night. I wanted to reach a villa I owned before the Sabbath. My horse was weary, and when the hillside above us collapsed in the late evening he couldn't jump away quickly enough. When all the mud and rocks stopped moving, I was trapped with both legs wedged under a large boulder.''

"The horse was dead. It had fallen off the trail and down to the bottom of the pass," Modesto said. "When I found Robin, he'd been there all night trying to push that boulder loose. I was in a hurry to get to church on time and had been traveling since nearly midnight. It was almost dawn."

"I was ready to cut off my legs. There wasn't any way for me to get leverage. All Modesto had to do was get around on the other side and give it one good shove."

"It wasn't really hard to do. The boulder rolled off and on down the hillside."

"You were truly a good Samaritan," Val said.

"Yes," Modesto said, "but he was a desperately hungry fiend and very nearly killed me."

Robin shrugged. "It was nearly dawn, there were pink streaks in the sky."

"He left me for dead after I'd rescued him."

"I didn't have a choice. I had to have shelter. Of course, I felt bad about draining a human, especially under the circumstances. I went back that evening. He was still alive."

"A miracle," Modesto interjected.

"Were you really as angry as you sound?"

He laughed. "Yes. I resented Robin for years, even though he gave me more than my share of life. And it's been a good life, all in all. I wouldn't change what I've become for all the bell, book, and candle."

She felt his statement was a personal favor to her in a way. "Thank you," she said and leaned over and kissed the monk on the cheek. "For saving him." Modesto blushed with heat until he glowed slightly to vampyr eyes.

"She could seduce a saint," Robin said, "even one

like you.''

"A real saint?'' Val asked, sitting back in her chair. They laughed and the talk went on to other things, but the idea had stayed with her through all the years— Robin thought she was irresistible to any man, even Modesto. It was a power that she drew on now and then.

She wrote another letter, much kinder in tone. It would be mailed in the morning, when they planned to close the red brick house.

Chapter X

At dusk Theo and Val drove to a small wooded park on the north side of town, to say goodbye to Sarah and to pick up Wolf. Sarah and Bart were waiting at a picnic site with a fifty-pound sack of dog food on the wooden table, and the big dog at Sarah's feet. Wolf raised his head like a furry sphinx when they drove in, then came to Val in great bounds as Theo helped her from the car.

"Do you think he'll fit behind the seat, Theo? He's awfully big." She reached down to pet Wolf's back as the dog's thick tail brushed against her legs in greeting.

"There's room on the floor," Theo said. It was now almost totally dark, except for the street lights on the road.

Sarah ran up to meet them, hugging Theo, then Val. "Can't I go with you? I'll be good. I'll do everything you say."

"We've been over that before," Theo said, a bit sharply.

"I hate Houston!"

"It'll only be for a while," Val told her, trying to

163

smooth over what was turning into an unpleasant scene. She took Sarah's hand and they walked away, out of the halo of the streetlight, down the path that circled the park.

"Poppa says it's too dangerous for me to go with you. I just don't believe it." Her voice wavered even though she held her chin up defiantly, daring Val to agree with her.

"He's right, you know. And your safety is very important to us." Val sensed that under her rebellion Sarah was feeling vulnerable and rejected, but there wasn't much anyone could do about it. There was no way they could take her with them.

"He still sees Nicholas and that fat guy, Smith, behind every tree, even though they're gone." She looked down and kicked some pebbles with a quick scuff of her foot.

"Sarah, the danger is for you and it's real. It isn't the hunters. It's what's happening to your father. As time passes, he'd going to become less human and more like me. The most severe changes are happening now. In a year or two he'll have everything under control and it'll be safe for you to be with us.

"You're used to me being very calm and rational but it isn't always like that. If something happens and he loses control, there's no way to stop it. And no way to predict what will happen. He won't hurt me, because we're alike. But how he'll react to humans when he's under stress is a big question mark. We can't let you be the guinea pig."

"So make me a vampyr."

Val shook her head. It seemed that a perverse streak ran through the entire James' family. "You're far too young."

"I'm nearly sixteen. That's old enough."

Val shook her head again. "No, I was nineteen and that was too young."

"I never thought you'd try to take Poppa away from me!" The words exploded from Sarah. She pulled her hand away from Val's. "I trusted you!" She ran back to Bart's car and got in the back seat, sulking. She wasn't crying, Val was sure, but she was very close to it. She'd never looked more like a child than at the moment when she turned away. Val felt helpless and fatalistic as she walked back to the picnic table where Theo and Bart were sitting.

"Any luck?" Theo asked. He had both elbows on the rough boards of the table top and his forehead resting on his clenched fists. He didn't look up.

"Perhaps when she's had time to think about some of the things we talked about . . . ."

"It won't work," Bart interrupted. "She's as stubborn as her mother and spoiled rotten." His voice was astonishingly like Theo's, a bit deeper perhaps, but the similarity startled Val. She stared at him wide-eyed, barely managing to shift her gaze when his good-natured face turned to meet hers.

"Theo, you're a sly one," he said. "I was expecting a femme fatale with long white fangs and a black satin gown, not an angel in blue jeans. Is this whole thing a hoax?"

Val laughed. He was about ten years older than Theo, but the blarney was familiar. "Unfortunately not," she said sliding in next to Theo. "Do you really think we'd leave her if there were any way to insure her safety with us?" Theo put his arm around Val.

"Without Valan and what she's done to me I'm

absolutely certain I wouldn't be here now. I'd be dead. You saw the medical records."

Bart sighed and stood up. "Why don't you go tell Sarah goodbye one more time? Let me walk Valan back to your car." He picked up the large sack of dog food, and they started off.

"She feels helpless and left out," Val said as they approached the white car. She walked slowly, swinging her hips, with Wolf at her heels. "I can't change that. When we're settled we'll be in touch."

"Don't worry about her. We'll get along just fine. But why exactly does Theo fear letting her go with you?"

"He fears himself. In fact, you'd better go now and tell him it's time to go. He's hungry and upset. That's a bad combination." But when they looked back, Theo had already left Sarah. He came up and slid in behind the wheel without a word. Wolf curled up on the floor at Val's feet, and she had to sit crosslegged to avoid stepping on him. It was crowded.

"Take care of him," Bart said when he shut Val's door. Then he stepped back and watched as they drove away.

They drove through the night toward Austin, Waco, Dallas, and further north. Wolf rode easily, with his great head coming up in front of Val when he'd sit up to watch the darkness. One stop near a small town was sufficient; they satisfied themselves with blood from plastic packets out of the cooler.

Theo stared ahead mechanically most of the time, his face empty of life. He was in a dark mood. He was wondering if Val was the biggest mistake of his life; Val, what she stood for, and what he'd become because of her.

166

And, as they traveled the dark, never-ending ribbon of pavement, Val wondered too. What would he decide? Could he accept what he'd become? Strangely enough, she wondered most about his beast. What would it be like? She doubted that it would be a hungry one like hers, cruel like Arthur's, or even love-starved like Claire's. His beast would be something different, fierce and rare. But it would be a mystery to all of them until it took command.

Monday, December 1

It was too crowded in the Corvette, so they traded it for a twenty-six-foot long motorhome as soon as they reached Kansas City. Wolf would prowl the aisle, or sit silently between them in the front, or sometimes occupy the dinette in the back and stare out at the traffic behind.

They traveled mostly at night with frequent layovers in parks. Then Theo's moody withdrawal from the world would dissolve in Val's arms and release his desperate need for her.

They visited San Francisco, but Modesto was gone, to Mexico. Then they went on to Las Vegas, Reno, and Portland, touring the west and visiting vampyr colonies in most of the major cities. While Theo tried to find himself in meeting the others, Val tried to find the key to security, but no one had the answer.

Winter finally caught up with them in Colorado.

It stormed for four days, dumping nearly three feet of snow on the ground and effectively cutting the small campground off from the outside world. Then the skies cleared, and in the crisp night air Val could hear snowplows on the Interstate nearly a half-mile away.

Val was restless. She had wakened before sundown,

and now was moving from one end of the motorhome to the other, unable to relax.

"What's the matter," Theo finally asked, "cabin fever?"

"The snow," she said, "is so deep. I'll leave tracks. And, it won't be dark out."

"There are two packs in the fridge, you don't have to go out."

She stuck her hands in the back pockets of her jeans and turned to face him. "Theo, it's not fresh enough for me. You can have it, it won't hurt you, but it'd make me throw up. It won't digest."

"I'll go," he said.

"You've never done it."

"I guess it's time to start. You've done more than your share for a long time."

"We'll go together, then," she said and started dragging their coats out of the tiny closet by the door.

He stood and took a blue nylon backpack from the top shelf of the closet. He was surprised by his own willingness to go. His aversion to hunting was another thing that had been eating at him. Val had never complained, never seemed to notice his reluctance. As long as Wolf went with her, she seemed to enjoy the midnight forays for their sustenance. Theo, in the time they'd been together, had found himself unable to imagine what happened between Val and the beasts she met. He had dreaded knowing, but now he'd find out.

"How far do you think we'll have to go?" he asked when they headed downhill away from the camp. The powdery snow underfoot was making little squeaking sounds with every one of their steps.

"Not far," she buttoned the top button of her coat

168

and pulled the collar up. "There are a lot of cattle around here."

"Are you really that cold?"

"No," she shook her head. "It's just the mood I'm in, a little fearful. I don't really like deep snow." She touched his arm, stopping as she did.

"There," she whispered. "Concentrate. What's in the air?"

The wind blew uphill; the air was crisp, and sounds carried well. He closed his eyes, cocked his head and listened, but it was a rich pungent animal scent that he caught, rather than the sounds of creatures moving in the night.

He turned to face the wind directly, and the scent was stronger. "What is it?"

"The cattle. Let's go."

Wolf barked and pranced around Val when he saw she'd located her quarry. They walked slowly toward the scent, the huge dog leading the way, skirted a snowbank and came within yards of·a dozen white-faced Herefords in a hollow. They had their rumps to the wind and were staring directly at Wolf. They snorted and backed up, preparing to turn and run.

"Talk to the leader," Val whispered. "Tell her not to be afraid."

"How?"

"With your eyes. Concentrate."

He didn't think it would work. The cattle were too skittish, too wild. Then he caught the foremost beast's eye and saw the simple terror there. "Be at ease," he told the beast. "We mean you no harm." He repeated his thoughts over and over until the cow relaxed and took a step toward him.

"Now the next one," Val said. Within ten minutes they were standing surrounded by the thick-coated cattle.

"The best place is here," Val touched a spot on the nearest cow's neck just above the shoulder. Theo nodded and worked to attach the plastic bag to the tube and needle. The tube was stiff and unwieldy in the cold, but gained flexibility when warm blood started running through it.

"It isn't nearly as bad as I thought it'd be," he said. They went from one cow to the next.

"Oh?"

"I had visions of hypnotic coercion, or having to wrestle animals into submission. It's not that way at all. They really understand what we are, that we won't hurt them."

"They're only afraid of humans. They know we're different. Vampyrs don't kill."

"It is a lot different than I'd imagined," he said as they finished and he pushed the last bag into the back-pack.

"How?" She stopped scratching a cow's back, turned and took his arm. "Let's go back."

"You made being a vampyr look so easy, but I lost everything, my home, my job, my friends, everything, even my daughter. I feel like a refugee."

"But you have life and time and all the wealth you could ever want. Millions of other refugees have nothing."

"They had no choice. I did, and that leaves a big hole in my life. I put it there. I don't know what I am or who I am any more."

"So what do you want to do about it?"

170

He looked up and saw the camper lights ahead; they'd come almost all the way back. He shook his head. "I don't know. What can I do?"

"Valan," he stopped, faced her and took her shoulders. "I keep thinking if I could turn around, go home and just be good old Theo James, M.D., everything would be like it used to be."

She reached up and touched his chin. "If only time could run backwards."

He looked at her face, but she stared past him, lost in thoughts he couldn't share. He knew then that no matter how much they loved each other or how long they were together there would be parts of her hidden from him.

Finally she said, "Let's go in." Then, when she stood in the open doorway: "Let time pass, Theo. Time can solve almost any problem if you let it."

He wanted to ask her what she meant but she seemed preoccupied with her own thoughts again. He felt very much as he had on the first day of medical school when he'd stood outside the anatomy classroom door, wondering what mysteries lay in store for him and knowing that nothing he dreamed of would come close to reality.

When the road finally cleared, Val called Corey Madison and had her mail forwarded. Most of the letters were routine messages. Val found it a bit startling to realize how well the group business concerns ran themselves. Either, she concluded, she'd done a good job of setting things up, or big business, like an ocean liner with the engines suddenly turned off, just keeps on going on its own inertia. There was only one letter in the whole lot that burned in her fingers for immediate action. It had been written a month before.

Dear Valerie,

It is with deep regret that I have to inform you of the disaster that has befallen our colony here in Tres Rosas, Brazil. As you know, we came here fourteen years ago to set up a cattle station and safe house for South American vampyrs in Rio de Janeiro. We did so, and we flourished. Now I am the only survivor.

Life was kind to us until we were visited by a vampyr known to us only as Potchnick. After staying for a while with apparent sobriety and good judgment, he went berserk and drained a half-dozen natives in less than a month. As a result, the station was attacked and everyone beheaded except Potchnick, who escaped into town. I was away on a shopping expedition or would have suffered the same fate.

Eight fine young vampyrs were killed, in all, and the station burned to the ground. All of our efforts here have been in vain. Don Alba will take over the stock, but I am leaving Brazil forever. I am coming to you personally to insure that justice is done. My mate and sister were among those slain. My heart cries for vengeance.

Sincerely, Agapito "Pete" Garcia

When she'd finished reading the letter, she sat at the dinette table lost in thought. Wolf came over and nudged her several times with his cold nose before she realized that he was there. The news was a terrible blow. So many years of hard work, so many lives, lost for nothing.

She put on her coat and went to use the phone.

When she called Corey, the maid answered the phone. At least three minutes passed before he picked up the receiver and greeted Val with a gruff hello.

"I have to see Pete Garcia," she said, as soon as the

pleasantries were over.

"He's been looking for you, too. I called around when he showed up in November. No one had seen you in months. The woman you've got managing your Chicago house, Pearl, said you'd probably be along to visit her, and I sent Pete Garcia out there. Where've you been?"

"On a vacation, just traveling around in the mountains. Do you happen to know where Salvatore is?"

"Paris."

Sal was sleeping when she called. Eudora answered the phone at Chateau Robinet and while she went to get him Val wondered, idly, if they were sleeping together. The thought of sleek Salvatore and fluttery melodramatic Eudora in the same bed brought a smile to Val's lips, but it didn't last.

"Where have you been?" Salvatore demanded without even greeting her.

"With Theo. Where's Potchnick?"

"He's sleeping until February's full moon in Arthur's wine cellar."

"In New Orleans?"

"Yes. Everyone in the group has had it with him this time. Where have you two been hiding out?"

"We've been camping in the mountains. This business has come at a bad time for us. Theo's got the worst case of identity crisis I've ever seen."

"It's a little late for that now."

"I know, but he has to work it out. Will you set up the Cabal?"

"It's all ready. We were waiting to hear from you."

"Who's involved?" Val asked.

"Arthur, his ladies, and Clive; they're in New

173

Orleans now; also, Claire, Eudora, and me. There'll be three coming with Pearl when she takes Pete to New Orleans. That makes the thirteen, unless you want to sit in?'' He let the last statement stand as an accusing question, but Val wasn't sure who or what he was accusing. It might have been her disappearance into the mountains with Theo or his own rage at what Potchnick did.

Then he said, ''I guess hypnosis just doesn't work on vampyrs. At least, it didn't with Potchnick.''

''I'm responsible for letting this thing get out of hand,'' Val said. ''We should have taken care of Le Guignol years ago. I'll be there to take part.''

''Fine, I'll bring the ax and robes. When and where will we meet?''

''In ten days in New Orleans. We may as well have it there, that's the most convenient place, considering what the outcome will probably be.''

When Val got back to the motorhome Theo was sleeping in the bed above the cab with the curtains pulled snugly all the way around. His little buzzing snores only made her restless, so she and Wolf went for a walk in the snow and gathering darkness.

Her pockets were filled with bags of fresh blood when they returned to the darkened camper, and Wolf's fur was damp and smelly.

Theo woke and turned onto his side to watch her stack the darkly bulging bags in the vegetable bin of the tiny refrigerator. The rest of the space was taken up with beer and other human food they left in there in case they had to feed someone in the course of a day's activities. It happened often enough on the road that they stayed prepared.

"The butane is getting low," he said as Val hung her coat in the narrow closet.

"It doesn't matter. We have to leave tomorrow, anyway."

"Why?"

All the bitterness that had been building up inside her since she'd read the letter came out as she said, "Get out of bed and I'll tell you the whole gory story." She was upset and knew he could sense it. She wanted him to know that she had problems, too, sometimes.

He rolled over the edge of the mattress and dropped feet first to the floor. When he took her in his arms he was deliciously warm, his nude body radiating heat built up from hours under the covers. She ran her hands, still icy from outdoors, across his finely muscled back and down to his hips.

"Mmm," he murmured, stiffening.

She laughed. "Don't you want something to eat first?"

"In a moment," he kissed her hungrily, taking her tongue into his mouth, then caressing it with his. They concentrated on the kiss until the tastes of their mouths were indistinguishable. Then he started stroking her hair and brushing the curls back with one hand. She tilted her head back, knowingly and eagerly accepting him. His other hand slid between them, touching her breasts, resting there for a moment, then loosening the top buttons of her shirt and gently pushing the soft cloth away from her shoulder.

"I want you," he said. His lips played across her cheek, down her neck, leaving a warm damp trail before coming to rest on her bare shoulder for a moment. Then, with a deft touch of his tooth, he nicked the skin

175

so that a large drop of blood welled up, warm and fragrant. He touched it with the tip of his tongue, slowly savoring the taste, his warm breath blowing across the nape of her neck.

The smell of her own blood, the fierce but tiny pain of the wound, his radiance in the darkness; she couldn't control the desire that overwhelmed her. She moaned and her head came up until her lips brushed his chest and a tooth scratched him above the nipple as her mouth rubbed hard against him. Slowly she sucked the sweet hot blood from his breast, a drop at a time, and they stood there, his hands holding her close against his pale skin. He fed her those few precious drops of blood and she gave as she received, a prelude, a consummation, an affirmation of their love.

The complete trust it took to offer herself to Theo and the restraint necessary to take just a drop or two of his life in her mouth forged a deep bond between them.

"Now then," he said, releasing her and touching her chin with the tip of his finger. "What's wrong?"

"We have to be in New Orleans by the fourteenth."

"We or you? Is it part of your group's operations?"

Val nodded. "A Cabal. Please come with me."

"Do you think I'd let you go alone if you needed me?" He tapped her nose affectionately. "What's a Cabal?"

"It used to mean secrets within the Jewish faith, then it meant a group of plotters of a conspiracy. With us it means an odd number of older vampyrs, usually thirteen, who form a court of judges to rule on a problem. It's our only legal system."

"Any Cabal can rule on any problem?"

"Just problems of an unusual nature that can't be

resolved any other way."

"And the decision is binding?"

"Absolutely. It's a court of last resort. But it's difficult to get thirteen vampyrs to sit in Cabal, let alone come to an agreement, unless it's very important. Most vampyrs prefer to live and let live."

"And this time, what's the problem?"

She told him what she knew of Potchnick, of Pete Garcia's story and her conversation with Salvatore. All the time she felt herself sinking into a depression, sliding down the slick sides of a bottomless pit, because she would probably have to say the words that would bring death to a fellow vampyr. It wasn't, she thought, that Potchnick didn't deserve it. He probably did. She didn't know.

Tuesday, December 2

On the road the next day, Wolf sat in the passenger's seat next to Theo and stared at the mountains while Val tried to catch up on her correspondence. They planned to take a week to reach New Orleans.

Chapter XI

Tuesday, December 9

Theo and Val arrived in New Orleans on December ninth. They had done most of their traveling in the dark but a different kind of darkness had surrounded Val during the trip, covering her and poisoning the air she breathed. Yet the more she had withdrawn into herself, the more Theo had taken over. He had done all the driving and the hunting, and had even taken their clothing to the laundromat the day they spent in Kansas City. The only constructive thing Val had done was wire Don Alba.

DON ALBA JAVIER RODRIGUEZ
RIO DE JANEIRO:
INVESTIGATE TRES ROSAS MASSACRE STOP
ATTEND CABAL ARTHURS NEW ORLEANS
DECEMBER TEN STOP

                                        VALERIE

She told Theo that she felt much better after that, although she had no idea what would come of it.

Arthur's home in New Orleans sat on a sleepy side street. It had once been a brothel. When he bought and remodeled it, he kept the bordello motif of scarlet, white, and black in most of the rooms. There were fifteen bedrooms on the second and third floors and a wine cellar taking up most of the space in the basement.

Arthur's ladies came running out into the twilight to greet them, hanging on Theo, patting Wolf and hugging Val warmly. Tammy, a bottle blonde with painted lips and a sinuous, slinky way of moving, proudly announced that she was sleeping with Arthur. But it was Rosa, a dainty hispanic, who managed the place, bossing the others with her sharp tongue.

Maria, an elegant mulatto, showed Val to the second-floor rooms Arthur assigned her and Theo. The suite had a balcony that overlooked the street. Maria stayed to open the windows and adjust the drapes.

"Let me get these clothes up so the wrinkles come out," she said, opening Val's suitcase on the bed and shaking out the clothes. She spoke with a slurred soft accent and odd grammatical forms that Val found fascinating to hear.

"Thanks," Val said absently.

"You sad now? That man do right by you?" She meant Theo, who had stayed downstairs in the front room to meet the others. Almost everyone had arrived; Salvatore and the others from Paris would arrive in the very early morning.

"He's a good man, Maria. I'm sad because I have to be here and sit in judgment on the old vampyr."

"There's an extra man coming from Chicago. You can sit out."

"No, it's my responsibility. Would you follow me if I

backed out on something as simple as this?''

Maria looked at Val carefully from where she was standing halfway in the closet. "Valerie, I follow you 'til someone with a stronger eye comes along. Because you're a good person. I hope that never happens while I live."

Val was moved by her simple declaration and went to the window. There was a man pacing the yard in the dark. "Who's that?"

Maria came over and looked out. "That just Clive, my twin brother. He helps around here, too lazy to make it hisself." She turned away and pretended to listen carefully. "I got to go now. Rosa be calling if I don't. You be feeling better, hear."

There were voices rising from downstairs, where the others were socializing. Val wanted to go down and visit, but her unwilling body refused to take the first step until Arthur came to lead her around his home. The rooms were beautifully furnished with antiques and satin drapes. They bypassed the parlors, with the clicking sound of billiard balls and the tinkling notes of a clavicord coming from behind closed doors, and he led Val down to see Potchnick. Le Guignol lay on the brick floor of the old kegroom in the basement, with his head pillowed on his rough black coat and his wiry beard sticking up over his thin chest.

"Why is it locked?" she asked. "He won't wake up, will he?" She touched one of the latticed iron bars set in the heavy wooden door.

"To keep Pete out. He comes down here and stands looking in." He shook his head thoughtfully, and his nearly silver hair sparkled in the glare of the bare light-bulb overhead. "The door will hold. It's built to my specifications."

"I hope he sleeps until it is all over one way or another."

There were times when Arthur, as arrogant and willful as Val knew he usually was, could be tender and considerate. As Val took his arm to leave the cellar, he covered her hand with his and patted it gently. It was his way of telling her he understood her distress.

Wolf followed Val out onto the balcony, where they sat together in the darkness and cool breezes long after Arthur had driven away to meet the plane. The great grey dog was warmth and comfort at her side as she listened to the Louisiana night, letting it chill her until she felt at peace. Then there was a knock at the door.

When she opened it Pearl stood there, majestic nearly six feet tall and handsome. She came in and sat with Val on the red-and-white striped love seat at the foot of the bed.

"I wanted to thank you, and Claudius, for helping me last summer."

"It was nothing."

"We feel we still owe you. When school is out this spring, he's moving to Chicago to live with me. There's another vampyr in with the hunters already, so he isn't needed. He says they don't do anything except talk now."

It seemed to be Val's night to notice people's speech patterns. Pearl's voice, while still mellow and deep, had lost all traces of the black accent she'd used so heavily when they'd spoken on the phone last summer. It bothered Val.

"Your voice—it's so different from before. Why?"

Pearl laughed and leaned back against the couch. "Honey, I wanted you to know where I was coming from. I know how and when to speak the language."

"Oh," Val liked her immensely; the directness and pride impressed her and she felt there would be complete honesty in anything Pearl would say. "Tell me about Pete Garcia."

"Child, you're the simplest creature I've ever met. By that I don't mean simple-dumb, I mean simple-straight-forward." She patted Val's knee. It seemed to Val that she was getting a lot of compliments and petting since she'd arrived. Whether it was the seductive whorehouse atmosphere or their collective nervousness that caused it, she couldn't tell.

"Now, that Pete's a strange one," Pearl said pursing her lips. "He's here to kill a dragon, like it's a holy quest. Of course, he's been through enough to make anyone act a little crazy.

"We went to a downtown disco last night, the whole houseful, and he tried to make it with a human girl. He even got her out in the alley. I sent Mark, one of our men, after them. Mark said Pete was all over the girl and ready to take a bite. Mark broke it up and Pete was pretty quiet today. But still—what do you think of that?"

"I don't know. Things like that do happen." They sat in silence for a long time until the sound of Arthur's car arriving from the airport could be heard. Val went to the window in time to see Salvatore, Claire and Eudora get out and come toward the house.

"Could you ask Claire to come to me when she gets a few minutes?" she asked Pearl as she shut the windows and pulled the drapes.

"Sure." Pearl took it as a signal to go and closed the door gently behind her as she left. Val scarcely noticed her departure.

Wednesday, December 10

By the time Claire came up, Val had taken off her shoes and was lying on the bed, wearing just jeans and a sweater, her head propped up on all the pillows and her journal balanced on her knees. Val had given up trying to write, turning off the lamp, and was just staring into the darkness. Then Claire opened the door, and stood there, a black-lighted silhouette as she let her eyes adjust. She closed the door, kicked off her high heels, and came to sit beside Val on the bed.

"It'll be all right. Don't worry," she said, stroking Val's hair.

"It's open and shut, Claire," Val said sadly. "He was a grand old bogeyman, the kind good nightmares are made of."

"I know. The last of the Titans."

It was four o'clock in the afternoon, overcast and nearly dark outside, when Val woke up. The telephone on the table by the head of the bed was ringing and Claire had gone.

"Valerie, you have a call from Javier. He insists on speaking to you personally." It was Arthur's voice and he seemed peeved that Don Alba wouldn't give him the message.

"Put him on," she mumbled, not quite awake.

"Valerie, Javier here. I did what you wanted but can't get there until early tomorrow morning. Can you hold off the Cabal? I want to speak to it. Pito Garcia will be there?''

"Of course. Pete's already here. What's the problem?''

"Nothing serious, something mechanical on the Learjet.''

"I warned you not to buy that thing.''

"Hah! I love that plane. It's just routine. Give my regards to the others.''

"No, I want your presence to be a secret. Only Arthur and I know you're coming. It wouldn't do to let Pete be on guard. It might destroy his honesty.''

Javier chuckled. "I see. Then I'll arrange to have a car of my own at the airport.''

When he hung up, Val buzzed Arthur downstairs and told him to forget that Don Alba had called.

Maria carried in a tray with goblets of blood and some fresh towels just as Val finished changing her clothes. Maria was in a bad humor; her eyes flashing and her lips tightly pursed together.

"What's wrong?''

"This whole house, that's what.'' She dumped the towels on the bed. "That coonass man, Pete. He's got no right to yell at Clive just because we sleep together. It ain't his business.''

"Of course it's not his business,'' Val said. The relationship between Maria and Clive was a surprise to Val, but their incest really didn't matter to her. With vampyrs there were never any children. But the relationship was unusual. Most vampyrs Val knew retained enough human training to keep the taboos.

"Where's Theo?''

"In his room,'' Maria nodded toward the closed door at the far end of the bathroom which led to the next bedroom. "Arthur put him in there."

Val took the tray from her and carried it through the door.

Theo was lying on the bed, fully dressed in jeans and a flannel shirt, his hands tucked behind his head.

"When are you going to kill that old fellow?" he asked as she put the tray down on the table at the head of the bed. The bitterness in his statement was a measure of the helplessness he felt. He'd figured out what would happen to Potchnick, and he'd realized how dependent he was on Val's experience and strength. Without her, he knew, his chances of surviving as a vampyr were practically nil.

Val cocked her head.

He sighed and moved over to the middle of the bed. "Come here," he said gently and reached for her. "I'm as tense and frustrated by this whole mess as you are. At least you know what's going on."

"The death of a legend," she whispered, pressing herself full length against him.

"Potchnick, that crazy old man in the cellar?"

"Le Guignol's scary and repulsive, and he's done a lot of terrible things, but he's never done anything to hurt another vampyr before. We all rather looked up to him for staying alive so long."

"Why do you call him that?" He stroked her back.

"Have you ever watched a Punch and Judy show? Punch always winds up killing everyone until he can't get away any more, and then he's executed. There was another puppet show, long ago, featuring le Guignol. He made Punch seem like a model citizen. Perhaps Potchnick made the rest of us feel like model citizens."

"You fit here in my arms," he said, squeezing her lightly.

Arthur pounded on the door in the other room, and when there was no answer, walked in through the bathroom and stood lounging against the wall looking down at them. "Javier's pilot just got a patch through from the airport. They'll be getting in about one; he'll be here before two this morning. I don't know why you want to keep him a secret, Val, but I'll go along with it."

"He's going to speak to the Cabal about what happened down there. His estancia is practically next door to Tres Rosas. I don't want Pete, or anyone else, to be on guard."

He shrugged. "You can lock this room and keep him in here. Maria has the rest of the group convinced that you two are having a lover's quarrel, so no one will notice that you're not using this room.

"I've invited everyone out for a night in the old town. Some others will be there from Atlanta. We probably won't be back until dawn." He scratched behind his ear. "Just one thing is bothering me. Don't you believe Pete? His sister and mate were killed down there."

"I can't condemn anyone, even le Guignol, on one person's testimony. And I know you feel the same way."

"What?" Arthur straightened up.

"Why else did you lock the door on Potchnick? The formalities of justice never stopped you from doing anything you thought right. Why not let Pete in and save us all a lot of trouble?"

"Humph!" He turned and headed out. "By the

way," he called from the other room, "Sal wants to see you."

"Any time," Theo called back. He was strangely at ease, as though he was finally in control of himself for the first time in months.

Thursday, December 11

The traditional Cabal robes were nothing more than circles of coarse white cotton, about two meters across with a hole in the center large enough for a head to pass through. The edges were neatly turned under and hemmed, but they had no decoration. The cowls were similar circles of finer, looser cotton, a little more than a meter across, that merely draped over their heads like the cafe tablecloths they resembled. The front half was kept folded back unless the Cabal was in session. Then the members covered their faces.

Theo had gravely watched as the other vampyrs donned the ritual garb, then took his place as doorman.

The crescent-bladed ax, forged during the Spanish Inquisition, lay on the center of the mahogany dining-room table. The sides of the polished steel blade had been worn smooth by the years, and the cutting edge was sharp and pure. It was usually kept in a specially made box in the Chateau Robinet armory and was brought out only to be cleaned and cared for periodically—or to be used.

Val sat in the center of the long table on the side against the wall and listened as the young vampyr, Agapito Garcia, retold his story. The others sat around the table, leaving an open space about eight feet long across from Val for the witness. Pete sat there with Arthur and Salvatore flanking him. He was nervous, speaking hesitantly to the thirteen figures who had hooded their faces minutes after his entry. They could each see him clearly through the thin cloth.

His story was essentially a repeat, highly embellished and emotional, of the letter he had written to Val. He described the angry villagers and Potchnick's excesses, then his own shopping trip for salt and new tools for the station. He paled when he described his horror at coming home to find his sister and lover with their heads severed, and all the others brutally killed, each body described in bloody detail. His voice quavered as he finished by recounting his flight to town and escape to New York.

When he was done he buried his face in his shaking fingers and wept.

"Any questions at this time?" Val asked. There were none. Several of the robes were fluttering; Eudora had wormed her hand up through the neck hole and was dabbing her eyes with a tissue.

"Pete." Val lifted the front of her cowl so he could see her face. "We're finished with you for now. Go back to your room and lock the door. We'll call you again when we need you." Theo, acting as doorman, led him away.

"Do we vote now?" Tammy asked, raising her cowl. "It's stuffy under these things." Her voice was petulant.

"There are others to hear yet," Arthur said. "Be quiet, drop your cowl, and think about his story."

After nearly half an hour, there was a knock at the door. "Lift your cowls. Another witness is coming in," Arthur said rapping the tabletop.

Don Alba entered, six feet of Castilian royalty

dressed in a black, continental-cut suit. He gazed slowly around the room, examining each face without changing expression. "Perhaps you are right, Arturo, I should return to the North. There are so many new faces." He came to the table and bowed to Val before he sat down.

"Shall we begin?" He put his elbows on the arms of his chair and delicately positioned his fingers to meet their mates in front of his chest. The others dropped the cloth over their faces.

"I am Don Alba, currently of Rio de Janeiro. I am a vampyr of one hundred and ten years. At this time I operate a large estancia near Tres Rosas. It is one of many business interests that belong to the group. Valerie, is it not so? I am your agent in South America."

She nodded silently under the cowl.

He continued. "I first heard of the Tres Rosas massacre in November when Pito Garcia came to me. He said villagers had destroyed the cattle station because of the depravities of a guest, one Potchnick. He asked me to maintain the herd while he hunted the murderer. I agreed.

"Last week I received a wire from Valerie asking me to look more carefully into the matter and attend this meeting. I went to Tres Rosas and interrogated the entire village of thirty-two persons.

"I put all of them in the church and let them out one by one to see me. Of course, ten of my vaqueros helped. There were no incidents and there will be no repercussions. The local police are entirely on my payroll.

"This is the story they told me. No villagers were killed by vampyr attacks, but in the month preceding

190

the massacre two young maidens were bitten by a dark young man. They were not drained or seriously harmed. They thought he was a handsome fellow and wondered when he would return.

"The farmers found the bodies at the cattle station several days after they had been killed because birds were circling overhead. They notified the police and buried the remains. I saw, in the cemetery, only eight new graves. They were all young vampyrs, evidently, since none of the bodies disintegrated on exposure to sunlight.

"A thing of interest. All were slain in their beds. The farmers insist that the girls known as Merida, Pito's sister, and Elena, his lover, were found in the same bed.

"I am finished. It can be verified, if you like. Ten human vaqueros heard the same story."

"Any questions?" Val asked.

"What do you think happened?" This came from Mark, who was sitting at the end of the table to Val's right.

Javier shrugged. "Is it not obvious? Either Pito killed them out of some anger, or Potchnick killed them. He is a man of awesome reputation for loving to kill."

"Who do you think did it?" Mark insisted.

Javier shrugged again. "You have heard of Pito. In all fairness shouldn't you listen to Potchnick? Is it right to judge and execute a man in his sleep?"

Val smiled beneath her cowl at his voice of reason. Javier stood up, bowed to her again with a whimsical expression. "Invite me to drink at the bloodletting. I will come willingly." Then he left the room.

Silence prevailed for another half-hour. Then Salvatore came in and sat down without any ceremony.

"I know everyone," he said, waving his hand as they started to lift the cowls. "I don't have much to say.

"Valerie asked me last night to tell you about my work with Potchnick. "Last spring he agreed to let me hypnotize him to reduce the murderous tendencies he's never been able to control. We worked together for nearly six months, and both thought we had accomplished some good. Evidently not. He's old and set in his ways." Salvatore shook his head and looked sadly at Val. "But to me it is a personal failure. I don't know why this is important, Valerie."

"Can you hypnotize him now?"

"Probably. He's used to me waking him up about halfway. He'll just fall asleep when I'm finished."

"Will you do it? We want to hear from him; the truth."

They retired, *en masse,* to the corridor of the wine cellar, leaving the cowls and robes on the backs of their chairs. Arthur unlocked the huge door. Potchnick lay unmoving and unaware, just as he had when Val had seen him before. As the group came in and stood crowded against the wall, Salvatore knelt beside him and shook his shoulders; all the time whispering into his ear.

"Blood! Blood!" Potchnick muttered the words and tried to twist away from Sal's voice.

"Where?"

"Everywhere." He licked his lips.

"In Tres Rosas?"

"No, just *los vacas.*" The cows; Potchnick rambled on in Spanish.

"Did you kill in Mikros?"

"Yes."

"In Paris?"

"No."

"In Dolblinka?"

"Yes." Potchnick twisted his head and started gasping for air. Salvatore sat back on his heels and let his subject relax.

"In Armenia?"

"Yes."

"In Tres Rosas?"

"No."

"What happened in Tres Rosas?"

"Nothing. I just went away. You told me to."

"What did I tell you?"

"Go and kill no more!"

"Was everyone alive when you left Tres Rosas?"

"Yes."

It was a grim and somber group that filed out to the corridor.

"It will be finished here, tonight," Val said pointing to the ground at her feet. "Does everyone agree?" Each person nodded as she looked from face to face.

Then Arthur spoke. "Maria, Tammy, go get the cups and ax. Rosa, invite Javier to join us; I'll put the block over here."

She pushed the two-foot-square block of wood out to the middle of the corridor from where it had been stored in a side room. When everything was ready they sat down against the cold brick walls to wait, with Javier sitting inconspicuously next to the stairs.

Pete came down the stairs quickly and rushed past the others to stand in front of Val. There was an eager look on his face that roused the others to sit up straighter. "You've decided already? Will you let me do it?" He was already reaching for the ax.

Val stood up. "Pete." The word was soft, seductive. He glanced at her for the briefest moment, but it was enough. She held him in submission. He stood and stared at her transfixed, his lower jaw relaxing enough to let his mouth droop open. The truth was burning in his mind, the lifting of the sword to slay the girls, the flies buzzing over the freshly spilled blood, the heat of the evening when everyone slept and died without waking. Even the reason was there. Merida and Elena had decided to move back to the city, together. Fourteen years at the primitive cattle station were enough for them. Pete, rejected and full of rage, struck out, not an act of his beast, that might have been understandable, but a carefully planned vengeance. He had calculated carefully to involve Potchnick, the guest with the terrible reputation. He hadn't known about Salvatore's experiment.

Val nodded. Javier and Sal moved to his side, taking his arms. Pete growled and tried to wrest himself away, his eyes never leaving Val's, as they bent him over the block until his chest was hard against the wood.

Arthur's aim was sure. The head rolled off the block and lay, still staring at Val, while Maria held a plastic bucket to catch the blood spurting from the severed arteries of his neck.

The cups were filled before the heart stopped pumping. Even then there was a great pool of blood on the floor. They drank of the cups. Val's shook so that she had to hold it with both hands and bite the rim with her teeth, but she did drink.

The Cabal was over at midnight. Val and Theo went out to the motorhome; she didn't want to stay in

Arthur's house any longer. While Theo sat up in the bed watching a monster movie on TV, Val tried to get the Cabal out of her mind, but it came back like a play seen through the wrong end of opera glasses, and with an unsatisfactory ending.

There was the smell of blood on her hands, though she washed them twice. It clung there, mouthwatering and sweet. She knew they would have to leave there as soon as possible.

Friday, December 12

Mark came out to see Val and Theo just after the TV station went off the air for the night.

"I was going to be a priest," he said, frowning intently as though it was difficult to remember why. "And was made a vampyr by a repentant rogue in a flophouse down on the L.A. waterfront. We were doing mission work.

"I guess I went crazy when I realized what I'd become. I had constant nightmares of being forced by my unholy nature to mutilate young maidens. It got so bad that I couldn't tell what had actually happened, and what I had been dreaming about." He laughed a little, nervously. "Pearl found me."

"Then what?" Theo asked. He'd been lying on the bed above the cab but rolled over, propped his head up with both hands, and looked down at Mark and Val sitting at the dinette. He liked the boyish young vampyr with his dark blond tousled ringlets and naturally downcurved mouth. It gave him an air of sensual innocence; a purity that would have become a priest.

"I'd just jumped out a window down by the docks. She patched me up, put me to work and told me to quit feeling sorry for myself. That was six years ago. I followed her to Chicago last spring. She's a wonderful person." He stared at Theo, then Val, with what seemed to be an habitually worried expression.

"Why are you telling us all this?" Theo asked.

"Well, Rosa said you're leaving soon. I want to go along." He waved both hands while he talked, a sign of nervousness, Val thought. He continued. "Besides, I wanted to get to know both of you. Everyone knows about your group and admires the things you're trying to do. I'd like to be a part of that. I think it would be great if vampyrs could live normally with people, instead of having to sneak around all the time." He paused and sighed deeply. "Do you mind?"

Theo glanced at Val. She shrugged. "Why not?"

Thursday, January 15

They went east to the Atlantic coast, then meandered west, stopping occasionally in the large cities along the way. Each of the three was moody in a different way. Mark was shy and uncommunicative, hagridden by the nightmares he couldn't control. Theo wrestled grimly with the alien vampyr ways he knew he would have to accept—violence, lust, strange bedfellows, and all—if he intended to survive. He missed his house in San Antonio, his university friends and colleagues, and even Mrs. MacMullin; and while he and Val were indescribably close, he longed for Sarah. Somehow in his campaign to stay alive he hadn't reckoned the cost of becoming a vampyr.

The physical problems were difficult enough, with the ever-present need for fresh blood, the growing strength and alertness in his body, and the awareness that a beast lurked inside of him, prowling, looking for a way to escape. But it was the growing tension in his mind that dragged him into despair.

He knew the Cabal had been necessary, the judgment just, the punishment correct. He knew, also, that the vampyrs were not responsible to humankind's laws and courts, yet the horror of the beheading intruded during every idle moment. He worried, also, that Val would leave him and turn to Claire as Pete's sister Merida and Elena had done. There seemed to be odd gaps in vampyr morality that he couldn't reconcile with his own upbringing.

The incestuous relationship between Maria and her twin had startled him, not as much by its existence as by the openness with which Val, Arthur, and the others accepted it without comment. He repeatedly examined his own love for Sarah, looking for the minutest sign of unnatural affection, and doubt froze him. He found himself unable to call her or to write her. Sometimes, on the long hauls between cities, he would stare at the road without seeing it, then look down and find he was gripping the steering wheel so hard his knuckles were white.

Mark wasn't the only one whose sleep was marred by nightmares. Val's came with great intensity, and passed as quickly, wakening her to see nothing but ribbons of daylight streaming in at the bottom of the curtains. Then she would try to concentrate on the present, but her mind faltered. New Orleans burned in her mind.

By unspoken mutual consent they changed campsites frequently, as though looking for a place that would bring peace of mind.

Monday, February 16

Val's nightmares kept coming back. Things out of the past came to her during the restless days when the wind blew around the edges of the motorhome and shook it. Visions of events that happened long ago with Robin intruded at the most unexpected moments; in the middle of a conversation, or during a walk. Sometimes she saw Robin in the corners of her eyes; he faded to nothing when she turned to face him. He came unbidden, even when Theo held her as they rested together, even when they were making love. His vividness startled her.

Yet she couldn't control the visions, couldn't erase them. Perhaps if she concentrated on them, wrote them down and saw them in the light of logic she'd be able to free her mind. Perhaps—tomorrow.

Tuesday, February 17

The moon was full and the nights bright, and the days dragged endlessly. Val envisioned the same memory over and over until it seemed like a filmloop showing repeatedly in her mind.

It was Paris; spring. There was a lot of moisture in the air, which made her skin feel fresh and soft. Fog every morning gave way to rolling clouds in the afternoons.

And, then, she was wearing a black velvet dress, cut low across the shoulders and the back, hanging straight over her hips and accentuating them, yet giving her an air of such richness and glamour, that whenever she wore it, she felt good about herself. It had been a gift from Robin, as were the pearls, the size of her thumb, strung in a choker that rode high on her neck and shone with a pink luster that complimented her pale skin.

They walked together down the cracked and uneven sidewalk. She had to take his arm to balance herself. Her teetering high heels made her slightly nervous; but they were fashionable. They went into Maxim's and sat at a table where Robin would order strange and exquisite dishes. He knew everything about food, although he never ate, and hadn't in centuries. He would watch her taste the delicate cuisine and have a small glass of wine. That was long before she started throwing up all solid food.

They laughed together at a multitude of little jokes that no one else would have found funny. They were still enamoured of each other after ten years together. Val smiled and raised her face with a sense of the fulfillment his love had brought her.

How soon it was all to end. How sharply doom hung over them.

They were staying at the chateau north of Paris, one of the very few places where they were at peace. Robin and Val had one of the larger suites. There was an air of permanence and warmth in their rooms because they'd left things there over the years; paintings, books and knicknacks. Whenever they arrived, they felt they'd come home.

Then it was that particular night again, very near the morning. Val was getting ready for bed, and streaks of orange and red were already appearing in the sky. Dense fog hovered over the lawn below. Robin stood there by the window. He was still dressed for evening in black and white, with a top hat in one hand. There was a faraway look on his face.

It was a bad omen, she felt, to stand looking out a window; waiting. Waiting, usually for the unexpected. Somehow the expression on his face moved her. She went to him and took his hand, and together they stood there listening to the earliest birds. They were raucous in the morning, always making more noise just before the dawn than they did once the sun had risen. But they listened. The wind stirred the leaves on the branches and whisked at the fog. They saw farmers in the fields down the road moving about their morning chores, as farmers have since the beginning of time.

He spoke. "I've seen all this. I've done all this. What's left, Val? There's nothing left for me to experience, save death." And his hand tightened on hers, squeezing her fingers and her soul at the same time. She knew then that he'd already made up his mind that this would be the dawn; the last one.

As the sun began to rise they turned away from the window and went downstairs. He led her out on the porch, and they waited for sunbeams to light up the yard. Then they walked into the garden, where the grass was still very damp. Val was barefoot, wearing only her nightgown. They embraced one last time. His skin was already hot and she was crying. She remembered that; standing there watching him with tears streaming down her face.

And as the sun came further up, his visage darkened. The skin on his hands withered, tanning and wrinkling. The flesh shrank away from his fingernails, leaving them curved and yellow like the claws of some fearsome animal. His face, too, aged six hundred years in a matter of minutes. With an almost inaudible moan he began to smoke. Tendrils of it curled from beneath his cuffs, around his collar. His hair turned white and fell in powder on his shoulders. He stood there for what seemed an eternity. Finally, with one last burst, a bit of flame, he was gone.

Small bits of grey ash floated in the air, picked up by the gentle morning breeze. Completely gone. Gone forever. Val sank to her knees on the grass.

In the motorhome it came back to her, over and over again, the same intensity of feeling that tore at her soul. She woke moaning in bed next to Theo, and he wanted to know what was wrong.

"A nightmare?" he asked, holding her tight.

"Yes," she said.

"Talk about it," he crooned. "Talk about it, and it'll go away."

"I can't."

"Is it about what happened in New Orleans?"

"Yes," she lied. She lied to the man who loved her, and that too brought anguish. But she could not bear to tell him the truth.

Chapter XII

Thursday, February 19

Early in the evening Val pulled on her jacket and called Wolf to the door. They were parked in Kansas City, less than a block from the Missouri River. The medley of odors coming from the river had intrigued her all day; she wanted to see the water close up in the twilight.

"Where're you going?" Theo asked, looking up. He was working on a pile of papers at the dinette.

"Down to the river. Want to come along?"

"Maybe later. I want to finish this article," he said. He'd been writing whenever they parked somewhere. He planned to send it to a colleague in Austin who would try to publish it under his own name.

Mark stood up and stretched with a long, sinuous twist. "Valerie, do you mind if I go along?"

"Of course not. Come on," and they walked side by side up the hard-packed footpath that led to the river's edge. The Missouri flowed by darkly in the gathering twilight, surrounded by mounds of rolling damp air that would become fog in a few hours. Wolf wandered off ahead of them, intent on his own business.

"How do you like traveling?" Val asked.

"All right, I guess," he answered, then hesitated. "It's all the girls we keep meeting."

"Does that bother you? I thought most of them were quite attractive." Val slipped a glance sideways at him. She had been curious; why did he back off whenever the vampyrs they'd met along the way showed much interest in him? She didn't think he was overly shy.

His chin dropped onto his chest as he hunched his shoulders and clasped his hands behind his waist; the classical contemplative stance. That in itself was interesting.

"Yes, they were," he finally blurted out, "but I can't handle girls like that."

Val was surprised. He was nearly thirty, actual age, and handsome in a classical way. Mark possessed a soft petulant boyishness that most women found irresistible. He could have had almost any girl he wanted. "What do you mean? They practically throw themselves at you!"

"That's the problem, Valerie. I was raised to be— pure. I've wanted to be a priest ever since I can remember." He raised his head and looked out over the water. "It's been happening to me ever since I've been a vampyr. I used to be able to control situations like that with prayer, but now—Pearl says it's the nature of my beast. I can't resist. It isn't even me doing it. I'm just along for the ride. I don't feel as guilty about it since she explained it to me, but I still don't like it."

"I think I understand. Every vampyr has a beast that embodies his mortal weakness. I don't dare miss a meal. Mine's a hungry beast."

They watched as a string of boats drifted by, a long

procession of shadows dotted with running lights, on their way downriver to meet the Gulf. "She said it wasn't sin if my beast does it, because even though I know what's happening, I can't stop it. I have trouble accepting that. If I do it, I'm responsible."

"I'm no theologian, and I don't know much about what makes something a sin," Val said. They started walking again and skirted a group of skeletal willow trees, their leafless branches arched out over the bank and dragging in the water. "But it seems to me that you have to learn the limits of your beast's power and live within them. If you can't resist a girl, why not stay with her for a while until you're the one in control of yourself? Don't just panic and run."

They walked a little further, and Wolf barked in the darkness ahead of them. Moments later a jogger, clad only in shorts and a tee shirt, trotted breathlessly by.

"He's working too hard at it," Mark said, watching the flashing white of the tee shirt disappear beyond the willows. "I used to jog, don't have to anymore. I think we are the way humans were meant to be; in perfect condition without having to work at it."

Wolf came out of the underbrush toward them, padding slowly, his tongue lolling out to the side of his mouth. He was ready to go back. Mark took Val's arm as they turned around.

"All the great thinkers have been celibate."

Val laughed. "Mark, there's a big difference between inspiration and frustration. Come on."

When they got back, Theo was sitting in the driver's seat staring out into the darkness. He hadn't even turned on the lights in the camper. "I called Bart in Houston while you were gone," he told them. "Things aren't going well for Sarah there." His face was pinched, full of anxious and tender concern.

Val touched his shoulder. "We'll go right away, if you like. There's no reason to stay here any more."

He nodded.

Sunday, February 22

They arrived at Bart and Nancy James' home in Houston at six-thirty in the morning. Theo parked the motorhome at one end of the huge one-story ranch house, its rear window to the backyard tennis court and swimming pool.

"Too bad they don't have kids of their own," Theo said, killing the motor.

"What do they do with a place like this?"

"They have a lot of company. Nancy's a compulsive party giver." He grinned and waved at Sarah, who came running out the front door toward them. She was still buttoning her blouse. "She's looking good."

"Hah! She's looking gorgeous," Val said, and she was. Sarah was taller, blonder, and more mature than she had been six months ago. There was still a coltish quality about the way she moved, a promise of even more beauty to come.

"Hi!" she yelled and pulled the door open before they were even out of their seats. "Oh, I'm so glad to see you!" She grabbed Wolf and hugged him; then Theo caught her up in a warm embrace. Val noticed he was holding his breath. She did the same thing when Sarah hugged her, but it was hard to keep the pungent warm human smell out of her nose in the closeness of the vehicle.

"Come on outside." Val led the way and took a deep

206

breath of fresh air. As they stepped down, Bart and his plump wife came around the front of the cab. They were fully dressed despite the early hour.

"Nan," Bart said, "meet Valan." He guided his wife toward Val. "And who's this?" Mark was descending the steps.

"Just Mark," Theo said and introduced everyone.

"Come on," Nancy took Val's arm, "I'll show you the guest house." Mark tagged along after them, leaving Sarah and the brothers talking on the dry grass of the winter lawn.

Nancy was nothing like what Val had expected. She looked ten years older than Bart, warm and motherly, with little rolls of flesh escaping above and below the too-tight confines of her undergarments. "You'll love it here. We have lots of room."

The guest house was on the far side of the tennis court. It consisted of two suites joined by a common living room and kitchen area, very comfortable in an old-fashioned, overstuffed way. "It'll be nice to use a real tub," Val said as they inspected one of the bathrooms.

"Towels and things in here." Nancy pulled open a closet door. "Is Mark your little brother?" She fluffed her greying hair with one hand and watched as he carried in the suitcases and hangers full of clothes from the motor home.

"We're sort of remotely related. He's just staying with us for a while."

"Well, come on up to the house when you get settled. Just walk right in. We'll have a little get-together with the neighbors this evening to introduce you."

Val thanked her, closed the door to the living room,

and took a long hot bath in the tub. Theo would have to take care of his own problems. He hadn't been specific about what Sarah had been doing; she felt that he didn't want her to get involved.

It was good to be warm and clean and calm, instead of bouncing about in the drafty motorhome. The bed looked so inviting, in spite of its worn blue chenille bedspread, that instead of getting dressed she closed the blinds and slipped under the covers for what turned into a full day's sleep.

She woke up about four in the afternoon. The TV was on in the living room; she dressed and found Mark sprawled there alone on the couch.

"Your meal is in the refrigerator," he said.

"Fine. Where is everybody?"

"They went to Mass this morning, and now they're at the supermarket shopping. Mrs. James has asked half the countryside over tonight to meet you and Theo. The caterers are barbecueing the fatted calf already."

"Good grief!"

"That's not all. You missed a dandy scene when we were trying to avoid eating lunch." He slouched further down on the couch.

"What happened?"

"Mrs. James asked Theo why you weren't married yet. Sarah and Dr. Bart started giggling and Theo told her it wasn't any of her business."

"What did you do?"

"I just sat there looking stupid. Mrs. James cleared the table without a word, but I don't know how those dishes made it to the kitchen. She was really put out."

"I imagine so. Thanks for the warning."

An hour later, Nancy was all smiles and small talk

when she took Val on a guided tour of the main house. Val would not have known that she'd been angry. The house was opulent—the bricks a little too pink, the shrubbery a little too thick, the carpets a little too plush. No detail was obviously out of proportion, but the total effect was, Val thought, overripe.

The gathering of neighbors turned into a pandemonium. Over a hundred guests wandered in and out; the stereo music was turned to full volume. Val found it ghastly. She mingled, apprehensive and alone among the humans, pretending to drink Perrier and lime. Theo, Bart, and a bunch of other men had disappeared by nine to the den to watch TV. Mark had vanished to the guest house a little later, leaving Val to cope with Nancy and the chattering hordes. Even Sarah had deserted her. "I have homework, you know," she said as an excuse. She'd been following Mark and Val around all evening with none of the sulking pettishness of last summer. Whatever problems Bart was having with her seemed to be under control; she seemed genuinely cheerful.

Bart emerged from the den at eleven to turn the poolside stereo system down, and that seemed to signal the end. By midnight the last dozen or so guests had retired to the living room for coffee. The evening of mingling with the mildly drunk humans left Val tense with unidentified fears. There was something wrong with the situation that she couldn't put her finger on. Something she should have noticed but had missed. So she sat outdoors at a poolside table and watched the caterers clean up the mess.

They were packed and gone within forty-five minutes, and she was still trying to figure out what was bothering her. As she started to go indoors, Theo and Bart met her. "We're supposed to fetch you in," Bart said, holding the doorknob.

"Fine. Did you know your wife has been introducing me as Theo's fiancée all evening? It makes me uncomfortable."

"I told her you weren't planning on getting married, but once she gets an idea she's kind of hard to stop." Bart shrugged. "Do you want me to tell her the truth?"

Val shook her head as Theo put his arm around her shoulders. "Have you had any luck with Sarah?" she asked him. "She seemed content to just follow me around this evening."

They were at the living room door by then, so he said, "I'll tell you about it later. It's strange."

"Here's the loving couple," Nancy called, clapping her hands. "Come on in and meet our closest neighbors." Val wished she was out in the guest house playing gin with Mark. As soon as possible she headed for the kitchen for a glass of water.

Nancy followed her. "I do hope you set a date soon. We'd love to have the wedding here, maybe at Easter."

"At Easter we plan to be in Paris," Val said abruptly.

Nancy's face took on a genuinely worried look. "What is it you're not telling us? It isn't like Theodore to live with a woman without marriage."

Theodore, she called him. Val had never heard anyone use his given name before and Nancy's sincerity moved her. Val took a sip of water and decided to give her a reason.

"It's money. I have a trust fund that pays me nearly a quarter of a million a year as long as I'm legally single. It's a bequest from a maiden aunt who believed in women's lib long before it became fashionable. We can't afford to get married." Val shrugged.

"Oh," Nancy said. That was the end of the conversation.

"Money talks," Val thought on the way back to the living room. She caught Theo's eye before she sat down; he got the message.

"Val, you are tired." He stood up and addressed the remaining guests, who were languidly finishing their coffee. "She's just getting over the flu, you know." He was getting to be such an accomplished liar, Val thought wryly. "Let's go." Polite mumbles, a few good nights, and they left.

As they went out the patio door, Val heard a humming noise and splashing coming from behind the cabana on the other side of the pool. "What's there?" she asked.

"The Jacuzzi. Is Mark over there?"

"Probably. Let's check." She took Theo's hand and they headed toward the noise. It was getting cool, perhaps in the mid-forties, but the evening was mild. The idea of splashing around in the dark sounded like fun.

But what they found when they came around the end of the cabana wasn't fun. Mark and Sarah were standing close together on the steps of the tub, barely illuminated by a single light on the patio cover overhead. They were dripping wet and glistening in their swimming suits. She had her hands on his pale shoulders pulling him to her, and her head was stretched back, exposing her throat to the fullest. She was moaning, making little crooning sounds, and her eyes were closed. Mark was holding her, his back moving, swaying back and forth

211

as though he was rocking a baby; his mouth was on her throat, drinking.

Theo squeezed Val's hand hard, then dropped it. A primeval sound rose from deep in his throat, exploding from his mouth. He ran to them with his hands outstretched and pulled them roughly apart. As Mark's supporting hands left Sarah she slumped down weakly at the edge of the tub and sat there staring glassy-eyed while Theo spun Mark around and hit him in the face hard enough to throw him against the cabana nearly eight feet away. Theo stood poised to attack again, his teeth bared, but Mark collapsed and slithered down the wall, a blank expression on his face and blood dripping from his nose.

Val grabbed a towel from the back of a lawn chair and wrapped it around Sarah's neck.

"Let's get her into the guest house before anyone sees her like this."

"Go ahead," Theo said, straightening up, his attention still focused entirely on the young vampyr's motionless form. "Mark, get your things together. Pack everything."

"Theo!" Val protested. Mark was still sitting there, not trying to move. His tongue, moving in and out, absently licked the blood off his upper lip.

"He has to go; to Arthur, to Pearl, anywhere he wants. But he can't stay here with Sarah." Theo started to turn away. "Not now. She's only sixteen." He walked away, back toward the main house.

Val took Sarah to her bathroom and sat the dazed teenager on the closed seat of the toilet. Sarah was shivering and covered with goosebumps, so Val draped a blanket over her shoulders. It was nearly ten minutes before the bleeding from the thin slit in her neck stopped.

There was a medley of odors around Sarah; of blood, of fear, of woman aroused. Any would normally have awakened hunger in Val, but she was unmoved.

Mark came and stood at the door with a hand on each side of the frame. "I'm packed," he said. "I know I have to go. I agree with Theo. I'm sorry." He didn't try to come any closer.

"What happened?"

"She came out when the party was nearly over to watch TV and talked me into trying the Jacuzzi. It sounded harmless enough. I thought she was just a kid. Then she really came on strong. It all happened too fast."

Theo appeared behind Mark, much calmer. "I've got Bart's car keys. How is she?" He pushed past Mark, knelt beside Sarah, briefly pushed open one eyelid, and held her wrist for a few moments.

"Weak, but steady. Put her to bed in here. She'll be all right." He stood up. "Let's go."

"Theo," Val pleaded. "Will you listen to Mark's version of what happened?"

He put his hand on Val's shoulder, kissed her lips gently and turned to face Mark. "It wasn't Mark's fault, Valan. He just happened to be there. But I can't let it happen again." Then they drove off, leaving Val to wonder what was going on that she'd missed.

Monday, February 23

Sarah woke up shortly after dawn. "Am I a vampyr now?" she asked when Val brought her a salami sandwich and a glass of milk—all she could find in the refrigerator.

"No. It doesn't work that way." Val sat on the side

213

of the bed and held the plate for her. "Be patient, Sarah. You can't have what you want yet. Give human life a chance. Wait about five more years; then no one will object."

She pouted. "How do I get to be a vampyr like you?"

"First, you have to know a vampyr who loves you. You've got that. Then you have to be an adult."

"Why?"

"Do you really want to be sixteen forever? You would never be able to pass yourself off as an adult; never own anything, legally or otherwise. How would you get a driver's licence or a passport that would be believable? It's too much trouble. For pushing too fast now, you'd be stuck forever having to work hidden deals for everything. How could you buy a home or even a car? Who'd sell one to you?"

"If I wait, then what?"

"Then your vampyr has to get two others to agree that you're worthy."

"In all the stories, if you're bitten by a vampyr you're doomed to become one. What did I do wrong?"

"That sounds like rabies to me. How did you know Mark was a vampyr? It's almost impossible for a normal human to spot one unless they've been bitten."

"His eyes. Do you remember how Poppa always used to look everyone directly in the eyes? He doesn't do it anymore. He sort of looks at faces without focusing on the eyes, the way you do. Most people wouldn't notice, but I do. Mark looks at people the same way. I used to think you were just being shy, but now I know it isn't that at all."

"Did Mark look into your eyes?" Val asked, dreading but already knowing the answer.

"Yes," she whispered. "I'd give anything to do it again, anything." And that, Val realized, was why Theo took Mark away. She should have known. It had been so long since she'd felt the rush a vampyr's eyes cause in a human. Theo knew. It had been less than a year for him.

"You're going to have to wait. If you behave yourself, maybe you can come to Paris this summer."

"Really? I'd love that, Valan. All right. I promise to be good until this summer." She blinked her eyes and stifled a yawn. Just staying awake seemed to take a terrific effort.

"You lost almost half your blood last night. That was very foolish, and it'll take a day or two before you feel well. Try to rest. I'm going to get some sleep, too."

"Stay here with me, Valan. This bed's plenty big."

Val smiled. "No, you'll rest better alone."

Bart came over at two in the afternoon, four hours after Theo came home from the airport. Sarah was still sound asleep in the master bedroom.

"Nancy's out all afternoon; Monday is her bridge day," Bart said, after he'd peeked in on Sarah. "What did you do with Mark?"

"Sent him back to Chicago. What did you tell Nan?"

"Just that Sarah wanted to stay with you overnight."

"I talked to Sarah this morning," Val said. "She's still obsessed with wanting to be a vampyr. I think you'd better tell me what's been going on. I wasn't going to pry or try to interfere but I need to know if we're going to protect her."

"Bart?" Theo cleared his throat. "Tell her what you told me."

"It started about Christmas," Bart said. "You were

pretty regular with the phone calls and letters up until then, a different place nearly every week. It all sounded so romantic to her. Even Nan and I envied you."

"Then the letters stopped?" Val said.

Theo nodded. "After we went to New Orleans."

"Sarah started staying out late," Bart continued, "wandering around downtown. She'd take the car, no driver's license, and just cruise around. She's been picked up and brought home twice. She said she was looking for her people, meaning vampyrs.

"About two weeks ago the neighbors' pet angora goat died in its pen. Its throat had been cut, but there wasn't enough blood on the ground. On a hunch I found a mason jar full of it here in the guest house refrigerator. Sarah admitted she'd done it. She was trying to become a vampyr.

"It made her so upset that the goat had died—she hadn't figured on that—that she wouldn't go back to school until I helped her buy a kid to replace it. The neighbors think she's just kind-hearted; they have no idea that she actually killed their pet."

"She's promised to behave," Val said. "At least until this summer."

"How did you manage that?" Theo asked.

"I held out a visit to Paris while we're there."

"At the chateau?"

"No, that wouldn't be safe. But we can get a hotel suite for a couple of weeks and play tourist."

"Sounds like a good idea," Bart said. "Theo, what do you think?"

He just nodded. As though he was too tired to care.

Theo went back to bed and slept the rest of the day. When Sarah woke up, she was very quiet. Nancy popped in and out when she came home from her bridge game. A half-hour after sunset, Val walked down to an ice house with Wolf and called Corey from the pay telephone.

Wednesday, February 25

Val was curled up on the large living-room couch and reading a frivolous book about a lovely maiden, a handsome man, and living happily ever after. Wolf was near the other end of the couch, dozing on the floor with his nose between his outstretched forepaws. Hazy sunlight fell on him through one of the windows.

Sarah came out of the bedroom in blue jeans, her hair up in huge rollers made of tincans with both ends cut out. "When do you think you'll be leaving, Val?"

"Perhaps next week. This isn't a good area for us; not much livestock around here."

"There's an Arabian horse farm about four miles down the highway." She sat down at the other end of the couch and extended one hand along the back, as though she was reaching for Val. "They have over a hundred horses, mostly grey. Valan, they're beautiful. I'd like to have one someday."

"When they were desert horses, they lived in the tent homes of their Bedouin masters," Val said. "Because of that, Arabian horses were bred to love people. That was just as important to the desert wanderers as endurance and beauty. I think dogs are probably the only creatures that care more for their masters."

"Will you take Wolf when you go to Paris?"

"I'd rather not. He's old." Val looked down at him sleeping there, oblivious to the conversation. "The vet said he's about nine, give or take a year."

217

"He could stay here. Aunt Nan won't mind. I'll take care of him."

Val nodded.

She patted her hair, uncurled one of the rollers, frowned because the hair was still wet and wound it back up. "I don't actually want to go to school tomorrow." Her voice was sad. She looked back at Val. "If you really care so much about Wolf, why don't you make him a vampyr? Does it only work with humans?"

"No, it'll work with any creature that can easily digest meat. But, as usual, things are more complicated than you think. The most difficult thing for any vampyr is maintaining self-control. You saw how Mark and your father lost theirs the other night."

She shrugged. "What about you? You never lose yours."

It was Val's turn to shrug and grin ruefully. "I've had a lot more time to practice. People are supposed to be rational beings, and look what happens. A dog, made vampyr, would be completely out of control, driven by urges he couldn't understand or cope with.

"It would be that way for Wolf. Do you see? It's because I love him that I'd never even consider changing him into an unnatural thing like that. With conscience and intelligence we can control the vampyr beast, without it . . . ." She glanced down at Wolf again. "It's better for him to live his days with love and die at his proper time."

"I see," Sarah said, but she was frowning.

Thursday, February 26

It stormed all day. The sky was black even at noon. Clouds poured over the whole region and filled the air

218

with heavy rain. By evening there were pools of water all over the tennis court.

Val liked rain, but this awesome storm left her depressed and longing for freshly blooming flowers. She was looking forward to spring much more eagerly than she had for the last few years. Perhaps because it had been such a hard winter in so many ways.

She had received a packet of letters from Corey in the mail. He enclosed a brief note asking her visit him at her convenience so they could go over some business details. She would stop there on the way to Paris at Easter, she decided. His letter worried her—its tone was unusually imperative.

She read Salvatore's letter next. It was very brief. If she approved, there would be a general meeting of the group at the chateau at Easter. Several hundred, he wrote, were making plans to spend part of the spring there. Val was excited by the prospect of the meeting and wrote immediately approving the idea. There were so many she hadn't seen in the twenty years since the last meeting. She found it a comforting prospect; all around her humans changed so visibly from month to month that she would often feel a sense of loss long before they were gone.

Chapter XIII

Friday, February 27

Dear Valerie

I must tell you what I've heard about the Canadian vampyr named Georges. A visitor to the chateau told me that on two separate occasions he destroyed vampyrs and brazenly took rings off their fingers and money from their bodies for his own use. No one in Canada dares challenge him. He even has Carlotta under his thrall. She walks behind him with her eyes downcast and serves him like a slave.

The visitor said all the Canadian vampyrs shun him. Valerie, I know you don't like to interfere with other groups, but please consider what might happen if he threatens us.

I shudder to think of it.

Claire

Val folded the letter and carefully shoved it back into its envelope. Somehow Claire's doomsaying didn't seem important. It was too remote in time and place.

Saturday, February 28

Bart and Nancy had gone to a party. "Probably an all-night affair," Bart had said. It was the third one that week, not counting the one Nancy had given in Val's and Theo's honor. They were included in the invitation but had declined. Their supplies were low, and they needed to hunt. They would visit the horse farm.

Before they left, Theo looked in on Sarah. She was sprawled on her back in the middle of the double bed sound asleep. The faded blue bespread was rumpled over her legs and Wolf was curled up beside her, his head draped across her arm. He waved the tip of his tail in greeting but didn't leave the warmth of her bed to go with them. "Guard her," Theo told him.

The night was overcast and humid, with shadows stirring where there was nothing alive. They left Bart's Porsche concealed in a brushy copse just off the highway and walked along between the road and the smooth wire fenceline.

"It's dark tonight," Theo said.

"Good for hunting."

He spread the wire for Val to slip through into the pasture. "Valan, something's been happening to me lately."

"What?" She ducked under the top wire, turned and held it for him, one foot on the lower wires to push them down. "It sure saves on clothes when they don't use barbed wire."

He grunted in assent and straightened up beside her. "Just how well can you see in the dark?"

"On a night like tonight, when the moon's not out?"

"Yes."

"Pretty well. The colors are different. Things

222

shimmer with heat or glow sort of blue and violet. It's not as it is during the daylight."

"That's it," he nodded. "Things shimmer in the dark. I thought I was imagining it."

"No, it's the infrared and ultraviolet light. Your eyes are starting to pick up a broader range of light waves. Most normal people can't see them at all."

"My sight is getting better all the time." He stiffened and pointed. "Look, there go the horses."

The Arabians were restless, trotting in great circles in the middle of the pasture, tails held high like banners in the wind, their hooves dwelling for an instant at the top of each stride. Then Val and Theo stood just inside the fence, in the protective cover of a clump of small trees, and watched them come.

"Wait until you develop the far sight. That's fun. You'll be able to read a newspaper from across the room, like Superman."

He shook his head. "I wonder how it works?"

"It has something to do with the lens inside the eye."

"Inside the eye?"

"It takes a long time for the eyes to change compared to some of the other things that happen when you become a vampyr. Your vision alters as the lens does. Most of the other changes have already started. Did you realize that you were moving so fast the other night, when you were reaching for Mark, that you blurred?"

"Really? That's interesting. Did you know that the inner parts of the eye, like the lens, don't get blood?"

"Maybe that's why the eyes change so slowly."

The horses' grey coats gleamed with warmth; their dished faces turned intently on the strangers.

"How does the hypnotic eye power work?"

"I have no idea, except that it's an expression of inner strength and personality."

The horses snorted and came closer. All of them were broodmares, great in the belly with their unborn foals, standing poised on long slender legs, ready to wheel around and flee. Val and Theo waited until they offered themselves with gracefully arched necks and gently searching eyes. A grand old mare bumped Theo with her delicately flared nostrils as she stood at his shoulder, and he could feel her warm, grass-scented breath as the plastic bag swelled to fullness with her blood. It was the last they meant to fill.

"Do all vampyrs have nightmares?" Theo asked. He spoke casually, but it had been bothering him for some time.

Val glanced at him. "No. Why?"

"No real reason. You seem to be plagued with them. So did Mark."

He saw her hands shake as she pulled the needle from the old mare's neck; it fell from her fingers. Theo took the bag out of her other hand, sealed it, and put it in the pocket of his jacket. He sensed that something was wrong, and wondered if it had to do with her nightmares.

The mares went away, snorting and kicking up their heels with the joy of being alive. Val and Theo watched until they were nearly out of sight, far across the pasture, their hoofbeats fading away in the dark. Then Theo reached down and picked up the needle she'd dropped, wrapped it in a bit of paper and tucked it in with the rest of the equipment.

She had turned and walked away. He was still trying to decide why his question had affected her so strongly.

He caught up to her and took her hand as they walked back to the car.

Suddenly Val blurted out, "It's getting to be more than I can bear."

"Your work? Or the memories?"

"Everything. There are just too many things that I can't forget and can't let go of."

"If you share them, it'll be easier." His arm slipped around her shoulders and she leaned against him.

"Perhaps." But she didn't, and he didn't push it.

Theo felt different. He had changed a lot in the last few months. He found it difficult to explain, because he wasn't sure what had happened. But as time went by he wanted more and more to take control of difficult situations for Val. It would be interesting for him to see how the others reacted when he went to Paris with her. A strength seemed to be growing in him, coming from some hidden source.

They were back in the guest room before midnight, settled down in the living room and buried in their own interests.

"There's one thing I'd like to try before we leave for Paris," Theo said. He was sitting in front of the TV, where he'd been watching the late show.

"What's that?" Val looked up from her newspaper.

"What if Sarah happens to come across a local vampyr? What do you think will happen?"

"Well," she paused. "She told me she would give anything to look into vampyr eyes again." Val found the want ad section, folded it open, and handed it to him. "Read that fifth ad. It's been in every paper since we've been here."

" 'Midnight's Children Discotheque, four to four.' Is

that a vampyr place? If we tell them about her, will they stay away?" He frowned in concentration, deep lines forming on his forehead.

"Perhaps. Do you want to make contact? The local leader is an old acquaintance. We aren't on the best of terms, but it probably won't hurt to talk to him."

He nodded, and Val called the number given in the ad. The man who answered on the second ring spoke with a harsh guttural accent above disco music in the background.

"Midnight's Children, Quintus here."

A shudder shook Val. She recognized the voice even though she hadn't heard it since 1948.

"Plutus," she said, not bothering to use his alias. "This is Valerie. I'm coming to see you tonight."

"I've been expecting you." Val's hand shook as she replaced the receiver and told Theo what had been said.

"What was that all about? How did Pluto know to expect you?"

Val stood up abruptly and grabbed her jacket. "Is there a map in the car? Let's go."

"I think so." Val started out the door and he followed, pulling on his jacket. As they were walking down the drive, he said, "That's an odd name. Pluto, the god of the dead."

"It's Plutus, not Pluto, and oddly enough that's his real name. He was the illegitimate son of a Greek financier and an Egyptian dancer. His father's only legal heir was a daughter, so they siphoned most of the family fortune off to Plutus before the old man died. It worked quite well. The daughter married well, and Plutus is incredibly wealthy."

"Then it is a Greek name?" He started the car, and they rolled out to the main road.

"The Greek god of wealth, a blind god. It's an appropriate name. Plutus was blinded by an infection before he was a year old."

"A blind vampyr?"

She pulled her denim jacket around her, perhaps because the wind coming in from under the dash of the Porsche was chilly. "He can't see anything except infrared. But if you look he will suck you in and drown you before he'll let you go. Everybody avoids his eyes except the strongest vampyrs."

"Are you warning me?" He thumped the dash. "Does the heater in this thing work?" His fingers twisted knobs randomly in the dark until a gust of warm air swept across his feet. "There."

"Plutus was different. He would always wear dark glasses. When he took them off onlookers would stare, and he'd be in control before they could defend themselves. His eyes are striking. They're pale milky white, almost as if the iris and pupil are missing. It's eerie—repulsive and fascinating. Other than that he's quite attractive, like most vampyrs." She shivered.

"Val, are you afraid of him?"

"In a way. I've come to dread challenges from other vampyrs. They're nerve-racking. I'll probably have to face him down, even though he owes me a favor. He knows his power and likes to use it. If we're lucky he might agree to insure Sarah's safety. He can do it."

"We'll be careful. We have to try. Are you stronger than he is?"

"Probably. I bested him in 'forty-eight but things change with time." She didn't tell Theo how nervous the prospect of a confrontation was making her. But he knew. What he didn't know was how immense the actual stakes might be.

Midnight's Children was a huge square castle made of white-painted cinderblocks. There was a sawtoothed turret at each corner, a drawbridge and a two-foot-wide moat across the front.

"We probably should have changed clothes." They were still wearing jeans and denim jackets, and Theo had on cowboy boots.

"It doesn't matter," he said. "They'll just think we're ranchers."

The parking lot was large, paved, well lighted, and nearly full. They were greeted just inside the main door by a teenaged human with a bald, painted head, his face a death's head of artfully applied makeup. His body was completely covered by a black bodysuit and gloves.

"We've come to see Quintus," Val told him.

The Death's Head bowed politely. "Ten dollars." He took their money with a bit of a smirk. "This way, please." He turned and led the way into the castle. They entered a sloping stone-walled corridor illuminated only by black lights. The head floated on before them, glowing, drifting above its dark-clad body. Humans would have seen only the disembodied head. But the ultraviolet light flooded the corridor for Val and Theo and much of the intended effect was lost.

Death's Head had evidently decided they deserved the royal guided tour for he talked almost nonstop as they followed him into the bowels of Plutus' domain. "We opened for business in November, and Midnight's Children is the most unique disco in town. Houston has never seen anything like it." Off to the right portals opened through the wall to expose alcoves overlooking the dance floor. "The booths are for the patrons who just want to watch the action." The music was deafening, almost drowning out his voice. "At Christmastime we strung thousands of Christmas tree lights all over the ceiling. It was beautiful."

They approached the level of the dance floor. Fashionably dressed people were wandering around, going to the alcove booths or to the bar. Many of them held exotic drinks in their hands.

The bar, located in a simulated dungeon just off the dance floor, was guarded by two Mexican suits of armor nearly eight feet tall. They reminded Theo of Don Quixote.

"We go in here," Death's Head said. "But take a look out on the floor first. It's quite a sight."

The light show was an impressive kaleidoscope of motion. There were strobes flashing and slides of winter scenes projected on the walls. The ceiling was completely covered with realistic plastic icicles sparkling like diamonds with reflected light from a giant mirror-covered ball in the center. "We had the icicles 'specially made for this winter. At Easter we'll use a sunburst up there."

He led the way through the bar and into a small hallway used for hanging coats and storing boxes. The back wall was dominated by a steel door, complete with a locking wheel and combination dial.

"It's Quintus' rule," Death's Head said. "You can go in if you can open the door." His grin seemed to grow larger, perhaps with malice. Theo wondered what they would find on the other side of the door and stepped back slightly, a reflex action. The whole adventure was becoming unpleasant, the blinking lights, the noise, the patronizing attitude of Death's Head. He didn't like any of it—and they weren't even close to Plutus.

Theo glanced at Val and nodded. He was determined to see it through. So she went to the door and pressed one ear to the cold steel. Within a minute she straightened up and turned to Theo. "It's open."

He pulled the heavy door open. Beyond was a sharply angled hallway; a different atmosphere, cooler air, muted voices, and no music.

"It's a simple but effective way to keep out pests," Death's Head said, bowing again and retreating, leaving them to enter the hallway alone. At the end of the short twisted passage was a large open gaming room, filled with cigarette smoke and bustling with activity. There were Faro tables on a slightly raised railed-off balcony at one side and baccarat, roulette, and twenty-one in the pit. No one seemed to notice their arrival.

"No craps," Theo said.

"Craps in the room to your right," a voice spoke behind them. They wheeled around. A chubby white-haired man was sitting in a teller's cage beside the door. He smiled at them.

"We came to see Quintus," Val said. Her voice was a bit higher-pitched than usual.

"Upstairs." He pointed; across the pit a spiral staircase wound around the inside of a turret wall. They'd walked nearly to the far corner of the castle from the parking lot.

"Curiouser and curiouser," Theo said as they began ascending the coiling steps.

"What?"

"Like Alice in Wonderland, we've gone down a rabbit hole full of the unexpected."

230

"I don't like the way Plutus is playing with us. It's more like mice down a cat hole." Under different circumstances and a different mood it would have been fun to explore the castle, but she was tense. It was going to be unpleasant.

They stepped onto a landing and went through another door, into a sumptuous room filled with dancing forms. The lights were comfortably dim and the Hugo Montenegro stereo music was soft and slow.

The blind vampyr sat in the solitary splendor of a white velvet couch to the left, between the door and what looked like a bar, but there were no liquor bottles visible.

"Plutus," Val said, her normal conversational tone almost lost in the hum of activity in the room.

"Valerie?" He raised his lean, close-cropped head, weaving it back and forth like a serpent, trying to pick out her cool shape from the throng in the room. He waved his hand gropingly toward her; she took it in her own. He grinned tightly, pulling the skin on his cheeks into hundreds of tiny wrinkles. Quickly he slid his dark glasses off with his ring-studded left hand. He was going to try to take her.

For an instant she floated away from her body toward his milky eyes, but the pull wasn't strong enough to hold her. She pulled back and drank of him instead, taking knowledge without giving in return, as he would have done to her. "Kiss my hand," he tried to will her. She knew what he wanted, submission in front of his followers. She might have acquiesced, if her patience had not worn thin in the noise and confusion of the castle.

She smiled stiffly and watched his face contort with effort as he stood up from the couch and tried to gain control. His hand lifted hers inexorably until his lips brushed her fingers. Then she let him go. He sank, pale and trembling, onto the white velvet.

The music continued to play, but the room had grown still. The vampyrs were staring at them motionless.

Theo and Val sat down on either side of Plutus, and the crowd relaxed. The talk resumed with an ugly buzz.

"They didn't like what you did," Plutus said petulantly.

"That their god isn't as omnipotent as they thought?"

"You didn't have to do it."

"Who challenged who, Plutus?" She spoke softly, trying to put a touch of menace in her voice. "You know I don't play games."

"What do you want?"

"Not your castle or your group," she said. "As if you didn't know. I've come to call an old debt due."

"Name it and it's yours," He spoke quickly, quietly. They both knew he was honor bound to obey.

"I want you to guarantee that no vampyr in this area will touch a certain human girl under any circumstances." He looked puzzled, but once she told him the entire story he nodded with visible relief.

"Of course I'll help. It's a small thing to do to cancel a debt." He grew expansive. "I'd have done it for you anyway. It's nothing."

"It means a great deal to us," Theo said as he leaned back, relaxing. The dancers were swaying to a waltz.

"Will you be coming to Paris this spring?" Val asked.

"Not unless I have to. This place takes all of my attention."

"Aren't you pushing your luck with that casino downstairs?" Theo asked.

"Not really. The police commissioner's wife and son are down there tonight, and we're very lenient with certain patrons when it comes to paying their tabs." He shrugged. "Anyway, the ownership is well disguised and I have ways to get out in a crisis. Don't worry about me."

"When will you be leaving for Paris?"

"In a few days. We just have to pack," Val said.

"Carlotta will be there. Do you know her?"

"We've never met."

"We were lovers once. We still correspond. She's bringing your group a real surprise this time."

"Oh?"

He laughed. "A new member, one you'll find fascinating. By the way, his name is Georges." He laughed again, in an ugly way.

Theo and Val stood up together as though they'd planned it.

"It's time to go," Theo said, and they left.

Val was more uneasy after listening to Plutus than she had been on the way to see him. She was not worried about Sarah; he would do what he said. But his attitude toward Val personally was ominous. He'd been unpleasant, threatening, and she didn't know why. And Georges kept popping up. This time it worried her.

Chapter XIV

Monday, March 8

Val and Theo arrived in New York safely. At the airport was Corey Madison, a wide smile on his deeply tanned face. Val could see changes in him. Grey had begun to show at his temples and he looked at Val with an odd longing in his eyes. She wondered what he was thinking about. Corey had a calm and gentle manner that hid solid steel. He could be ruthless, she knew. She'd seen him in action on behalf of the group.

His office at home had a mahogany desk the size of a small boat, framed by a picture window overlooking the ocean. They sat informally on overstuffed easy chairs in the other half of the room and dealt with business papers most of the day. Theo sat in on the meeting. His quick grasp of the group's financial arrangements surprised Val until she remembered he'd been a very successful physician.

When they finished, Corey invited Val, not Theo, out to dinner, something he had never done before. He'd been content to take her money, do her work and keep the group at a great distance from his personal life. Val was curious. "Was there anything special you wanted to discuss?"

"Well, Ann," he answered. He always called Val that no matter what identification she came with. It was the name he had first known her by, Ann Turner. "Well, Ann, I'd like to talk to you alone, not about your business affairs, about mine."

"What, then?" Val asked.

"It's about my arrangement with you and the group."

"I'll wait outside, if you like," Theo said.

Val nodded and Corey said, "Yes. It won't take more than a few minutes. But it's important to me."

Corey looked straight at Val as he spoke. "Ann, do you recall that once you asked me if I ever wondered what you were?"

She nodded. "Yes. I was curious. You see us coming and going and you never ask who we really are."

"It never occurred to me before that. I thought you were merely rich people who liked an excessive amount of privacy. But I've been thinking about it since then. I see you, Ann, every few years, just as beautiful and vibrant as you were the first moment I met you. That was nearly fifteen years ago.

"I'm forty now. You still look like a teenager."

Val laughed. "It costs a lot to stay young in this world. But you know we have more money than we can ever use."

"Yes, but that's not the answer." He frowned and shook his head. "I think I've finally figured it out. You and Salvatore, Arthur; some of the others that come through now and then, that beautiful Frenchwoman, Claire. I've been keeping track of all of you. There are

236

others I've only seen once or twice so I can't be sure. There is something different about you. I'd like to venture a guess. Please be honest with me."

Here it comes, she thought; we're the Mafia, smugglers, or illegitimate children of jetsetters with an immortality elixir. "All right, Corey."

He nodded again, leaned back in his chair with his fingers together. "OK. Ann, are you some sort of vampires?"

She smiled at him, an innocent smile, but her mind was reeling. Then she decided to level with him. "Yes. We're vampyrs. And . . . ?"

"All right, Ann. I'd like a change, a new business deal with you and the group."

Val arched an eyebrow. "Yes?" This was potentially disastrous. If he was going to be completely unreasonable she wouldn't be able to let him leave the room alive. He could ruin the group in minutes.

"I'm forty, not getting any younger. I've no family. I'm a financial genius. I've earned you many times more than my fee, which is overly generous. I'm not complaining about it." He ticked each point off on his fingers as he spoke, building his case professionally.

"Go on," Val said. She didn't want to kill him.

He continued gently. "Ann, I see the grey on my temples coming in thicker all the time. Soon I'll be an old man sitting here in my office signing papers for you with a trembling hand, going senile with the knowledge that my most valued clients have eternal life."

She knew then what was coming. "You've been a good friend, Corey. What do you have in mind? We'll consider any reasonable request."

"Ann, make me one of you. I'll still serve another

237

twenty years in this capacity. I know all the angles, and when it's time for me to disappear, the way you do, we'll have it set up here so we'll be protected forever. I can do it. The computers we've put in can handle most of the business without any interference already. I want to trade that million a year to become one of you."

Val leaned back in her chair. "It's always been important to have at least one human emissary, Corey. I'll have to talk to the others. Most of our membership's deliberated on in advance, chosen with a great deal of affection and most often with love. Theo and I would back you, but it takes three. Is there another member, Corey, who loves you enough?"

"I don't know, Ann. I really don't know. But I'd give anything I have to join the group." He was deadly serious.

"You'd give up a cool million taxfree a year, for the dubious pleasure of not being able to eat as others do, of not walking in the daylight, of being feared and hated by most of the earth's population? When you see us come by, Corey, sometimes we're full of joy, going to new adventures or old friends, but more often we are running away from death and terror. Running away from people who have discovered what we are. This is what you want? It's a world of secrets."

"I've lived in New York all my life. I've seen you come and go since I was just out of law school. As a group, you have impressed me more with gentle manners, sensitivity, and good sense than the so-called normal people I deal with on your behalf.

"Yes, I want to be one of you."

"Corey, listen to me closely. Secrecy isn't always enough. There are humans who hunt us actively. Darrell, from Los Angeles, was attacked and killed last year. Sometimes we've been forced to retaliate. Most of us are murderers too, in self-defense.

"We rarely drink human blood. We don't do the things you see in the movies. We try not to bother people and we try to go on our own way.

"You know that many of us live on ranches or in the wilderness country. There are nearly five hundred in Canada alone.

"It's a violent life, and often lonely. Do you really want that?"

"Ann, I look in the mirror in the morning and see a man growing old. What do you think?"

"All right, Corey." Val nodded. "We're on our way to Paris. There's to be a meeting there of some of the older, wiser ones. We'll talk about it and I'll send you the answer. Soon, I promise."

They stood up then and Val reached over and took his hand. "Corey, if it were up to me only in this case, there would be no hesitation. Be patient."

He nodded, and they went out to meet Theo.

Wednesday, March 10
There was a throng of vampyrs already in Chateau Robinet when Theo and Valerie arrived, too many for Val's comfort. She preferred the silence of her rooms.

Val went upstairs and sat at the desk that Robin had used years ago. She wanted time to rest and to get her thoughts together. The paintings on the walls were old friends and the view from the open window so familiar that without looking she could picture the hedgerows and farms as they spread out in the distance. There was a breeze blowing in, and she could feel the heavy moisture in the air that heralded fog before morning.

Downstairs, Theo and Salvatore were playing billards and enjoying each other's company when Val joined them. The oldest vampyr of all, the Countess Carlotta, was coming soon.

"She's over five hundred years old," Salvatore told Theo. "That's unusually old," Val added, knowing that although vampyrs are immortal physically, a longing for death comes after two or three hundred years, overwhelming the normal urge to live with a growing sense of doom until suicide becomes the only solution. It was a measure of Robin's strength, Val thought, that he had lived so long. For many years he was the oldest of them all. Now Carlotta held that honor.

Chapter XV

Thursday, March 11

Carlotta arrived, veiled and silently regal. She didn't stay downstairs long enough for anyone to speak more than a word with her. A handsome, young-acting vampyr came with her.

"And that's Georges," Val thought as she watched them walk upstairs. "We shall see."

There were over fifty vampyrs in the house, mostly watchers, not leaders. Val told the handful who were leaders that they would meet some time in the coming week to review group activities and set the course for the next few years. A sense of well-being seemed to pervade the chateau.

Val met Carlotta just before midnight near the fireplace in the parlor. The wood was set on the andirons but not lit, even though the night was cool and damp. Val didn't notice the atmosphere.

As she sat down across from Carlotta, the Countess said hello but wouldn't meet Val's eyes. "I'm Valerie," Val responded. "I've waited a long time to meet you."

Carlotta sat in the easy chair like a copy of Whistler's

Mother. Her posture and expression were ancient in contrast to her appearance of youthfulness.

Finally she said, "Yes," her face hardened as though she was only slowly growing aware of Val's presence, "you were Robin's last mistress."

It was meant to be a cutting remark, as if she wanted to insult Val with the tone of her voice, but Val was too curious to be intimidated. She had learned long ago that personal attacks usually concealed something of greater importance. Val needed to find out why Carlotta was so hostile toward her, a stranger. She refused to rise to the bait.

"The last of many," she replied with a smile.

"It was you who drove him to suicide."

Again her remark was designed, Val thought, to draw her into an argument. "I think not," Val answered, trying to understand her emotions. "He'd made up his mind before I met him, that his time was soon to end. I had very little to do with it."

"Are you so sure?" Carlotta asked, her voice dripping with acid. Her black eyes flashed up to Val, then dropped. "He was once the most powerful of us all, but in his last years with you he let everything go."

That wasn't true, of course. Val knew it was time for a frontal attack. "I'm sorry, Carlotta," she replied. "Something is bothering you about Robin, about me. Is it something I should know?"

She laughed bitterly. "No, Valerie, not from the past, anyway. But there's something you should know about the future." She sat silently for several long minutes, thinking, considering what she felt and what she knew, making up her mind. Then she looked up, and Val saw, in the swirling, sucking darkness that held them together, nothing but pain and sorrow and regret where there should have been joy.

Val understood what Carlotta was trying to tell her. It was Georges, her young vampyr companion. He would be at the meeting, not invited or wanted, but so powerful that he would control the group against their wills, against their best interests. She was warning Val to beware; she was frightened that the handsome, curly-haired man who traveled at her side would have them all helpless before him.

After the moment of understanding, Val reached across and covered Carlotta's hand. It felt frail, far older than she'd expected.

"How did it happen?"

"We found each other in Montreal and went to stay in his cabin. At first he didn't seem so powerful. At first he was gentle. As we came to know each other more and more, he grew stronger, until it was I who did his bidding. It's never happened before, never. There are very few who've been able to rule me that way." At that she bowed her face into her hands and sat there silently, shaking her head. There were no tears, no sobbing. It was more as though she was full of wonder that someone so young could be strong enough to overcome her age and defenses.

Val rose and stood next to her, her hand on her shoulder. "Carlotta?" she asked. "Is he stronger than Salvatore?"

"I think so," she whispered.

"And me?"

She was silent for a moment. Then she looked at Val and said, "Valerie, ten minutes ago I would have laughed at you for that question. I hope not, I sincerely hope not. He wants everything, ownership of all the property, control of all the money."

"Who can stop him?"

"It's up to you and Salvatore."

"I see." Val patted her shoulder and turned to leave. "I'll go talk to Salvatore. And I'd like another chance to talk to you later, but before the meeting."

"I'd like that."

In the corner of her eye, Val saw Georges approaching, tall, blond, and confident. As he came up he stared boldly at her. "Are you ladies having a nice chat?" His voice was a little too loud.

"Yes," answered Carlotta, barely above a whisper. "Quite nice."

Val didn't look at him. She didn't want to test him until they were in the meeting. The time wasn't right. If they faced each other, it would be in mortal combat. They had to meet formally, not in the casual setting of a drawing room.

As she walked away he chuckled, and Val felt his eyes boring into her back. She walked proudly, but she was worried.

Val strode across the main hall and out the front door without looking back. As she went down the marble steps in front of the chateau she heard a familiar bass voice call from the darkness.

"There you are. I've been looking for you." It was Modesto, the monk, all grey-haired but no longer tonsured.

"Yes," she answered. He was sitting on a marble bench by the door. "You haven't changed."

"Of course not. It's only been twenty years since we've been together."

244

"At least twenty years. What's happened to you and the temple of Rhapsody?"

"I left. You were right what you said in your letter, but the temple is simply not for me. I have been traveling from place to place, living alone for the most part. It's getting harder and harder all the time, Valerie, with these modern record-keeping devices. It used to be I could go anywhere and be accepted. Now they want identification. Does that happen to you, too?"

"Yes, we all spend a great deal of time just building up identities, making false histories. Life was a lot simpler before they had computers."

"You said it." He laughed his deep laugh. "Come sit with me for a few minutes." He patted the bench. "I like Theo. Is he what you were looking for?"

"Perhaps," she said cautiously. "He has the knowledge that can find a control for our most dangerous urges. In time, who knows?"

"That's not what I meant," he said. "What's going to happen here next week?"

Val sat in silence for a moment. "I don't know, Modesto," she said hesitantly. "Everything has suddenly lost its focus."

"It's that new fellow Carlotta brought, isn't it?"

"Yes, is it that obvious already?"

"He is a man to be feared," Modesto said in slowly measured tones. "Beware of that one." He nodded his head and closed his eyes. So she rose from the bench and left him.

She strolled out to the gardens around the side of the house, stopping beneath a large linden tree to listen to the rustling leaves. She stood with her head bowed, her fists clenched at her sides, drinking memories. That was the spot where, years before, Robin had died.

She sank to her knees and knelt for a long while. Tears welled from under her closed lids in silent tribute to their time together.

When she opened her eyes and looked up, Theo was standing there, in the exact spot. He held his hands out to her and she took them and let him lift her to her feet.

Later they lay in bed, the full length of their bodies touching. His arm was across her breasts.

"Valan, what is it? What's wrong? Is it just this place or is there something else?"

She turned, rolling to face him, and looked at him with longing desires that didn't have names. He read everything in her eyes. She knew that he understood then what was happening. His body grew tense.

"Why didn't you tell me some of this before?"

"It wasn't important, not between us. It doesn't make any difference, does it?" she asked.

"No, Valan, it doesn't make any difference in the way I love you. But you have responsibilities that I should share with you. That's why we're together, to share things, everything. I thought we were on a vacation here. It turns out there's work to do."

"Theo, I never wanted to be responsible for all this. It was dropped on me when I didn't know any better. It just happens to be the way we do things. I'm glad that you know. It does make it easier."

His arm relaxed and began to stroke her. She touched him, their lips met, and they shared each other easily and slowly, as though they had all the time left in eternity.

Claire caught Val's hand and led her away from the crowd that was gathering in the downstairs rooms. They went into the garden behind the house and walked up and down between flower beds. Claire's face was downcast. "Look." She pointed at the ground. "The plants are coming to life. They know it's spring." Small, pale shoots were coming through the bare ground, barely visible in the dark.

"Why do you wear black so much nowadays?" Val asked. "Is it for Darrell?"

"No."

"Then what?" Val asked. "It isn't like you, Claire, to be so sad and silent."

She squeezed Val's hand. "We've been friends a long time. I can talk to you about it. It's a sickness of the soul." They stopped walking and faced each other.

"But, Claire, you're hardly older than I!"

"I know," she said. "I don't understand it either. I've tried everything. Nothing seems to help. It's been coming on for a long time." She shook her head.

"Dear Claire, do you think your time is actually coming? Isn't there anything we can do?"

"I don't know," she said. "What do others do to hold it away? I've lost the joy of it all."

"Perhaps a new place, a new man," Val said quickly, trying to banish Claire's all-too-familiar words, so much like the words Robin spoke the morning of his death. "Something entirely different. You've always been," she paused for an instant, "a little kinky."

Claire squeezed her hand again and laughed. "I know. I've terrible taste in men. You've told me that often enough. Valerie, I don't want to die. It seems inevitable, out of my control. Choose someone for me, someone who'll make me want to live."

Val thought about it as they continued their walk. "A man who would make you want to live. It isn't easy, choosing for someone else. But there is one man."

There was curiosity in Claire's face. Val felt better about her already.

"Who?"

"I'll tell you later. I want to prolong the suspense. You already know him."

"Who, Val? Who?"

Val smiled at her. "It'll be a surprise for both of you. Now, you owe me a favor. I have an important question."

"What is it?"

"Have you ever found a way to weaken a male vampyr?"

Claire let go of Val's hand and walked on, her head bowed.

After a few steps she turned to Val. "They sometimes seem weaker after a long night of lovemaking."

"Oh? I've never noticed that myself. Is there anything else?"

She shook her head and smiled. "No, but that should do it."

As soon as Val could, she sought out Carlotta and told her what Claire had said. Carlotta looked up at Val enigmatically, close-lipped and bitter, and shook her head. "He's a homosexual," was all she said. Val stared at her, round-mouthed. It was inconceivable to Val that anyone as beautiful as Carlotta could spend even a month, let alone years with a man who could not bring her comfort or satisfy her needs.

"You begin to see," Carlotta said, "what Georges

can do."

Val passed the information to Salvatore. "It's interesting," he told Val, "that we who live for so long in bodies so young eventually experience all the things that are normally reserved for the youthful. It's a rare one of us who hasn't made love at least once in every way imaginable. So there will be many who will welcome a chance to weaken Georges, now that he is making his unpleasant presence known."

Eudora followed Val when she went upstairs, and asked if she might come in to spend a little time visiting. Val assented; she was willing to listen to anyone.

They sat in the soft cushioned chairs by the fireplace. Eudora began, "It's not easy for me to come here and bother you, but I have to talk and give you some words of encouragement. You are the strength and moderation of the whole group."

"It wasn't something I asked for."

"No, no," she said. "I realize that. But I want you to know that all of us appreciate the time and effort you take on our behalf. We want you to know, Valerie, that you're very much loved. No matter what happens next week, we prefer you." She shook her head.

"Thank you, Eudora," Val said, much moved. She knew Eudora was overly emotional at times, but the encouragement made Val feel better.

"I fear if that monster takes control of the group, there won't be any group left. We'll all wind up dead or destitute."

Val was silent, full of foreboding.

"Listen," Eudora said, waving a hand in the air. "The rules are unwritten. We can change them any time."

"I know the rules are unwritten, but Georges plans to

change them. If he's as strong as Carlotta says, and as even Modesto has warned me, I'm afraid we're in for a bad time of it.''

"Oh dear, oh dear," she said. "Valerie, we can't let that happen. No one, especially that blond devil, will treat you the way they treat me. We must find a way. We will find a way to stop him. He's not going to take all our things away. No, no. We've worked far too hard to establish our security and safety." She stood up with a theatrical flourish, swishing her skirt around her legs. "Something must be done," Eudora said and strode out of the room.

Several hours later Val and Theo were at the window staring into the predawn darkness and saw the headlights of the limousine on the drive. A solitary man dressed in grey got out. "Javier!" She spoke his name to the night and gathered her white lace robe close to her body. "Thank goodness you've come."

Within an hour there was a knock at the door. When Theo opened it, Javier and Salvatore were standing there. They were wearing business suits, with silk ties.

"We had to see you," Javier said. His face was stern as he frowned across the room to where Val was sitting in deshabille on the bed.

"Come on in," Theo said, waving them to the chairs on either side of the fireplace. He started to pull the chair from the desk over for Val.

"I'll stay here," she said, moving to the center of the bed and arranging the lace of her negligee around her. He nodded and sat next to Salvatore.

There was something about the men, something out of the ordinary, that Theo couldn't quite put his finger on. He looked at them. They were handsome, lean and dark-haired; other than that, they really seemed to have little in common. Then Salvatore smiled at him and let Theo read in his eyes the bond that held them all together. He glanced toward Val, then Javier, and they confirmed what Salvatore had revealed.

"It's unbelievable," Theo thought. "Here I am, sitting with Valan's ex-lovers, and there isn't a speck of jealousy in either of them." He wondered about that, knowing he would be unable ever to share her that way. Then he caught another glance from Salvatore.

"We still love her," the message came. "We'll do anything to help her. But, no one, not even you, owns her."

"I'll come right to the point," Javier said out loud. Salvatore has told me what's been going on. I don't like it, Valerie, and it should not be allowed to continue." Heads nodded.

"What do you intend to do?" Val asked, looking at each of the men in turn.

"That Georges is a monster." Javier spat the words out with determined finality. Val didn't reply. Theo watched silently, concentrating on each of the speakers in turn, waiting to form his own opinion. Their seriousness warned him of the importance of the meeting.

"It would be simple to Cabal him." Salvatore leaned back in the soft chair and crossed his legs, obviously relishing the idea of George's head coming off at his feet.

"Or a sudden thrust of the knife in the dark." Javier placed his hand over his chest, volunteering.

"Javier, I don't understand your anger."

"Georges is arrogant, a bully and a cheat in the gameroom. That is an unthinkable and unforgivable offense."

"You are too proud, Javier," Val said. "You let a

matter of small importance cloud your judgment." She held up her hand, palm out, to silence them. "You would justify murder on grounds that you dislike him, that he is a bully and a cheat and has insulted us all?"

"He intends to take over the group," Salvatore spoke earnestly as he rubbed his lapel. "It isn't a prospect I look forward to."

"We stand to lose everything we've worked for over the centuries." Javier spoke quietly, but his hand made a sharp slashing motion downward that revealed his tension.

"Think of it as preservation—" Salvatore began.

Val interrupted. "He hasn't done anything yet except talk and bruise your feelings. It is a measure of our strength to follow our own ways of justice. There are no grounds to justify Cabal on Georges at this time without destroying our own standards of conduct. If justice is meted out for Potchnick and Agapito Garcia, it must be the same for Georges. Remember how I took control? He is doing nothing different, except that this time you don't like it."

"The moment he makes a move, we will be waiting." Javier stood up. "He won't get away with it."

"Thank you. That's all we can do," Val said, dismissing him with a slight nod. He wheeled and left the room.

"What do you think?" she asked Salvatore once the door had closed.

He had calmed down. Now he hesitated before he spoke. "What we've built is more than a financial empire. Our ethnics are in danger as well as our livelihood. I don't see a simple solution. We have to wait for his first move. It may be nothing but talk."

"Are you aware that Eudora's asked Renoit to come here?"

"Lui Renoit?" Val frowned. "Why?"

"She seems to think that he may be useful to you."

"Ha!"

"Renoit has a great liking and respect for you, Valerie."

"Unfortunately it is not mutual."

"Besides, she thinks you should introduce him to Theo."

"How long have you know Carlotta?" Val asked, dismissing Lui Renoit from the conversation.

"Nearly a hundred years," Salvatore answered. "Why?"

"I met her last night. She tried to dislike me at first and was rude. Then she did a complete reversal. Now she wants to help us instead of Georges."

Salvatore smiled. "She wanted Robin and he wasn't interested. She made Don Alba, and he left her for you. And evidently you knocked the stuffing out of her old darling, Plutus, in Houston. Is it any wonder she was prepared to hate you?" He shrugged. "She's avoided you for years because she's been jealous. But who could hate you?"

That, thought Theo, was interesting. But he was concerned about Valan. She was evidently in grave danger. Whatever was involved, and whatever the others had in mind, he would be there when she needed him.

Val got up without answering Salvatore and wandered around the room touching objects here and there, a black-and-white Grecian bowl on the mantel, a Tiffany lamp with coral-and-cream glass, the leather-bound books lying on top of her desk. "I need time to think," she said, absently picking up an overflowing folder of notes and correspondence.

Salvatore stood up. "I'll go then," she said, and went out the door.

Theo went to Val and took the folder from her. "Let me take care of this mess. Go, relax a little." He kissed the end of his finger and touched it to the tip of her nose. She nodded and walked back to the fireplace. She picked up the bowl that had rested there for nearly thirty years. It was a black on white *kylix,* a wide-mouthed drinking cup, with a parade of stylized chariots racing on the outside, horses following wheels following horses all the way around. The inside displayed the youth Narcissus, reaching for his unattainable reflection in a limpid pool.

She carried it cradled in her palms to the sheepskin beside the bed and sat crosslegged on the white fur, nestling the bowl carefully on her lap and surrounding it with the lace of her robe. She stared into its depths.

"It's strange how things work out," she thought. "Events, innocent at the moment or intended to have a specific effect turn and change in the course of years, twisting through time to coil back into the course of my life with new meaning, new importance and unforeseen consequences."

The bowl had been formed and fired in the Golden Age of Greece and discovered in a crypt near Corinth in 1947 during an insurrection that involved everyone imaginable, including the United States Army. She had come in from the west, over rocky unpaved roads to negotiate the purchase of the bowl and two small bronze dolphins recovered in the same crypt.

Their vehicle was a converted Jeep, modified to hold

extra gas tanks, each with hidden compartments for holding contraband safe from the prying eyes of border inspectors or mountain guerrillas.

Her human driver, Nikko, was a professional brigand and smuggler. Except for the overpowering reek of the garlic cloves he chewed like gum and the decay of his yellow teeth he was a presentable renegade, complete with gunbelts crossing on his chest and a knife as long as his forearm tucked into his boot top. Nikko was better than life insurance.

They had arrived in the village with an unpronounceable name before the afternoon sun began casting long shadows over the bleak landscape. Their business was conducted clandestinely in the basement office-wine-cellar-goathouse of Andros, the local artifact dealer and smuggler, over chunks of cheese and innumerable cups of strong Turkish coffee. Once a considerable amount of gold had exchanged hands, Val was the proud possessor of the bowl and the bronze dolphins.

Nikko had barely managed to stow them securely within the compartmented gas tanks when they heard angry shouts and the sounds of many feet approaching. Andros hastily crossed himself and Nikko, startled, repeated the ritual. Val followed suit. "When in Greece do as the Greeks do," she reasoned.

A group of heavily armed men, dressed in rough peasant garb, appeared. They were dragging a well-dressed civilian over the cobblestones. He was kicking and writhing, trying to get away.

"*Vrykolakas*," Andros said, spitting on the ground. The Greek word for vampyr—the only Greek Val knew. He continued with a long explanation, but Val didn't understand another word.

He yelled in English, "Help me!" But she did not recognize him.

The peasants reached the center of the village square and threw the captive into a deep well. Immediately they started heaving rocks down the shaft. The sound of the rocks ricocheting off the stone walls and thudding against living flesh sickened Val. There was nothing she could do without seriously endangering herself.

Nikko motioned urgently for her to come to the Jeep, so they could leave. Val shook her head, held her stomach, went to the side of the house and threw up all the cheese she'd had to eat. It would have had to come up anyway; but her nausea was effective now; it convinced Nikko and Andros that she needed to rest.

They trooped back inside. Andros' fat, garlic-breathed wife wrapped Val in a goat's-wool rug on the floor before the open fireplace.

Towards dawn she crept out of the house. The village was sleeping soundly. The vampyr in the well was not. She could see his eyes palely in the glimmering light.

"Are you alive?" she asked, over the edge of the shaft.

"What a stupid question. What took you so long?" His whispering voice echoed up the well.

"I was sleeping; ate too much goat cheese and got a stomach ache."

"Get me out of here. These walls are covered with slime. I can't get a handhold. They'll come again at dawn and I won't be so lucky. Greeks torch vampyrs."

Val went and got Nikko's tow rope. The well was nearly thirty feet deep but the rope should be long enough, she thought, tying one end to the back bumper of the Jeep, to reach the bottom. "How did they get the idea you're a vampyr?''

"I have weird eyes," he said. "Be careful."

She dropped the other end of the rope into the well and the coils fell in a clump. "Did it hit you?"

"No," came the peeved reply. "You just missed me."

Then there were scrapling noises in the well, then nothing. She waited. "What's the matter?"

"Those ignorant savages smashed my wrist. It won't support me yet."

"Tie the rope around yourself. I'll pull you out." When she pulled him up, he came over the edge dripping wet and clawing like a cat with his good hand. She moved back and let him stand up. As soon as he untied the rope he looked around and came at Val vampyr-fast, his milky eyes fastening on her as he moved.

She held him with all her power and he stopped in midstride. Then she made him take a step back, and another and another, until he was standing at the brink of the well. "One more step and you'll be back where you started." She was angry. "You've got a lot of nerve, attacking your rescuer," she said. "Give me one good reason why I shouldn't drop you back into that well."

"I haven't eaten in days," he whined. "And I didn't realize you were a vampyr, too."

"Go find a goat," she said and started coiling up Nikko's rope. "Then crawl under the tarp in the back of the Jeep and don't move. We'll take you out with us in the morning." He started to sidle away. "What's your name?"

"Plutus," he said, smiling crookedly. "No need to bother hiding me. I can manage." He started to go, then turned back to her.

"I'm grateful and I owe you one."

"Perhaps someday I'll collect."

"When I'm not starving, I'm honorable."

"Of course."

"Name it and it's yours."

He was gone by morning and so was Val.

From what she learned of him later, she should have left him there in the well. A few nights before he had drained and killed a child.

The Grecian bowl had sat on the mantel for thirty years, and she had seldom thought about it. Now Plutus was returning the debt.

Val felt caught, frozen like Narcissus in the glaze of the bowl, in her convictions and loyalties. She was surrounded by plots, emotions and ambitions that might shape the future of the group. There was nothing that could save her except her own strength. And she had doubts that it would be enough.

Chapter XVI

Sunday, March 14

COREY MADISON, SLOW HARBOR, NY: HIDE AS
SOON AS POSSIBLE STOP REMAIN UNTIL YOU
RECEIVE THE CODE PASSWORD I WILL SEND YOU
LOVE STOP ANN STOP

The younger vampyrs kept Georges occupied from
dusk 'til dawn and 'til dusk, but it didn't seem to
matter. Whenever Val saw him playing billiards or in
the midst of a mild flirtation or making ribald remarks,
he seemed as vigorous as always.

He was a real bully, Val decided, after watching him
playing with Salvatore. Elegant Salvatore, who played
billiards like a professional, let Georges win. He would
stand there in the shadows, just beyond the amber pool
of light on the table, and wait patiently for Georges'
clumsy shot, then take his turn, sinking one ball and
missing one the next. It was obvious to everyone but
Georges what he was doing. Once Georges saw Val from
the corner of his eyes while he was chalking his cue. He

straightened up, staring at her boldly, daring her. The voices in the room fell silent. She turned and went away.

She wondered what would happen when they finally met. She was afraid that she would be found wanting.

Everything was aware of what was happening. The gatherings took on an air of frenzy with too much laughter, too much aimless moving around. Val found it unnerving. She would retreat to the silence of her rooms or the peace of the gardens. Theo was always nearby, not always at her side, but he was there. She would glance up now and then and see him, not watching or even looking at her but talking to the others or sitting idly by.

In times of rest he was with her, with his arms about her. Then she felt everything would be all right.

Monday, March 15

The meeting was scheduled for Tuesday night. Many of the younger ones left to go into town to the opera. There were less than twenty left, mostly the quiet ones, the older ones. They wandered about aimlessly. Theo heard their footfalls in the hall now and then.

He was sitting at the desk writing a letter to Sarah when Salvatore came to see Val. Salvatore's feet hit the floor heavily, as though he was carrying a great burden, but his burden wasn't physical. He sat beside Val on the bed. "Valerie," he said, taking her hand, "If there is anything I can do, I'll do it."

She touched his cheek, just beside his mouth, with her fingertips. "Thank you. It means a great deal to know that so many of my old friends care." Theo watched, feeling the depth of affection between Val and Salvatore, yet aware that she had never loved Salvatore the way she loved him.

"I've always been thankful that there wasn't much that could weaken us." Salvatore's shoulders slumped a fraction. "Georges has seduced a dozen young men since he's been here, and it has not made the slightest difference. If only there were something else . . . . "

"I've asked Eudora to stay out of the meeting. If things go badly, she'll leave immediately, with my power of attorney. Corey should be in hiding by now, and will stay hidden until he receives my word from her. That way Georges will not be able to ruin the group; you can preserve most of our holdings. Tell the others to stay away from Georges until you find a way to stop him."

"And what about you?"

"There are ways to fight him, even if I'm gone. Things will work out. If they don't, if something dreadful should happen, promise me that you'll take Claire to Corey. Tell them that is my answer to their questions. They both have different questions, but there is only one answer. They'll understand. And remember, if Georges can't get to Corey you'll all have a measure of safety."

"I won't have to do it. But I will if it's necessary." He bent over and kissed her on the forehead. "Lui Renoit is here. He'd like to see you." Then he left without waiting for a reply.

She looked at Theo. "I don't feel indecisive. I know what's right. It isn't a sign of weakness to do what I know is right and stick with it. But why do I have such a strong urge to let them kill Georges in his sleep?"

"Self-preservation, woman's intuition, or fear perhaps."

She nodded. "I'm not exactly eager to be a sacrificial lamb."

He signed his letter, folded it, and inserted it into an envelope before turning and looking intently at her. Her deep green eyes were burning with distress. "Is it really that serious?"

"I don't know. Terrible things do happen at times during a battle of wills when both contestants are very strong. Only one can prevail. Georges is very powerful, Theo, incredibly so. I've been watching him. I'm frightened."

"What sort of things can happen?"

"If he turns out to be stronger, and it's a very real possibility, he could force me to be his slave, the way he's done to Carlotta. He could cripple me, or blind me, or kill me, if he's strong enough. It's hard to say. At best the loser will just go stark raving mad."

"And you're going to go through this? Why? You don't have to. We can leave. If he can't get to you, he can't hurt the group." His free hand came up in a fist and he struck himself lightly on the chest when he said "the group." It was the first time that he'd ever included himself.

"It's a matter of honor, I think. Running away never occurred to me as a solution. If you were in my position, could you run away?"

He scratched his chin and said, "No, I suppose not." Then he put the rest of his papers in a folder and came over to the bed and sat beside her. "Who is this Lui Renoit?"

"It's a long story." She lay back on the bolsters, inviting him to come by holding his hand but he persisted.

"Tell me."

"Well, you know it was Claire's idea for me to contact you last year in an effort to find a way to control the dracula syndrome."

"I have a lot of ideas that seem promising. When things settle down we'll start working again." His tone was slightly apologetic, as though he felt guilty about abandoning the research he'd done in San Antonio.

"It isn't easy turning into a vampyr. You can't rush it. All of your values and habits and preferences change so radically along with the physical things. I was a lot younger than you and it was terrible, even then, to give up my humanity. Most of us were a lot younger than you and without human ties.

"Valan, I'm grateful for your patience. I've had to do some pretty difficult things in my life, but they were nothing compared to what's happened to me this last year."

"Only the strong survive the first year."

"Or the fortunate ones who have wise protectors." He pulled the sides of her robe together at the neck. "You're lovely in lace. What does this have to do with Lui Renoit, and why are you so reluctant to talk about him?"

"He is a doctor, a hematologist, like you. Claire recruited him; he was competent in his field, which was treating rich ladies for anemic conditions. That generally means boredom. Anything serious he had the good sense to refer elsewhere. He was not a researcher, nor was he ambitious. Claire decided to underwrite a small general practice clinic for him in a fashionable suburb. She tells me he's been there nearly a year now."

"What is so strange about that?"

"He's half Indo-Chinese. That's where the name Lui comes from. And he's fluent in seven or eight Asiatic languages. Claire met him nearly twenty years ago when he was fresh out of medical school. He's spent the last ten years in Viet Nam and India victimizing the natives, and he came back to France only when things got too hot for his comfort."

"So?"

"He's a ghoul. He thrives on human suffering. I don't know how he keeps it under control here in Paris. It's only a matter of time before he gets caught."

"It rather wounds my pride that I wasn't the first doctor on your list," he teased, tapping her nose.

"You are the first. He was merely another of Claire's mistakes." She reached up and covered his fingers with her hand. "You can go talk to him if you like. I'd rather kiss a snake." She licked the palm of his hand and nibbled at the fleshy part just below his thumb.

"Perhaps later, green eyes," he said, leaning over her with a slight smile on his lips. "Right now I'd rather be a snake."

Tuesday, March 16

As the evening progressed they went down to the central wine cellar one or two at a time.

Theo escorted Val to the meeting, holding her hand on his arm as they negotiated the steep stairs. A tiny muscle at the edge of his jaw was twitching. It was the only sign of the tension in him. Val was unnaturally composed, unafraid, as if it were merely a dream. The walls around her were cool and dry, the air fresh and moving slightly through the maze of subterranean chambers.

He pushed the door of the low-vaulted cellar open for her. The wooden wire racks had long since been removed. All the others were there; they were dwarfed by the huge polished table and the ten massive chairs that crowded around it. Georges was already there, sitting next to Carlotta, across from Salvatore and Claire; Salvatore's face was dark with anger, as though they had already exchanged harsh words.

"Aren't we having the meeting tonight?" Val asked, pretending innocence. "I thought it was supposed to be tonight."

"Yes," whispered Carlotta.

"Then Georges will have to leave. He wasn't invited."

He stood up and said, "I'm staying."

Val ignored him and addressed Claire. "Is anyone else coming?"

"I don't think so," she replied.

"All right," Val said, taking her seat at the head of the table.

Theo didn't move to leave. "As long as there is one uninvited person," he said, "there might as well be two." He sat in the chair at her right hand.

There was silence all around. No one seemed willing to speak.

Georges stood glaring at Val. At the far end of the table Modesto sat as though in prayer with both hands on the table. The knuckles of his fingers were white. Carlotta's head was also bowed. "She's ashamed," Val thought, "of what she's brought upon us all."

Lui Renoit glanced apologetically at Val, then hid his half-moon eyes behind his hand. Georges slowly sank back into his chair. Javier let his upper lip drop slowly

265

to cover his teeth. He'd been snarling tensely.

The expressions on their faces were tight and fearful. Hands were moving on the table with a restless force as though they possessed life separate from their owners.

Val opened the folder that Salvatore handed her and spoke. "The first business before us . . . ." They went through the items, carefully chosen for their unimportance, slowly.

Finally, silence reigned and Val asked, "Is there any other business?"

"Only mine," Georges said. Once again he stood up, using his thick hands on the arms of his chair to push his body up. There was a droplet of orange spittle at the corner of his mouth. Val couldn't help staring at it.

"Look at me, you bitch," he said. "Let's settle this once and for all. I'm tired of playing around."

There was nothing left but to face him. She stood up, pushing the chair away with the backs of her legs. She arched her back stiffly, defiantly, and raised her eyes to meet his. They were grey and hollow, like the gates of hell. An eternity of darkness came swirling from him; choking and foul. It poured over her, formlessly, and tore her apart. She struggled, but there was no defense. Parts of her flew off like roof shingles during a tornado until there was nothing left but her naked soul.

Then there was nothing.

It was dark when Val woke, in her own bed. She was alone, and the house was unusually quiet. There had been so many noisy nights before the meeting that the silence was eerie. She tried to remember what had happened in the wine cellar, when Georges had sucked her soul out of her body. She was sure that she had died, at least for a while.

Eudora came in with a goblet of blood. Val was so weak that Eudora had to hold her head.

"What happened?"

"Hush," Eudora said. "Just rest. Everything's all right."

"Tell me. I'll only worry until you do."

"Shhh. You're very weak." With that she left. Val drifted into sleep.

Val woke and slept, woke and slept; she could hear people in the room, but whenever she tried to recognize them their faces would vanish. She couldn't tell whether they were real or dreams.

Sarah came, in blue jeans and with tears on her face, to tell her she'd broken up with another of her boyfriends. And Modesto, wearing his brown monk's robe with the hood, came to pray for her soul.

Theo would come to the door; Val recognized his step. But when she'd try to see his face it would vanish like smoke. Darrell came and asked her to intercede with Claire. He wanted another chance with her. "Strange," Val said, "I thought you were dead." She wondered whether she had gone mad.

And always Eudora came. Though she only stayed for a few minutes at a time, drinking was such an effort for Val that when Eudora left she would fall into a deep sleep almost immediately.

Whenever Val would ask her what happened, Eudora would shake her head and say, "Later. Everything's all right. Don't worry."

Val didn't have the will to make Eudora tell her, and Eudora was the weakest of them all. It was hard to accept or understand.

She had gone mad; no doubt about it.

Sarah came in again. She adjusted the drapes.

The sheets were clammy and cold.

Val awoke in the night with tears on her face and looked around the room. There was one light glowing—the Tiffany lamp on the desk. Theo was dozing in the chair by the fireplace, and Val was content to study his familiar features until he roused. He came to her, and she couldn't look him in the eye. Instead she stared out the window. He said, "Valan, Valan." She closed her eyes as he touched her face. "I love you very much," she heard him say. Then she fainted.

It should have been summertime, but it was cold. Modesto had just walked around the room swinging a smoking ball on the end of a chain, chanted three Hail Mary's at the foot of the bed, and left.

Eudora brought Val her drink. "Valerie, you've a visitor," she said.

Val's heart started beating faster, and her arms grew cold. She shook her head and handed Eudora the goblet. "No."

"It's Theo's daughter. You've called for her again and again."

"But she's been here with me. I've seen her."

"Not until today."

Val was silent then and let Eudora move her about in the bed. When she'd adjusted everything to suit herself she turned, and Sarah came in, just as Val had pictured her, with jeans and a yellow sweater. Lovely Sarah, with her long blonde hair and graceful walk. She sat on the bed beside Val and smiled at her, and Val could look her in the face. She bent over and kissed Val's cheek. "Oh, Valan, it's so good to see you."

Then Val's sight faded as she wondered whether Sarah was real or not. Her dreams seemed to have more substance than the lucid moments.

A sound wakened Val. Sarah came in and sat down with a book. She began to read.

There was a fire in the grate now and the room was warmer, though it seemed a pale fire, lacking substance. Val turned to look at the windows. They were shuttered and the drapes partly drawn, yet a draft of chilly air touched her now and then.

Sarah saw that Val was awake. She put down her book and stood up, "How are you, Valan?"

"Very tired," Val said. "How long has it been?"

"Since when?"

"Since I've been sick?"

"I don't know," she answered. "It's November now."

"Then the year's almost over."

"What happened to you? No one will tell me what's wrong."

"I don't remember." Val shook her head against the pillow. "Why is it so quiet? Where's everyone gone?"

"There's only me and Poppa and Eudora here now. There's not another soul in the house. There hasn't been anyone since I got here."

"Where is Theo?"

"He doesn't stay here in the room much. His presence disturbs you."

"Could I see him?"

She nodded and went out quickly. But when Theo came in and Val reached toward him and he smiled, the wall became visible through his chest and everything vanished.

"Damn," she heard him say.

Sarah and Eudora made Val sit up each time she

woke. They bullied her, but gently, as her strength came back. The long sleeps were almost a thing of the past.

"Why is the last dormitory room in the attic locked?" Sarah asked.

"I don't remember," Val answered. Sarah frowned at her. Val sensed the girl was displeased.

Theo came in the evening. He wore a black suit that shimmered in the firelight. Val thought it made him look like an elegant vision from long ago. He stood quietly at the door until she smiled at him, then he came across the room slowly. He didn't fade away.

He lifted her from the bed, wrapped her blanket around her, and carried her downstairs and out to the gardens. He walked around in the night air holding her easily.

The trees were bare, the leaves all blown away, and the gardens were banked with mulch, covered with burlap, sleeping, awaiting spring.

The cold wind ruffled Val's hair. It felt good. She could look at his face, the strong line of his cheek and the expressive shape of his lips, but not his eyes. She couldn't force herself to seek his eyes. After they came inside he slept beside her. When she cried out, it was his hand that stroked her shoulder and his voice in her ear that calmed her.

The sun was high overhead when Val woke, standing barely a foot away from Sarah's bed. Her body was trembling all over. Her hands and forehead were wet with sweat and it was very cold in the room. The fire had died out, leaving only a pile of ashes on the hearthstone. A sliver of light came in the shuttered window and trailed across the floor.

Val stared at Sarah, feeling the hard coldness of the floor. The only warmth was in the tiny island her bare feet had made on the wood. She must have been standing there a long time struggling to wake up. A great terror seized her and her heart pounded out of control as she realized what she had been about to do.

A primitive urge had drawn Val to Sarah, the only human in the house, the only human that she loved. A conflict raged within her, her beast wanting to go and drink of Sarah's blood, herself cringing at the very thought of it. Sarah lay there sound asleep, the covers up around her neck, her long lashes falling over her cheeks. Val turned and fled from the room.

Val didn't know whether it was Sarah's innocent trust or Val's own disgust at her beast's desires that had stopped and wakened her. Perhaps it was both. Sarah's room was on the third floor. Val hadn't known where it was. But the beast had known and taken her there.

She slipped back into her own bed. She hoped that she wouldn't have to tell Theo what had happened.

The inhabitants of the Chateau were a quiet group. The days and nights regulated their activities even as the bells in the abbey regulated the nuns who lived there. When vespers rang in the distance Val would often wonder what their lives were like—the nuns'. They must dream sometimes, she thought, of the freedoms they never knew, as she dreamed of the peace of mind that filled them.

The days were gloomy. The farmers went out only to check the hedgerows and fences. The cattle stood in sheds, in groups to hold the warmth. The fields were fallow; the brown earth showed through the dry stubble of harvested hay.

Friday, December 10

It snowed. Great flakes, nearly as large as the palm of Val's hand, fell on her head and melted into her hair. Her cheeks grew ruddy from the cold. She and Theo stayed out for a long time, enjoying the bite of the night air. She was weary when they finally came in, and she fell easily into a deep dreamless sleep as soon as dawn was coloring the sky.

The unthinkable happened again. She found herself at Sarah's bedside, leaning over her this time with her outstretched hand nearly touching the girl's neck, trembling, waking at the last moment to overcome the beast within. She didn't know how long she had been standing there; her mind floundered in profound confusion. She tried to understand why the beast kept drawing her back to Sarah. It was not a matter of hunger, but something beyond that, deep in her nature. She wanted to fight it. The idea of using Sarah was abhorrent to her. Yet she had no control over what had happened.

Val held her arms tightly against her breasts, her long white nightgown swaying slightly around her legs. Theo came silently into the room and stopped. She turned to him, "I was sleepwalking. I can't help it." Her voice quavered. "It's happened before."

He had a strange look on his face. He was dressed only in his slacks and shirt; the sleeves dangled open as though he'd dressed hurriedly. Now he buttoned the cuffs. Val felt isolated, rejected, watching him. Then he came over to her; they stood together for a moment looking down at Sarah.

He touched Val and must have sensed how weak she felt, for he picked her up and carried her from the room. Her arms went around his neck and shoulders, her face pressed against him. Back in their room he stood beside the bed, holding her. As she kissed his neck he pressed his jaw against her forhead.

The room reeled from the closeness, the smell of him. Val couldn't stop. Her lips touched him again on the same place and she bit, piercing the flesh slowly, until the blood flowed from his neck. He held her without wincing as she took his sweet hot blood. A marvelous strength and warmth filled her.

They stayed that way until Val could feel the muscles in his arms slackening. Then he laid her on the bed. There was blood all over the front of her gown, and the front of his shirt. He hadn't tried to stop the flow of blood.

He knelt at the side of the bed with one arm over her waist and bowed his head until it touched the sheet. He was bleeding onto the white linen.

Val felt vibrant yet confused, not understanding why he'd done it. "Theo, stop the blood. Please stop it."

Slowly then, the flow ceased. His arm was heavy when she slipped it off and knelt beside him on the floor. She made him get up and come lie down.

He fell asleep almost immediately with one arm hanging limply off the bed. The sheepskin rug had a great pool of darkening blood on it. She called Eudora to help take the stained things away.

Wednesday, December 15

The ground was covered with fresh snow that glowed an eerie blue in the moonlight. Val stood at the window of her darkened bedroom. The caretakers hadn't been out all day; there weren't any tracks around their cottage down by the main gate.

It would be a peaceful night, she thought. But as she

stood there, the great black chateau limousine drove up to the gate and stopped with its headlights glowing through the bars.

One of the men in the cottage came out and peered through the gate. When he was satisfied, he nodded and opened the gates, leaving a butterfly pattern in the snow. The car drove on around the circular drive to the house. When it stopped in front of the main porch its bright lights cast a golden beam across the yard illuminating the frozen birdbath, which was all covered with snow like a fairy mushroom.

A man got out, bundled up in a heavy topcoat and muffler, but Val recognized him immediately from his springy stride. It was Salvatore. She knew Eudora would let him in, but she went downstairs to greet him. He'd already pulled off his heavy coat and gloves and was sitting in the living room. Eudora fussed at the liquor cabinet behind him, pouring out a glass of wine.

He stood up when Val came into the room. "My, how radiant you look," he said, and caught her by the waist and swung her around in the air. They laughed with the pleasure of it, and Val smiled with him. She did feel radiant, altogether different than she'd been feeling for months, and she told him so.

"Could you get me something a little more sustaining than this?" he asked Eudora when she handed him the glass of wine. She headed toward the kitchens. Val sat down with Salvatore, by the crackling fire.

"How's it been going with you?" he asked.

"Until just a day or two ago, not too well. But I think the worst is over. I'm recovering some of my strength."

"Fine," he said. "How have things been here?"

"It's been very quiet. We've had few visitors. Sarah's here. She's stayed with me and has been the best nurse I

274

could ask for."

His face suddenly became very still, as though he'd dropped a curtain over it. "Sarah? Here? In the safe house?"

"Yes. I trust her more than I trust most of us," she answered, sensing his unease.

"No, that's not what I meant," he said. "A human here with you . . . . "

"Why is that so important, Sal?"

"Didn't anyone explain to you what you'd have to do to get well?"

"Everyone's been telling me that it's just a matter of time."

"Valerie, you of all people—" He broke off, shaking his head. "Is Sarah all right? Have you done anything to her?"

"Why, no."

"But you've had blood; human blood?"

Suddenly she realized what he was getting at. "Oh," she said. "No."

He was puzzled and cocked his head. "Then?" His dark brows pulled together. "Ah," he said. "Even better than human blood. Theo? Vampyr blood is the best of all."

"How did you guess?"

"Human blood is the one sure remedy for anything that ails a vampyr. You knew that."

"No one told me."

"Valerie, if you'd realized that the only way for you to get better was to drink human blood, would you have done it?"

"I don't know. But when it happened it seemed a very natural thing, and I couldn't help myself."

He nodded. "Your body knows best. If we'd told

you, you probably would have resisted forever and never gotten well. You see, it worked out for the best." He shrugged and smiled at her again. "I've a letter for you."

"Oh, who from?"

They were interrupted by Eudora, bustling into the room with two goblets on a tray.

As soon as Eudora left, he took the letter from his inner pocket and handed it to Val.

The letter was on Claire's usual rich linen stationery and written in her careful hand.

Dearest Val,

We are here in upstate New York enjoying the most beautiful snowy winter ever. You were right of course, a new place, a new man, and a wonderful one at that. Promise me that from now on you will pick all of them for me.

Corey sends you his best. He's making the adjustment to his new life quite easily but works like a fiend in town taking care of all of us. He's a genius.

You were right. We suit each other. We are like two opposing pieces of a puzzle fitting together tightly along our eccentric edges. We both thank you very much. You've been in Paris far too long.

All my love, Claire

Val folded the letter and put it back in its envelope, enjoying the lift it gave her.

"Where is Theo now?"

"Upstairs, probably still asleep. He's been acting oddly, Sal. When he let me take his blood, he didn't try to stop the flow. It was as though he was trying to bleed to death."

"That's impossible, of course."

"I know, and I think he knows it too. But why?"

Sal pursed his lips. "Tell me everything that happened."

She did, starting with the weeks of hallucinations, the terrible days of sleepwalking and waking at Sarah's bed, the horror of knowing the beast was commanding her against her will. Finally she told him about Theo's bizarre sacrifice. When she was finished he said, "It's obvious, Valerie, he loves you. He loves Sarah. He felt you'd keep going there again and again in your sleep. So he let you bite him instead. He's hoping that will stop it."

"Will it?" Val glanced up sharply.

"Most likely, yes. You've always had strong self-control. Now that you're better, there's no reason for you to keep on sleepwalking."

"Thank goodness. It all sounds so simple and logical when you explain it. But what about the other? Why did he try to kill himself?"

"Oh, that," Sal said, waving his hand. "Hasn't he told you what happened?"

"What do you mean?"

"The night you and Georges met eye to eye."

"No one has told me anything about that night."

"And you don't remember?"

"No."

"Well," he said, leaning back in the chair, "that should be between you and Theo. When he's ready, he'll tell you. That will explain why he tried suicide."

"The most interesting thing isn't what he's done," Salvatore went on, "it's why you stay with him."

"I think you'd better explain that."

"It isn't like you to stay with a man without strong power."

"I think you're jealous."

He frowned. "And it's not like you to give in to someone the way you've been doing. You let him influence you against your instincts and better judgment."

"It's there, Sal, the power. He won't use it. He thinks cooperation is better than coercion.

"Besides," she went on, "good love is sharing more than just good sex. Would you have done that, offered your neck for me?"

"For you, Valerie, yes." He started to add something more but Theo came in then, looking healthy and relaxed in jeans and a pullover, an easy smile on his face. They shook hands and he sat down. They started to make small talk, so Val left and wandered about the house.

In the kitchen she found Sarah.

The teenager was fixing herself a grilled cheese sandwich. Sarah smiled when Val came in and waved the long two-pronged fork at the table. "Hi. Want to come with me to town? There are some clothes and things I want to get."

"The stores will be crowded. It's nearly Christmas."

"It doesn't matter. I may never get another chance to come to Paris."

"What makes you say that?"

"Aren't we leaving soon? Poppa said that when you got better we'd probably go back to the States. I hope so. I never imagined Paris would be so unpleasant in the wintertime. In the stories I've read it's always such a magical place."

Val laughed. "It is a magical place sometimes. It's a place where dreams can come true."

"Not mine," she said, taking a bite of her sandwich. "Not mine at all, and I've missed a whole semester.

Now I'll probably have to go to summer school to catch up."

"Oh, Sarah, I'm sorry. I never thought of that."

"Don't be silly, Valan. I'd much rather be here to help you." She glanced at Val with a guileless smile. "This house is fascinating. Do you own it?"

"More or less. It belongs to a business concern I control. We've had it for several hundred years."

"I love the antiques. I want to see all of them, but some of the rooms are locked. Could you tell Eudora to open them for me?"

"Just ask her. Most of the locked rooms are storerooms and not very interesting."

"Even the one in the attic?"

"Of course." Val couldn't recall any locked room up there, but if there was it was merely a storage room.

Val sensed there was something else Sarah wanted to say, but she held it back, talking instead of the clothes she was planning to buy.

Friday, December 17

Theo came up while Val was resting and rebuilt the fire in the grate. He was very calm, almost withdrawn, as he stoked the flames with steady hands. The room grew warm and pleasant.

They sat for a while in silence. Then Theo leaned back in the chair, almost slouching, one hand propped against his forehead.

"When we first met," he said, looking at the floor, "I was desperate. You breezed into my world with a strange offer of hope. You were so full of life. If you were surprised that I accepted you so quickly at face value, it was because I was grasping at straws. The remissions were getting shorter and shorter. There wasn't much hope."

"I know," she said. "We were suspicious. It was almost too good to be true. We decided to go ahead because what we were trying to do was so important that it was worth the risk."

"My only intention was to take advantage of you; use you to save myself. The research was secondary. But that didn't last very long." He paused and rubbed his brow. "You're far too beautiful and charming for any man to keep at a distance. I found myself unable to help falling in love with you.

"I was able to rationalize all the things that happened by saying to myself that it was the vampyrism, as if it were a thing separate from your personality. Valan, you're the gentlest kindest creature I've ever met."

"I," he sighed with his eyes closed, as though considering what he wanted to say next. "I've always been a healer of men. I thought it was beyond my nature to kill for any reason. But I found that I could kill for you." Val didn't understand everything he was saying but he was concentrating so intently that she didn't want to interrupt. He continued after a slight hesitation. "It's contrary to every moral value that I've held dear all my life. I even rationalized that, saying it was part of my vampyr nature now. I was able to divorce the things I did from my own personality, as though there were two beings inhabiting my body; the one I called myself and the other, the vampyr."

"I feel that way, too," she said, "that there are two beings inside me: my own self, quite unable to harm anything, and another, the strong and ruthless beast. I know what you mean. We all have the same intense sureness that we can keep ourselves apart from the beast, but it sometimes gets out of control. It happens to all of us now and then, through no fault of our own."

"Exactly. When we came here with all the other vampyrs I felt at home with them. They understood. I enjoyed myself until Carlotta and Georges came. As soon as they arrived things changed. All the easy control was gone, and everyone seemed to know what was going on except me."

Val clasped her hands on her lap and looked down at them.

"No one bothered to tell me," Theo went on, "until we talked the night before the meeting. When we went down those stairs together, there were two things going on in my mind. I was afraid for you, not knowing how to help. I was angry that anyone would dare to threaten us. My two personalities were disagreeing with each other.

"When you stood up to him, I held onto the arms of my chair so hard that I broke one off. You faced him with such calm dignity that for a while I was sure you'd overcome his eyes. He was arrogant. He stood there looking down at you.

"It must have been five or six minutes. It seemed an eternity.

"You were locked together there, staring into each other's eyes as though the rest of the world had stopped for you. There was a coldness and intensity on your faces that wasn't human.

"The rest of us, well, we sat there tense and helpless. I felt rage building up in me. When your knees knuckled and you fell to the floor, I jumped.

"Georges was standing frozen like a tree, still under your spell. I leaped across the table like a cat. I remember scraping against it with one foot. My teeth hit him hard on the neck and he fell over backward with me riding on his chest.

"Valan, I was completely out of control. The beast that's my vampyr nature took over completely. When we hit the floor I was still at his throat. He never came out of the trance, not even when I ripped his flesh open with my teeth."

"Your beast did it, Theo, you can't blame yourself."

"That wasn't the worst part. When I was through with him and raised my head to look around the room, like some wild animal, the others were gathered around me looking down on me with a blood lust in their eyes that I've never seen before. Yet, I'm sure it reflected the look in mine.

"When I moved away from him, they descended. He didn't stand a chance. I just stood there watching them. When everyone finished, Javier cut off his head with a switchblade knife he pulled out of his boot. He smiled like a demon when he snapped it open. He was still smiling when he used his foot on the handle to force the blade through the spinal column. It was deliberate murder.

"When my rational self took control and I realized what I'd done, I was in such a state of shock that Salvatore had to lead me away. There was blood on my hands." He rubbed them together as though it was still there, then shook his head. "I haven't been good for much for a long time. Especially since every time I looked in on you, just the sight of me was enough to make you faint.

"It was the first time that the beast ever took full control of me. It's incredible how powerful it is, and I feel helpless to keep it from happening again.

"When I followed you into Sarah's room, I understood that it was something you couldn't control, that it would happen again and again until there'd be another tragedy. That's why I let you use me instead."

"But why did you try to bleed to death? That's the part I don't understand."

"Well, I've felt so guilty about the whole business; using you, and killing Georges. There should have been something I could have done to stop it all. At the time I was kneeling there, it just seemed to be the right thing to do."

There was a vibrating resonance in his last words, a wistfulness for goodness betrayed and innocence lost.

An intense sympathy for him swelled in Val's chest. She went to him and knelt at his feet. "I'm a hollow shell of what I was. Physically I'm well, but the power that was in me is gone. You gave me your life blood. You have to be my strength now."

"I'll be whatever you need." He touched her forehead with his fingertip and ran it down the bridge of her nose. "Why don't you look in my eyes any more?"

She shook her head. "It isn't just you. I don't think I could bear to look into anyone yet. Even the thought is painful. I'm not strong enough to counter any threat or challenge at all, even a friendly one."

"There's no challenge in my eyes, Valan, just an irrational love for you." He tried to lift her chin, but she shook her head and closed her eyelids tightly.

"Not yet," she whispered. "Not yet." She shuddered as the awareness of total vulnerability swept over her. She dreaded the idea of having to grow used to weakness after so many years of complete control of herself and absolute power over the others. It was nadir.

Chapter XVII

Sunday, December 26

Dearest Claire:

Christmas was a quiet time here. We gave the usual gifts, books and sweaters and gold-plated pens, gestures of love more than anything else. I have owned and lost at least a hundred gold-plated pens.

We are packing our belongings. Theo has booked reservations on a flight to New York next week. It was the first one leaving with seats available for the three of us. At that, Sarah will be sitting across the aisle from us. We will see you in New York.

The chateau will be empty for a while except for Eudora. She plans to spend the rest of the winter here, then go on to England when the others return.

Theo and I will settle Sarah for the spring semester in Houston, at Bart's and Nancy's, then travel through the southern states.

We are looking forward to escaping the rain and snow here. There has been nothing but cloudy weather and drizzle, day and night, for over a week. It is oppressive.

We are feeling much more relaxed and like a family except that Sarah still finds it difficult to accept our differences; perhaps she never will until she becomes one of us. Theo fights the idea. He says, "Live a human life first, then, perhaps . . . . "

Give my regards to Corey. We wish you love and long happiness together. Until later,

Ciao, Valerie

Wednesday, December 29

Val handed Salvatore the stack of papers she had been going over. "All done, except I'd like to table the contract for the India imports for a while. Unless they can guarantee the gold content of the statuettes it isn't a good deal."

"Fine," he said. "I'll be glad when you take over completely again. All this high finance messes up my life style."

They were sitting in the downstairs parlor of the Chateau, side by side on the sofa, trying to catch up on the myriad of details that had been in limbo while she was unable to work.

"Watch out or we'll be putting one of those computers in here, the kind Corey has."

"Good. Then we'd both be off to the Riviera for the rest of our lives." He laughed, setting the stack of papers on the cushion between them.

"Don't count on getting off so easily," Val said. "Corey has nightmares about that computer." She leaned back, draping her arm over the back of the couch. "Do you really think I'm fully recovered?"

"Of course. There's color in your cheeks and a sparkle in your eyes. Is there any reason I should think otherwise?"

"Well," she took a deep breath and looked down at his shiny, mirror-smooth loafers. "It's hard to talk about, even to Theo. No, especially to Theo."

"What's wrong?" He leaned forward, looking straight ahead, with his hands clasped over his knees. There was a contemplative look on his face.

She felt that he would understand if anyone would and the words rushed out almost before she thought about them. "The power's gone, Sal. I can barely tell Eudora what to do."

286

"I find that hard to believe."

"It's true."

He picked up the papers and sorted through them silently. When he was finished, he put them in his brown leather briefcase and clicked it shut. "It doesn't work that way, Valerie. You can't get rid of the power inside you so easily."

"So easily? What do you mean by that?"

"You were hurt, grievously so, by Georges. You don't want to be hurt again. So, you refuse to be hurt by denying that you can be hurt." He punctuated each statement by ticking it off on his well-manicured fingers.

"You're wrong!" She shook her head furiously, letting her too-long curls fly about. They hadn't been cut in months and swirled heavily over her shoulders. "You don't know what's happened inside of me." She dropped her face into the crook of her elbow on the back of the sofa, turning her body so her legs curled up on the cushion, a purely defensive position. She wanted him to be wrong.

"Try me," he said gently, touching her shoulder. "Do we trust each other? How many times have you looked into my eyes?"

"Hundreds," she said, raising her head, looking past him to the Landseer painting of two wolfhounds which was hanging over the snowy Greek marble mantel, and at the same time fighting the urge to shut her eyes.

"Have you ever found pain there?"

"No," she whispered, shivering.

"What are you feeling right now, Val? Is it fear?" He stroked her arm.

"Yes, and much, much more."

"When you can conquer the fear of being hurt, when you can find the courage to look, your power will come

287

back. Do you think you're the only one who's ever been driven mad that way?"

She stood up and went to the window. The morning was clear and sunny, more so than it had been in weeks. "It's good to see daylight for a change."

"If it gets much brighter we'll have to close the drapes."

"Of course." She moved away from the window and walked aimlessly to the fireplace, leaned against the mantel, and kicked the grate with her toe, sending a cascade of sparks flying.

"We really should modernize this house, get a good heating system at least. It's too quiet here today, as if we've been deserted. Where is everyone?"

"Sarah's sorting her treasures. Eudora's in the wine cellar polishing crystal for New Year's Eve. Theo's gone to visit Lui Renoit's clinic, and we're here watching you turn your back on life."

She ignored him. She found herself listening without reason for the vibrant stillness of the house to break. "My internal clock is out of phase. I feel it should still be summer. Has that ever happened to you?"

"Not that I can remember. Is it important?"

"Listen. There should be wind and the sound of the house moving with the warmth of the sun. What do you hear?"

"Nothing."

"Don't you find that peculiar?"

He stood up, came to the fireplace, and put one arm on the other end of the mantel. "We look like a pair of bookends standing here," she said, trying to lighten the conversation. He would have none of it.

"Valerie, you have an eternity of life waiting for you. And if quality counts for anything, you are one of the best-loved beings on earth."

"And if fear counts for anything, and if humans knew what I am, the most hated and reviled being on earth. I am the leader of the ghouls, vampyrs, bloodsuckers, ravagers of maidens, things that go bump in the night."

"That is an unfair thing to say."

"Oh?"

"And if you really believed it, you'd simply have another reason to find the power you've buried somewhere inside yourself. If you really believe it, you must do something about it."

"Such as?"

"Prove to them that they're wrong."

"Now you're starting to sound like Claire. She'd like nothing more than to star on Broadway as Madame Claire, The World's Most Beautifyl Vampyr."

"It isn't funny, Valerie."

"Don't say any more about it right now," Val said. "I need time to think about it."

He nodded.

Then a supernatural sound filled the house, a groan of anguish that grew from a faint rumbling to a wail expressing agony beyond description. They stiffened simultaneously, their ears straining to identify the voice that uttered such a cry.

Sal's face grew ashen.

"What is it?" Val whispered. The sound was growing higher in pitch, breaking into yelps like those of a fearsome beast in mortal agony.

"Potchnick," he said, turning toward the hallway. Suddenly heavy feet were thumping down the stairs, coming faster and faster.

"What's he doing here?"

"He's been sleeping in the attic for months."

"In the attic? In the locked room?"

Salvatore nodded curtly and started toward the hallway. Val followed, with growing apprehension. He stopped in the doorway and blocked it with his arm, keeping her in the parlor behind him.

"What's happening?"

He shook his head. "Wait." Then Potchnick appeared, the cuffs of his baggy brown wool trousers flapping around his bare ankles, above his ungainly sabots. His loose grey shirt was covered by the tangled strands of his long black beard that flowed over his chest and shoulders.

Le Guignol's mouth was contorted, drawn wide open, surrounded by his thick mustache. His yelping cries were fading, being replaced by gasps as he reached the hallway in front of them. His dark eyes were unfocused, staring straight ahead; he showed no sign that he saw them. Instead he ran by, arms outstretched, and crashed through the leaded glass panel beside the main door.

Val pushed under Sal's arm and ran to the broken window. In the sunlight Potchnick had slowed to a staggering walk. He was smoking where his skin was exposed. He writhed and held his blackening hands over his face, burst into flames, and disintegrated.

She stepped back, bumping into Salvatore. "What made him do that?" she asked, still staring out at the empty driveway. Then it came to her with a dreadful certainty. Only one thing could have caused Potchnick to stampede into the certain suicide of broad daylight. Val moaned and started toward the stairs. Salvatore stopped her with his arms.

"Let me go," she cried.

"Valerie, don't go up there!"

"Sarah!" Val screamed. She broke away from him and ran up the stairs so fast the banisters blurred, yet each step loomed before her with photographic clarity, every riser a barrier. Val screamed Sarah's name over and over, knowing even as she did that it was too late. Salvatore's hypnotism had done its work on the old bogeyman; why else would he have run to a daylight death with such horror on his face? He'd done the forbidden deed.

Val hoped with all her aching heart that there would still be life in Sarah as she topped the stairs into the attic hallway. The last door on the right was partly open, swinging inward at an odd angle. Sarah was there, crumpled on the floor as though she had fainted and dropped limply from a standing position. Her long blond hair streamed out around her, partly concealing the plastic high-school identification card she'd used to pry open the lock.

Val fell to her knees beside the still form. There was no pulse in Sarah's pale wrist, no soul in her violet eyes.

"Too late," Val said to no one and settled back on her heels. "Too late."

The tiny gash on Sarah's neck looked far too small to have caused her death. Yet there it was, the mark of the beast, wakened from the long sleep, insatiably hungry, unable to resist the freely offered throat of the child who dreamed of becoming a vampyr.

The tears streamed uncontrolled down Val's cheeks, sliding across the corners of her mouth and leaving a salty taste. She held the limp hand, caressing it, trying to warm the cooling flesh, until Sal took her elbow and pulled her gently away.

"How can we tell Theo?" She looked at him and felt a flash of tender emotion there before she dropped her gaze. Love, concern, and pity were nakedly glowing from his warm dark eyes. He helped her to her feet and held her in his arms.

"Don't think about it, Val. I'll tell him. He knew the risk when he brought Sarah here."

"He brought her here for me." Val pulled away slowly. He let her slip from his arms.

She walked away down the hall, her sneakers making sad squeaking sounds on the polished wooden floor, down one flight. There Val hesitated, rubbing the newel post, then turned toward Sarah's room. Her clothes were piled on the bed, and a large steamer trunk, which Eudora had found for her, yawned open to receive them and the treasures she'd collected; a ceramic Panda bear, a jade necklace with an Italian cameo pendant, bottles of French perfume carefully sealed and wired shut.

The room was sunny, fresh with the scents of Sarah and waiting for her return. Val closed the door and sat on the edge of the bed. She tried to look at herself in the vanity mirror. Her reflection wore the face of a hag-ridden wraith, thin and pale, frightened beyond the edge of endurance. Her eyes glowed emerald, deep wells of pain.

She floated in them until she could stop thinking about Sarah, about Theo, about anything.

The sun had long since passed overhead and there were long fingers and pools of shadow in the room when Eudora shook Val's shoulder, breaking into her self-imposed oblivion. Val stared at her without thinking, meeting her, feeling the loving warmth and taking it, feeling the stirrings of the power buried deeply within. Then, as Eudora and Val shared their grief, Val realized that everything Salvatore said was true. The power wasn't gone, only the courage.

"You'd better go downstairs to your suite," Eudora said, still resting her hand on Val's arm. "Theo is taking it very hard."

"How long has he been home?"

"Several hours; since they took her into town. Lui and Salvatore have taken care of everything. They made it look as though she fell through the broken window and cut herself. Lui signed the certificate as an accidental death."

"She kept asking about the locked room. I should have guessed."

"There was no way for you to have known. Go to him."

Val nodded and they walked together down to the second floor. Eudora kept her arm around Val until they were at the door. There she left Val hesitantly reaching for the knob.

Theo was sitting by the cold dark fireplace. His back was to the door, his head bowed, his legs straight and crossed at the ankles. She came up beside him and slipped her hand over his head until it rested on the nape of his neck. "Theo?"

"Salvatore's going back with us."

"Back?"

"To Houston. I've talked to Bart on the phone, they won't know the real truth." He shook his head. "When is it over, Valan? When do I finish paying my dues?"

Her hand rubbed his neck lightly but she didn't answer. There was nothing she could say to take his grief away.

"I wanted life more than anything. I was ready, willing to accept my sacrifice. And now . . . . "

"Shhhh."

"Do you know what I did when I brought Lui home? He raised his hand, rotating it to expose a long gash on his wrist that was already healing itself at the ends. "In the morning it'll be gone," he said, "I cut it and tried to force my blood into her mouth. She could have had it all."

"Come with me," Val said, holding her hands out to him. They took their coats and went out along the road. The sun was nearly down as they slipped out the main gate.

The road was quiet, except for their footfalls. Only field mice crossed the pavement in front of them. They paced off the kilometers in the dark.

Monday, January 3

Salvatore drove the rented car onto the drive in front of Bart's Houston home. Wolf was the first living thing they saw. He rose, growling, from the shrubbery at the side of the front porch as fearfully majestic as Cerberus, the hound of hell. Then, through the predawn fog, he recognized them. He welcomed them, his long bushy tail waving gently and his ears submissively laid back.

"I am a juicy rabbit, a crunchy roach at your feet," he seemed to tell Val, bending his body with his muzzle over his hips as he spun in slow circles of adoration before her.

"We won't leave you behind again," she promised him while Theo rang the bell.

Bart came to the door long enough to give Theo the key to the guest house and a sleepy announcement that, as far as he knew, everything was arranged for the next day's funeral.

They slept most of the day with Wolf on the floor beside the bed.

Nancy came over to see Theo for a little while. She was full of a grief that somehow didn't seem quite real to Val. She insisted that Theo go over to the main house

294

with her to visit with Bart. He refused.

He listened to her pleas with a lack of interest that worried Val and irritated her. He wasn't moved. He could not accept the comfort of pity from anyone, even them.

Once Nancy even turned to Val for help in persuading him, but Val just shrugged her shoulders and looked helpless, not willing to get into the argument. Nancy did get him to agree to ride with them to the funeral. "Salvatore could take Val. The family," she said, "should ride together," clearly leaving Val out of her scheme of things.

"I will enjoy seeing her grow old," Val mused.

Theo, Salvatore, and Val spent that night driving about. The rented Chrysler had a full tank and they went a long way into the country where the land rolled away in long low waves in every direction and small herds of cattle roamed in the fields.

Theo talked of the dream he had carried since they had been together, of the lab and the work he wanted to do. "It's a matter of location," he said, "a place where we won't be bothered. We will start looking for a good place when we are finished here." But his voice was wooden; it lacked conviction.

Val found herself staring off into space without a thought in her mind. She couldn't concentrate on even the simplest things. Time crawled by with maddening slowness.

Tuesday, January 4

Early in the morning, before they dressed for the funeral, Bart came over. He asked Val, "What really happened?"

"She fell through a glass panel," Val said.

295

"Can you look into my face and say that?"

"Bart, you are human; you are my friend. But I could look you in the eye and tell you that cows have wings, and you would believe it forever after."

He thought about it without blinking, the muscles of his jaw working slowly as though he were chewing something tough and flavorless. "Then we'll never know?"

"You can only be sure about what you believe. But if you don't believe me, remember that belief seldom has any relationship to reality."

He shrugged and left. "Got to go change clothes," he said.

In the hour before the time came to drive to the funeral they drank part of their daily ration out of glasses from the kitchen. Afterwards Salvatore vanished to his room and Val sat on the floor with her head resting against Theo's knee.

"Are you sure you don't want to go?" he asked.

"It is a family matter. That doesn't include me."

"She loved you."

"I couldn't bear to hear a priest talk about her. It's too hard, dragging it out this way. I've already said goodbye. Can you understand?"

"I think so."

"When we choose to die it should be clean, a moment of rapturous agony, a cloud of pure smoke returning our spirits to the wind."

"The casket will be closed."

"Then why do you have to go?" Val asked, picking a bit of lint off the carpet. At least he wouldn't have to look again at the face they had irretrievably lost.

"She's my daughter."

"She doesn't care now. And if she knew what you

were setting yourself up for emotionally, she'd beg you to stay away."

"Probably." He was silent for a while, thinking. Val waited. Then he added, "Death wish, perhaps."

"Do you really want to die?"

"No." He shook his head and moved his hand over to twist a tendril of her hair in his fingers. "I want . . . ." There was another long pause. " . . .Absolution."

"Who's going to grant it, Theo? God or yourself? You haven't done anything that God wouldn't forgive. You're being pretty rough on yourself."

"Yes."

"Will doing this free you?" It was difficult for Val to follow his thoughts.

"Yes. I'm sure of it."

Nancy walked in then, without knocking, as they had told her to do, and found Val there on the rug with Theo's hand in her hair. Nancy looked down her nose at Val a trifle longer than necessary.

"Are you ready, Theo?" she asked, pointedly ignoring Val.

"In a moment," he answered, standing up and offering Val a hand, pulling her to her feet and into a close embrace. They kissed. Just one kiss, but full of warmth and promises.

"I'll be all right, don't worry about anything. Meet me with Sal and the car after the funeral; about three o'clock."

"Fine," Val said, lying like a trooper. Things were anything but fine as far as she was concerned. Her hands slipped hesitantly from Theo's chest.

As soon as they were gone she took the luggage to the door and waited for Salvatore to bring up the car.

Their dark blue Chrysler with heavily tinted windows nosed cautiously up to the door. A man got out. He was wearing a charcoal-grey suit, white gloves and a complete head mask, so lifelike that she had to look closely before she realized who he was, and why he was wearing it. Even though the day was cloudy with a bit of drizzle now and then, there was a lot of light coming from the Texas sun. Salvatore needed the protection.

It was the walk and gestures that reassured her. His brown eyes must have been twinkling behind the dark glasses as he loaded the suitcases into the trunk.

"Where'd you get that?"

"A Swedish makeup artist I helped get out of jail taught me how to make them. It comes in handy to have a second skin for these little daytime excursions."

"It's fantastically realistic, and much handsomer than your real face." Val opened the front door of the car; Wolf jumped in wagging his tail.

"Ha! Just for that I'll wear it forever."

"We're supposed to wait here until it's nearly over," Val said. "But I want to go now. Is that all right with you? We won't get out of the car."

He nodded and slipped behind the wheel. She locked the guest house door for the last time.

At the church, the lot was full of strange-looking vehicles of all kinds and colors, mostly belonging to Sarah's youthful friends; the Chrysler filled the last space.

Salvatore sighed as he settled back and draped his right arm over the back of the seat while they waited for the service to finish. "So Theo's done it to you again," he said.

"What do you mean by that?"

He turned and stared at Val through the dark glasses.

298

"How many times in the last two years has he brought trouble to your feet?"

"It's not his fault," Val protested. Wolf growled in agreement from where he was curled up on the floormat.

"No, it's his poor judgment. And you're sitting here like a ninny letting him do it again."

"What would you, in your superior wisdom, suggest?"

"Run. Now." He gave one of his continental shrugs, barely noticeable. "Cut it loose, Val, while there's still time. He isn't worth it."

"He's our hope for the future." Val shook her head. "That's not all. I can't leave him. I love him. What about you? You don't have to stay."

"Val, you're still my responsibility. Do you really think that I'd follow you all over the world all these years if I didn't love you for yourself?"

Val didn't answer. It had never occurred to her. He was always simply there whenever she needed him. Finally, she said, "I always take you for granted."

"You can. If something happens to him, it isn't the end of everything."

People were beginning to leave the church. Val's eyes strained for a glimpse of Theo. He finally appeared at a side door, flanked by Bart and Nancy. All of them got into the black limousine parked nearby.

Salvatore pulled in toward the end of the cortège and they rode in silence for nearly an hour. Then the procession made a sharp right turn onto the cemetery drive.

The drive curved around, doubling back on itself to form a large circle with a Y at the base. By the time they pulled in, the hearse had gone completely around, stopping near the left side of the entrance, and the youthful pallbearers were already unloading the heavy bronze coffin. Other cars in the cortège were parked along the road. Mourners were walking toward the green-and-white-striped canopy over the gravesite.

The drizzle was increasing. It was almost heavy enough to be called rain. Droplets gathered on the windshield and dribbled downward, leaving the view distorted. The older folks were opening umbrellas or covering their heads with folded sheets of newspaper. Only the students ignored the moisture.

Salvatore pulled the Chrysler out of line, swung around in front of the hearse, and parked it so they were facing back toward the main road.

A policeman came clanking over and stuck his head partly in the window on Val's side. He smelled of freshly shaved whiskers and bay rum. Wolf growled at him with fangs bared; he pulled back a bit.

"You'll have to move," the policeman said, tipping his hat slightly.

"We're only staying a few minutes," Salvatore told him. "This is Mrs. James. She felt she had to come, even though the Doctor asked her not to."

"All right," the policeman said, nodding and moving away, but not very far.

"Nice lie," Val said. Salvatore was immobile. Val sensed he was frowning behind the mask. She rolled the window down all the way and twisted her body to look out. The priest was still talking and moving his hands—the Lord's Prayer, she thought. His back was toward the road and his voice indistinct.

When he was through and people started moving back toward their cars Val got out and stood in the damp grass, waiting for Theo. Silver dots of water quickly covered her sleeves. They felt fresh and cool on her face. Theo glanced up, midstride, as the family headed across the soggy turf toward the limousine, saw Val and smiled slightly, almost drowsily.

"Excuse me, Nan," she heard him say.

"But, Theo, you're coming home with us!" Nancy whined petulantly.

"I'll call you later." There was something different in his tone of voice, an undefinable hardness. "Take her home, Bart."

"Theo, you promised." Her voice was still pettish and she tugged at his arm. "We all want you to come." He glanced at her with suddenly brilliant eyes.

He was turning toward her, his face tightly controlled, when a dove-grey Cadillac pulled up at the end of the cortège. He stared at it, frowning. Then he walked rapidly toward Val, ignoring Nancy. She started to follow, but Bart took her arm and led her away.

"What's wrong?"

"Did you see who just drove up?" he asked, stopping close to Val.

Bart had ushered Nancy into the black limousine, and their driver was easing out past the hearse.

"No."

The grey car was parked with the windshield wipers off, and the interior was concealed by the rain collecting on the glass. The cortège was steadily moving past. The somber-suited men from the funeral parlor finished talking to the caretaker and headed back to their car.

A slim young woman in a flashy pink miniskirted uniform and heavy makeup got out of the Cadillac on the driver's side, came around the front, opened the passenger door, and helped a man out of the car.

It was Plutus, complete with wide-brimmed fedora,

gloves, dark glasses and a white cane.

The hearse and the last cars were going, and the caretaker was clumping across the grass to his truck on a side road. The tent over the gravesite was sagging from the water and the flowers by the still open hole were the only touch of color. The sky darkened and the rain increased.

Plutus adjusted his jacket and frowned heavenward. Then he approached, coming slowly across the pavement.

"I came to offer my regrets," he said in his familiar harsh whisper, but the tone of his voice was anything but sympathetic. "Carlotta told me you haven't been yourself since you met Georges." He smirked. "Carlotta spoke quite highly of you and your efforts." It was clear that he hadn't come to offer condolences. He'd come to challenge Val.

Val's fingers grew cold. She reached for Theo's hand. It was warm and wrapped around hers calm and confidently. The car door slammed on the other side. Salvatore, in his latex mask and dark glasses, came around the front and stood between Plutus and Val. "Val, you can do it," he whispered.

"No."

He looked at Theo, then quickly back to Val, his mask unreadable. "You are surrounded by power. You're safe." Val thought he was referring to his own power.

"Then you take him."

"No, Val. Look." He pointed his gloved hand at Theo.

"Valerie," Plutus said, smugly, "I'd like to see you, now." His words faded out toward the end as a great thundering roar of blood pounded through her ears, filling her brain. Her head swung from Salvatore to Plutus and back in fear and confusion. The overpowering instinct to avoid a confrontation had paralyzed her from the neck down. Then through the vibrating maelstrom of her blood she heard the thrilling sound of someone calling her name.

"Valan," it was a command whispered with the gentleness of a master, calm and sure, the way Robin used to call her from across a crowded room. But it wasn't Robin. It was Theo. And the warmth flowing from his hand to hers filled her. The rushing noise faded, growing fainter until she could hear the sounds around her; the rain, a distant bird.

Val looked at Theo and into him, fearlessly, acknowledging the force she knew had been within him for a long time. He had somehow reached deeply within himself and brought it to consciousness with perfect control. He stood straighter, taller, as though the awareness of his newly recognized strength made him larger than life. It was an awesome power, yet familiar and gentle as she looked into what he had to tell her.

"Be strong and fearless," he radiated. "What you were you will be again." There were no words between them, only ideas and emotions flowing back and forth.

"And you? What of you?" She sent back her feelings and fearful doubts.

"With the sprinkling of the soil on the coffin's lid, I broke free of the ties holding me to the human world. There's nothing left now but you and me.

"We'll never know what destiny brought you to me, but it's my fate now to use what you gave me. Together we are free to seek control of all the vampyr beasts that dwell within, then offer immortality to the world.

"Turn around now, beloved green eyes, and show

Plutus that what was, is again—and will be, long after he walks in the sunlight for the last time.''

Something tightly crumpled and brittle deep within Val unfolded and vanished; the hold of Robin's power that had haunted her for more than forty years was gone, exorcised by the greater power of Theo's love. He squeezed her hand slightly and released it. There was a serene smile on his face like the smile of Buddha in contemplation of inner peace, and she knew that her own face reflected the same expression.

She turned and let her gaze travel up Plutus' grey suit-coat. She saw his hand go up and come away holding his dark sunglasses. There was a one-sided smile on his face, confidence in the forward thrust of his jaw, but Val barely noticed. She stiffened as though someone was pulling upward on the back of her head and looked directly into his milky eyes.

She didn't see his lips go slack with surprise or his glasses fall from his quivering fingers. All she saw was the dark well of his soul, hot with ambition, shrinking to a small black point, and then, as she drew away, the color of his eyes changing from milky white to an opaque blue.

Plutus moaned in anguish and fell writhing to the ground with his hands on his eyes. The water on the grass made dark spots all over the grey wool of his suit.

They left him sobbing in the mist and drizzle, the chauffeur bending over him, wringing her hands. Salvatore drove them away, slowly, without looking back at either the blind vampyr or the fresh gravesite.

Val took Theo's hand, but she didn't look at him. She stared ahead. It was the future she saw, not the highway disappearing into the mist. A faint smile played on her lips.